DRAGONCALLER

Published by Clockwork Dragon, LLC
www.clockworkdragon.net

First Printing, July 2019

Dragoncaller is a work of fiction. People, places, and incidents are either products of the author's mind or used fictitiously.

ISBN: 978-1-944334-39-0

STARDRIFTERS BOOK 1

DRAGONCALLER

LEE FRENCH
JEFFREY COOK

Lee wishes to thank Brendan, the best sounding board ever, for his relentless cheerleading and browbeating. Josh, Adam, Mike, DJ, and Colin comprise the crew of the *LSS Sanity* and perform their officer duties admirably. Special thanks to Connie for saving the day at the last minute, and to Stefan and crew for once again turning words into masterful audio artwork.

Jeffrey would like to thank Jennifer Wolf, Matthew Lewis, Sheri Budrow, Katherine Perkins,Aiden Manalang, Ken Lea, Richard Doyle, Kelly Hendrix, Beki Knox, Kaylin Anderson, Lora Abbeglan, Ivy Hope, and everyone who at conventions who assured us lesbian space opera… with dragons…really did need to be a thing.

CHAPTER 1

MADISON

Jets fired, shoving the last escape pod out of its berth to escape a Lakhan Oligarchy cruiser. According to their sensors, Madison sat inside the pod. Biological materials cloned from a swab of her flesh, sprayed two minutes ago, made sure of that. The real Madison watched the spherical pod leave to make sure it cleared the outer ship's hull.

Her uncle would kill her for stealing one of his ships and letting the enemy take it. But only if her mission failed.

She nodded her satisfaction as the readout beside the pod's sealed door reported a successful launch. Within the next minute, it would plot a course across the galaxy to the nearest known Stardrifter hideout and fire the engines to head there. Or the Oligarchy lackeys would catch it. Either option worked for her.

By now, everyone else should've assembled in the place she needed to reach within the next thirty seconds. She sprinted down the worn, aging steel corridor, following its gentle curve and hoping against hope she and the crew would see the *Wayward Scout* again. With luck, they'd all return to it in a few hours.

The soles of her leather boots tapped against the floor, their soft, repeating sound echoing enough for her to hear it and cringe. Not that it mattered. Without technological intervention, hevit shock troopers would sense everyone the moment they stepped onto the ship even if they stayed still and silent.

At the first intersection, she darted to the side. Jaco, her closest and most trusted friend, leaned into sight and waved for her to join the crew in their hiding place. Madison hurried through the gap in the wall. As soon as she passed him, Jaco hauled a concealing panel into place. Shmar flipped a pair of locks to hold the panel secure. Oolaang used three of his arms to hit a series of switches. The shielding mechanism hummed into life.

Locked inside a dark, cramped compartment in the guts of their small ship, they stood a chance of evading detection by Oligarchy ship sensors and hevit troopers.

Oolaang, one of only two nonhumans to back Madison's mad plan, pushed a button on a small device in his fourth hand. White noise buzzed low enough to ignore after a few seconds. Between that and the shielding, the hevit troopers shouldn't hear them through the walls.

Madison knew her plan would work. It had to.

Twelve members of her uncle's crew stood inside the compartment with her. Each had trusted their life to Madison. They believed in her as they believed in Captain Christopher Wayward, the man who'd raised Madison since her parents died ten years earlier.

They waited.

Madison had watched an Oligarchy cruiser take an enemy ship more than once. She knew what to expect.

The *Wayward Scout* rocked as foreign arms attached to the ship's docking collars and airlocks. For a normal ship assault, Oligarchy craft first used precisely fired blasts to disable a ship's transport engines. Under Madison's orders, Oolaang had sabotaged the *Wayward Scout* in a reversible way, making the ship appear damaged and unable to escape the cruiser.

As she'd hoped, the enemy had proven unable to resist a wounded ship drifting near an FTL jump point. For extra security, she'd chosen a specific time and date. 15:30 Stardrifter time equated to 06:21 Oligarchy time, otherwise known as both six minutes ago and four minutes before a guarded shipment of mithrite-reinforced steel passed through.

The arms dragged the *Wayward Scout* into the cruiser's assault bay. Madison and the crew held onto each other to keep their balance. Jaco wrapped an arm around her waist and pulled her close. Buckles on the front of his blue longcoat, the same style everyone wore as part of Captain Wayward's crew, pressed against her back. He rested his chin on her shoulder, probably to get her red ponytail out of his face.

They all knew better than to speak.

Muffled whirring announced the airlocks opening by force. No one in the compartment would hear the stealthy hevit troopers boarding. They had to rely upon the hevits performing a sweep and leaving. According to her calculations, that sweep should take no more than twenty minutes.

Madison wished she dared to use the wristband in the thigh pocket of her pants. With it, she could send a few specific kinds of signals to the ship computers and monitor the airlocks and outside cameras. She didn't know if the hevits could detect the wireless connection between the two. Odds pointed to yes, so she kept it shut off in her pocket.

She prayed to whatever might listen for her plan to work. Seconds crept past, each longer than the one before it. Madison kept her cybernetic left eye focused on the analog clock hung on a hook stuck to the wall. No one else could see it in the darkness. One more thing the crew had agreed to rely upon her for.

In the long stretch of forever, Madison imagined herself returning to her uncle in triumph. Armed with the knowledge she'd confirm on this mission, the Stardrifters could finally stand a chance against the Oligarchy. She'd light the spark of a true revolution.

Stealing from the Oligarchy kept the Stardrifters alive. A revolution would set them free.

Though no one knew what freedom would give them or mean, it had to be better than skulking through the galaxy, evading the Oligarchy ships and their soldiers, stealing whatever they could from the profiteers who flourished under lakhan rule, and living as isolated dots in the darkness.

She didn't enjoy living under the threat of capture at any moment. Becoming an Oligarchy slave promised a lifetime of hard labor, humiliation, and pain. Not that it would last long. Humans didn't survive that kind of treatment for more than a decade or two.

Though other races could wind up as slaves in the Lakhan Oligarchy, they had to commit crimes to do so. Humans only had to exist.

Time ticked on, slower than anything Madison had ever experienced. Ten minutes took ten years. Jaco kept his grip on her, providing a solid, comforting presence at her back. Whatever happened, he'd support her.

Someone burped. Everyone else held their breath in case the white noise generator didn't cover it.

The compartment warmed enough to make sweat bead on Madison's forehead and at the small of her back. They hadn't considered body heat. If she'd thought of it, she would've brought something to cool the room.

Maybe the hevits and their keepers wouldn't notice. Their reputation declared they would. Madison prayed harder for the walls and their shielding to block heat, smell, and everything else. She should've thought of all the senses. Jaco's breath smelled like the mints he liked and always carried in a pocket. If that revealed them, she'd never forgive herself for such a stupid oversight.

A thumping clang pounded Madison's chest. She hadn't expected that sound. Her gambit had relied on a lot of assumptions. Maybe she should've watched until she'd identified which class of cruiser had arrived. One big enough to fit the ship inside its cargo bay would still work but might have more hevit troopers than they could evade. The boarding sweep might take longer.

The time for that kind of thinking had passed. They'd all committed to this and couldn't back out now. Literally.

Ten more minutes passed with all the speed of an eon. Jaco shifted his weight. She swayed with him. Someone coughed. Every tiny noise shot more tension into Madison's shoulders.

For safety's sake, Madison forced herself and everyone else to wait another five minutes. Then she patted Jaco's arm. He released her.

"Let's move," she whispered.

Oolaang deactivated the shielding and tugged a pair of dark-lensed goggles over his large eyes to protect them from the bright lights. Shmar unlocked the panel. Jaco picked up the panel to keep it from scraping on the floor and opened a narrow slit. Madison pressed her face against it. If anyone had to risk an eye to see into the corridor, she would do it with her artificial one.

The cybereye's advanced cameras gave her a wider view than anyone else could manage anyway.

She saw and heard nothing moving. "Clear."

Jaco set aside the panel. Madison stepped into the corridor and slipped to the end closest to the port airlock. There, she leaned out and checked in both directions. The hevits had left all the internal doors open. On this level, they led to storage compartments.

Behind her, Shmar tapped on a wall console. "The airlocks are still open," he whispered.

Jaco thumped a spot on the wall to open a much smaller compartment. He handed out laser pistols, their blue casing a close match for the blue of their coats, and gave Oolaang his toolkit. They'd worried too much about accidental discharges or dropping things to bring them into the hiding compartment. Besides, the ship had these handy secret spaces too small for a person anyway.

Madison retrieved her wristband, a thin, white piece of flexible plastic, and powered it up as she snapped it onto her right wrist. As soon as it booted, it formed a neural connection through her skin. She commanded the wristband to show her the feed from the ship's outside cameras.

Holographic images sprang from the wristband, hovering in the air where everyone could see them. With mental commands, she cycled through the twelve views available.

From bow to stern, the *Wayward Scout* covered only twenty meters. Four thick mechanical arms, two from above and two from below, held the *Scout* suspended inside a docking bay at least five times its size. *Wayward Star*, the mother ship for the *Scout*, with a one hundred meter hull, would fit inside it with room to spare. Any Stardrifter ship would fit inside it.

Faced with this evidence of the size of the ship they'd encountered, Madison chewed her lip. Regular escort cruisers didn't haul ships inside enormous cargo bays. They clamped a ship in place, boarded, took prisoners, and left the emptied vessel to drift. Her mission didn't change, but their odds of success dropped.

That kind of thinking didn't help anything. She sucked in a deep breath and refused to let the fear dancing in her veins stop her.

Two tolos, members of another of the Oligarchy's lackey races, watched the ship through a force field. They had big, blocky bodies with turquoise and cobalt skin, and a ridge for gills along their jaws. Both tolos used heavy, full-body control rigs, which accounted for some of the mechanical arms moving to accomplish unknowable goals.

To leave the ship, Madison and the crew had to use one of the two airlock access bridges. Each bridge consisted of a transparent tube big enough for two hevit troopers to drag an unconscious prisoner of any race, including the ones twice as big as a human.

With no options for creating a distraction, Madison chose the port bridge. She couldn't be sure from extrapolating the camera angles but thought the ship would block any view of them by the pair of tolo workers.

Jaco handed her the last weapon. She strapped the gun to her left hand and wrist. Like the wristband, the pistol forged a neural connection. The link included her cybereye, which allowed her to use its superior capabilities for targeting. It wouldn't fire unless she really wanted it to.

"Port side looks safer. Jaco and I will go first, then the rest of the boarding team come across together." Madison shut off the camera feed and straightened the collar of her longcoat, then double checked the contents of all eight of her pants pockets. Everything was in order. "Those staying on the ship..." She smirked. They'd all memorized the plan. Nobody needed her to remind them. "You know what to do."

Shmar flashed her a thumbs-up. Several others nodded. Oolaang hugged his toolkit to his chest. Jaco patted her shoulder. Nervous energy danced between them. They'd never faced these stakes before. Captain Wayward had taken care of them all. He'd kept them out of this level of danger by not taking the big risks other captains plunged into. Other Stardrifters called him The Madman, but not for taking unnecessary chances.

"Let's move."

Four members of her team stayed behind to undo Oolaang's sabotage and get the ship ready to leave on a moment's notice. Jaco and seven others, including Shmar and Oolaang, followed her to the airlock. Nine lives to assault a ship of hundreds.

At the airlock, Madison and Jaco peered up the tube together. A metal catwalk ran uphill through the access bridge, providing a flat surface to walk across. At the other end, the tube spilled into the Oligarchy ship without a barrier. They'd left the door open at both ends, which Madison found interesting. She filed away the information for future missions.

"It's pokken huge," Jaco whispered.

"Don't think about that. Focus on the goal and keep heading toward it." She spoke the words as much for herself as for him.

He nodded and stared up the bridge. "Sprint or creep?"

The tube ran twenty meters or so. Madison thought she could handle that. "Sprint and stop at the other end before stepping through."

His brown eyes danced with mischief.

She snorted and launched into a dash. As expected, he charged past her, turning the run into a race. He won because he always won in a straight-up race. Jaco had longer legs with thicker muscles, and he'd spent most of his childhood running from everyone and everything on the backwater dump of a world where they'd picked up the skinny, hungry orphan kid. Eight years of regular meals on Captain Wayward's ship had solved all three of those last problems.

Madison reached the other end four paces behind Jaco. She counted it as a kind of win because he hadn't beaten her too badly.

Keeping watch, Jaco waved for the rest of the boarding party to make their mad dash up the tube.

"Getting slow in your old age," Madison said as she puffed to catch her breath.

His eighteenth birthday had passed a month ago. She'd hit nineteen ten months before that.

He chuckled, showing only minimal signs of exertion. "It's clear."

They stepped into a staging area with two exits, both closed. Under the usual grimy metallic smell of a spaceship long past its maiden voyage, Madison caught a vague whiff of something foreign. The odd, musky scent reminded her of nightmares.

The rest of the crew huffed and puffed into the room while Madison consulted her wristband. She'd spent months poring over every snippet of information she could find about the interiors of Oligarchy cruisers. Piecing it together had taken even longer. Her wristband displayed the results of that effort in the form of a rough schematic.

Knowing which way to find the stern from this room would've made their mission much easier.

"Maddie, we weren't expecting a ship this big," Oolaang said. "This might be a flagship cruiser."

The rest of the crew murmured their distress.

"Guarding a mithrite freighter?" Madison needed them to worry about completing the mission, not all the possible ways it could fail. "I don't think so. We're fine. Eyes and ears open, and stick together. Watch for places to duck into hiding."

She judged both unlabeled doors and consulted her schematic. Without a solid point of reference to orient with, she had to guess. The tolos worked to the left of their position, so the left door probably led to them. They didn't want to meet the tolos.

"That way," she pointed to the door on the right wall.

Her entire plan hinged on no one actively monitoring the ship's interior. Why would they? No one had ever boarded an Oligarchy ship and lived to tell about it. Watching all their soldiers, troopers, peons, and sycophants moving through the ship would take too much effort when they had no reason to suspect anyone would infiltrate.

Shmar and Jaco flanked the door. Dani stayed by Oolaang's side. The others lined up behind Madison. She nodded. Jaco waved a hand where the door's motion sensor would detect it.

The door slid aside. Jaco and Shmar checked outside and nodded. Madison slipped through with Faro at her back. The crew moved into a bright, well-lit corridor with doors at precise intervals. Madison saw nowhere to count on for hiding, but the hall did have plenty of intersections.

"I'm not picking the wrong direction," Madison whispered to herself. She led the crew down the corridor. At each intersection, she stopped and used her cybernetic left eye to check the other passage. Three intersections down, she saw a creature about a head shorter than herself, maybe a meter and a half tall, headed their way.

Madison had never seen a hevit in person. Pictures didn't do them justice. Tiny white feathers—capable of changing color to match their surroundings, she knew—covered it like shimmering, velvety fur, making it difficult to focus on and blurring the image in her cybereye. This one had two cybernetic legs, each moving with a bare whisper of sound. From study, Madison knew the elite troopers typically had internal enhancements, not visible external ones. Regular troopers, though, could catch or kill them just as much as elite ones.

She snapped her hand into the air and waved frantically for everyone to back up. They had to reach the previous intersection and duck around the corner to avoid this thing.

Dani hauled Oolaang around the last corner. Everyone else hustled as quietly as they could. Madison turned the corner as the hevit did. She held her breath and watched it stop at the previous intersection.

Its head, adorned with a small, hooked beak, turned toward her. One three-fingered hand waved at the air where Madison had stood moments earlier.

Terrified of getting caught, especially this early in her mission, Madison waved for everyone to keep going in the opposite direction.

The hevit took a step toward Madison. She turned and hurried to follow the crew. They ducked around the next corner. Ahead, she saw a door open, activated by Jaco slipping past it too close.

Everyone scrambled to duck out of sight, breaking the crew into two groups. Madison perched at a corner with Dani and Oolaang. Her cybereye picked up a hevit emerging from the open door and checking in both directions. It waved in the air like the other one had, making her think they smelled through their hands or fingers.

They still had that other hevit to worry about. Madison willed the second one to get bored and go back inside. The moment it did, she dragged Dani and Oolaang around the corner. As she yanked her head out of sight, she saw the first hevit turning the corner. One more second and it would have seen them.

The trio ran to meet with the rest of the crew. Jaco tried to apologize with his eyes. Madison shook her head to get him to stop. They had more important things to worry about. Like not attracting any more attention.

After darting across another intersection and reaching the next corner, Madison noticed the air cooling. Colder air told her two important things, each worse than the other.

First, tolos and hevits preferred similar temperature ranges to humans. This meant they had an actual lakhan on the ship, because they preferred cooler temperatures. Oolaang had guessed right. They'd encountered a flagship.

No one knew much about the lakhans themselves, other than their immortality. Captain Wayward's belief in a legend that humans had once killed a lakhan formed the core reason why everyone called him Madman.

Second, if she had her facts correct, the lakhans always stayed as far away from engineering as possible. Their mission objective lay in the opposite direction from the cold. In a ship this big, they might even need to descend a level or two.

Madison checked her schematic and made the best guess she could from what she'd learned. The stupid ship had no signs she could see, which made everything harder. But she'd seen some minor irregularities in the layout and had committed them to memory. The next time she did this, the mission would take less time.

Her crew followed her without complaint. Jaco did raise his brow as they turned in a circle. She ignored him.

At the next corner, she paused and caught sight of a hevit walking toward them. To her surprise, it stopped six meters before reaching the intersection, waving its hand at the air in front of it. Whatever it detected made it turn around and walk away. As soon as it stepped through a door, she led her crew across the intersection.

Ahead, she spotted the first signage. On a red door, a plaque announced they'd discovered engineering. Exactly where she'd expected. Had they gone the right direction the first time, they would've found it in five minutes.

Her gamble had proven correct. Oligarchy ships, unlike Stardrifter ships, all used the same layout. The flagship had a different scale than the craft she'd studied, but once she'd accounted for that, she'd had no problems. With this information, the Stardrifters could disable and destroy Oligarchy ships despite their inferior firepower.

She rushed to the red door and triggered it, then ducked to the side. The door slid open. No one stepped out. Jaco ran to the other side and nodded to her with a triumphant grin. Together, they triggered the door again and darted through.

Oligarchy ships used a vertical cylinder layout for their engineering sections to facilitate their long, thin fuel rods, which required a circular housing of a specific circumference. Rather than waste the space in the center, they lined the inner ring with consoles and put an elevator platform in the center so several could be stacked.

Madison rushed to the first console and issued a command to her cybereye to disengage and pop out. The device made a tiny click noise and slid out of its housing by a centimeter. As she plucked it out, she fished a cable from her pocket. One end of the cable fitted the socket mounted inside her empty eye socket. The other end split into four different connector types.

Behind her, Jaco grunted. Madison whirled in time to avoid a blow to the back of her head. A hevit she couldn't quite focus on drove a second thick fist into her gut.

She groaned and clutched her stomach. The hevit slammed an elbow into her back before she could react. Hevit fingers ripped the cybereye out of her hand. With her one real eye, she saw Jaco on the floor, already under control. This hevit had taken him down and moved on to her without a sound.

Hoping for a chance to run, Madison raised her hands in surrender. "Not resisting!"

The hevit wrapped a hand in her ponytail and dragged her through the door.

Her crew lay on the floor like discarded toys. More hevits stood among them.

There would be no escape.

CHAPTER 2

KIREHE

Kukiri dragons in a wide variety of bright colors filled the area with chirping chatter as Kirehe drank from the cool stream at the base of her home tree. The tiny flying reptiles, each small enough to fit in Kirehe's hands, dug with their tiny claws, searching for bugs to eat in the dim glow of pre-dawn. They spoke of simple matters—how they slept, what they wanted to hunt, and where they planned to go. Kirehe preferred this type of talk over their mating season drivel. Then came the egg-laying nonsense. After that, they spoke of nothing but the handling of hatchlings.

This time of year, though, when the sun rose late and set early, the babies had all left their nests and none of the kukiris wanted to make more. These shorter days marked the time to rest and save energy. Kirehe followed their example when she could.

"Food flying!" one kukiri whistled.

The flock leaped into the trees, eager to catch the airborne insects they preferred over the ground-bound ones. They flitted between hanging vines, thick branches, and tall shrubs, snatching their prey with claws and jaws.

Kirehe shook her hands, then wiped them on her knee-length pants, avoiding the sheathed machete tied to her rope belt. As she left the kukiris to find breakfast, one leaped from its perch and followed her.

Skila, a kukiri almost as old as Kirehe's seventeen years, liked to move between the kukiri groups and preferred Kirehe's shoulder as the means to do so. Kirehe didn't mind.

As soon as Skila landed, Kirehe reached up and rubbed under the kukiri's chin. The soft scales of her dark green underbelly stood out against the lighter green of her back. On her face, gold and rose feathers formed frilly curls around her jewel-blue eyes and matched the feathers of her wings. Though some kukiris shared similar coloring, only Skila boasted a dark green frill at the tip of her long tail.

They followed a narrow, winding trail through a dozen tall, thick trees connected by vines and wide-leafed shrubs. Along the way, Skila leaped into the air to catch her breakfast of flying insects and returned to Kirehe's shoulder half a dozen times.

"Good hunting," Skila chirped in her tiny, high-pitched voice.

"I'm glad," Kirehe whistled in response. Her voice could shift to match the kukiris and other dragons, a gift she shared with a handful of others across all the Iwa people. "May everyone's hunt be so fruitful today."

They reached a line of trees supporting thick, thorny vines, towering flower stalks, and woody shrubs. The plant life formed an impassable wall three meters high. Kirehe's path brought her to one of only two cultivated and maintained gaps in the protective wall for the village she pledged to protect.

Tosnorth, one of her hapa's villages, lay close enough to reach quickly, yet far enough to keep the larger dragons from causing trouble or eating foolish children. The villagers hunted the slower, meatier dragons and gathered what crops the jungle allowed to grow. A portion of their food returned to the TwentyOneSixteen Cave, the base for their hapa which they also called TOS Cave for short, where mothers raised their children under the tutelage of elders and craftspeople plied their trades.

Kirehe hadn't visited the cave since becoming an adult three years earlier. She visited the village every few days for her share of the food.

Stepping through the gap brought Kirehe into a different world.

Lines of flat stones marked the paths between gardens of herbs and roots the gatherers coaxed into growing where they wanted. They'd learned to do it from the sacred texts and paintings in the ThirteenFortyTwo, or TFT for short, Cave. Their ancestors had known many amazing things, few of which made much sense to Kirehe.

One member of the camp flock of kukiris, a blue-feathered one, noticed her and whistled a greeting. The rest of the flock, spread across the camp, echoed the whistle in a receding wave, creating a joyful chorus. Skila jumped off her shoulder to join them.

Trees with narrower trunks flanked a haphazard cluster of grass and leaf huts, and provided a protective canopy overhead. In the center, an open-wall cooking hut used a moving water and grass system to catch smoke and keep it from rising above the treetops. Near that central hut, one tree bore a large analog clock made of metal and plastic hanging on a hook, set to the same time as the sacred clock with the glowing red numbers in the TFT Cave. Everywhere between the huts, narrow sluices made from flexible, fibrous leaves, caught and carried water for people to use.

From the corners of many huts, strings of bones and bone fragments from the dead hung and swayed with the breeze. They served as reminders of the previous occupants. In Kirehe's tree, the bones of all those before her created a white curtain across the entrance.

Two men worked in the cooking hut, making flatbread on heated stones and stirring the contents of a large iron pot over the fire. When the hunters returned with kills, they cooked some to eat that night and the next day, and prepared the rest for transport back to the cave along with the other animal parts. Yesterday had seen no kills, so no one ate meat this morning. Instead, they filled the void with extra vegetables and bread made from the bounty of the gardens.

Kirehe preferred these meals. She could eat meat with the mara dragons, or with Nihan. All her dragons, though, turned up their snouts at soup and bread.

More members of the hunting pack, mostly men, sat with tools, repairing or making clothing, weapons, shields, or other hunting tools. During the long-day season, Kirehe's arrival often woke the camp. In the short-day season, she never did.

To one side, two men sat with a group of new hunters recently released from their childhoods. The skin around the fan-like tattoos on their bellies to mark their transition to adulthood still showed red irritation. They had arrived within the last few days.

One mentor beckoned her closer. Kirehe had yet to meet the new hunters. Not that she wanted to.

"Today, we'll show you the dragonline," the man told the new hunters. "Venturing beyond it brings you too close to Irondoom. What happens if you get too close to Irondoom?"

"The flying machines catch you," the girl said. "They take you to their altar and kill you as a sacrifice to their evil gods, which makes them stronger."

The mentor nodded. "Always remember that, no matter how good the hunting seems on the other side. This is Kirehe." He gestured to her. "She's one of our dragoncallers."

All four young faces, three boys and one girl, turned to regard her. Kirehe saw enough defiance among them to make her want to challenge them all to a dominance battle. But she'd learned not to do that in the camp. Instead, she stood straighter and planted her fists on her hips. Better to show them confidence than weakness or disregard.

"Is it true that dragoncallers can only talk to dragons?" one boy asked.

Kirehe scowled. She had no idea where such stupid ideas came from. Someone always had one, though. As a child, she'd heard the other kids whispering while she played with the kukiris. Their adult minders hadn't done anything about it and had punished her for trying to. "Yes." She turned her back on them and stalked to the cooking hut.

"No, Sanda," the mentor said with a sigh. "It's the other way around. Only dragoncallers can talk to and understand dragons."

Their voices faded into the background. The man tending the

bread nodded to her as she approached. He picked up a thin piece the size of his hand and offered it to her. "Kirehe." Unlike her and the other warriors, he didn't have the spear tattoo spiraling down his right arm. He prepared food, he didn't hunt it. Instead, lines, triangles, and circles ringed his left arm.

"Maton." She stuffed a bite of bread into her mouth so she wouldn't have to say anything else. As ever, the bread had the right blend of salt and herbs to tease her taste buds.

The other cook passed her a plastic bowl full of soup with a steel spoon. Her mouth watered at the aroma. They'd used bones to make the broth, something they didn't always do.

Several hunters sat on wooden benches near the cooking hut, enjoying their meal together. Kirehe steered away from them to sit on the ground among a scattering of kukiris. She knew the people glanced at her and didn't care.

Compared to people chatter, Kirehe preferred dragon mating chatter. She ate with speed, a habit she'd developed while training with the mara dragons. Those ravenous beasts would only wait until their kill stopped running before diving in and devouring it. If she wanted anything, she had to get it and gobble it fast. They showed no mercy. Not even after accepting her.

She returned her empty bowl and spoon to the wash basin and left the camp. They didn't need anything from her and had nothing else for her. Skila didn't join her this time, which happened. Kirehe didn't own Skila, and Skila didn't own Kirehe.

With a full belly, she took her time returning home. Halfway there, she heard her mara pack announcing their arrival. She turned off the trail to meet them. The local pack roamed a specific area, avoiding the scent of the flowers woven among the plant wall for that purpose.

The five-member pack drank from a spring-fed pool where Kirehe sometimes bathed. Standing two-thirds of Kirehe's height, bipedal, and wingless, the maras had deeper, richer voices than the kukiris and bigger skulls with bigger brains. Muted black and brown feathers covered their forelimbs, tails, and a frill down their spines. Mottled green and brown scales covered the rest of their bodies.

"Kirehe," the lead mara, Lipa, said as she approached, raising her head with a tinge of challenge.

Years ago, before reaching adulthood, Kirehe had learned the danger of letting any mara challenge, even a minor one, go unanswered.

She leaped at Lipa. The rest of the pack scattered to the sides to watch. Lipa hissed and raised her forelimbs, baring her thick, sharp claws. Kirehe snapped an arm to the side, blocking one forelimb. Slipping into the gap she'd created, she used her momentum to crack her knee against Lipa's jaw.

No dominance battle ended without a decisive victory. While Lipa reeled from the blow, flailing her forelimbs with their wicked claws, Kirehe ducked and snatched the mara's foot. She heaved. She also slammed her shoulder into the mara's body. Lipa toppled with a squeal and a whine.

Kirehe stood over Lipa, bouncing on the balls of her feet with both fists ready to deliver more punishment.

"Ki-Alpha." Lipa stayed on the ground, limp and pliant.

For three long heartbeats, Kirehe loomed tall and imposing. Then she crouched and petted Lipa's head with a grin. "Silly Lipa," she cooed.

The pack crowded close, eager for Ki-Alpha head scritches. She laughed and hugged them all, delivering scratches behind their neck frills. Tiny, loose feathers drifted in the air from her efforts.

When the pack pile had lasted long enough, Kirehe shoved maras aside to stand. "Run!"

She launched into a dash across the uneven ground, her toes digging into the ground with every footfall. The maras caught up in moments. They ran together, the pack forming a circle around Kirehe. Their heads bobbed in time, their feet landed in time, and their breaths puffed in time. When they needed to hop over a fallen branch or gnarled root, they flowed in a sinuous wave.

They slipped around trees and sliced through vine curtains.

Kirehe matched the pack's speed, turning the jungle into a blur. Though maras could run faster when fleeing in a panic, she'd trained with these and others enough to find their preferred travel speed no great hardship.

"Risi," Lipa hissed.

Maras found risi dragons delicious, and little could stop them from hunting once they scented one.

Kirehe laughed. "Go hunt." She slid sideways to leave the pack to their pursuit and kept running. She knew this place.

As she reached the edge of a cliff, she bellowed, "Nihan! Catch me!" Without pausing, she leaped off a twenty-meter cliff with no pool at the base.

Below, her krata dragon companion launched from his vine-covered hole in the cliff face. She landed on his broad, green back as he snapped his wings open. Thick muscles worked under her body, propelling the krata upward despite her impact.

Unlike most other dragon types, kratas had no feathers. Scales in green, black, and brown covered their bodies from snout to tail tip. Their bone-white claws worked equally well to rend flesh and handle delicate tasks. A lack of spines or frills, along with their massive size, made the kratas usable as mounts, and all the dragoncallers took advantage of that.

Kirehe hugged Nihan's neck, happy to see her best friend. Ten years before, an elder dragoncaller had introduced them as child and hatchling. She'd trained with him ever since. Many days, she'd snuck out of the hapa cave to spend an afternoon gliding through the jungle canopy.

Nihan purred in greeting, making his neck rumble under her body. Wind fluttered Kirehe's short, dark hair behind her. They swooped through trees, staying under the canopy. Nihan found a pool at the base of a waterfall and backwinged to land. Kirehe jumped off his back and dove into the cool, crisp water. Nihan plunged in next.

At the bottom of the pool, Kirehe swam through a wide passage and surfaced in a circular grotto. Nihan's head broke the surface as she reached the edge of the pool. Two years ago, she'd discovered this treasure trove by accident.

Ferns and vines grew from every crack in glittering black rock. Tiny white and pink flowers studded the vines. Water dribbled down the walls from the gaps between roots of a thick tree big enough to grow over the hole above. Flecks of metal in the rock walls caught and reflected tiny rays of sunshine. Along the rocky, silt-covered shelf lining the pool, small shrubs grew fat, juicy fruit the size of Kirehe's head. She climbed out of the water and checked the plants growing in the collected silt for the ripest fruit.

Nihan flapped his wings underwater, causing the pool to slosh and surge over the edge. "Treat!"

Grinning, Kirehe picked a fruit. She hefted the oblong weight and tossed it at Nihan's face. He snapped it out of the air. The entire fruit fit inside his jaws. He crunched the thick shell and chewed it into small pieces before swallowing. Sweet, fresh nectar filled the air, making Kirehe want some of the fruit.

She picked another one. "Share," she said, then she tossed it.

He caught the second and held up his claws. Powerful jaws broke the fruit. One half stayed in his mouth. The other fell into his claws, and he offered it to Kirehe.

Sitting on the edge of the pool, Kirehe took the fruit and scooped the red flesh with her fingers. She preferred not to eat the shiny black seeds inside and spat them to the side to make more of the plants in the sandy soil. They tasted bitter and crunched funny anyway.

While she ate, Nihan watched her, his slitted green eyes focused on the fruit in her hands. She scooped a few handfuls and devoured them, then tossed the rest to Nihan. The kukiris ate only insects, the maras ate only game meat, and the kratas ate whatever suffered the misfortune of falling into their mouths.

"Time to work," Kirehe said. She jumped into the water, letting it wash the sticky sweetness from her hands and face. Instead of swimming on her own, she hugged Nihan's neck and let him pull her back to the first pool.

Nihan climbed out of the water and let Kirehe situate herself again before launching into a lope across the jungle floor. He slowed to a stop as they reached the dragonline.

Dull metal stakes in the ground, each unassuming and easy to miss, marked the line. The dragoncallers had placed them according to where they and the kratas could hear the whine of the enemy machines. The first fifty meters beyond the line existed as a safety margin, though no one had ever told anyone else among the Iwa. If they knew, they'd insist upon foraging past the spikes.

At the starts of the long-day and the short-day seasons, the dragoncallers checked and moved and stakes as necessary. The enemy didn't stay still, so neither did they. They typically moved the line no more than a few meters in one direction or the other, though. Irondoom served as the enemy's base, and they only strayed so far from it to find their sacrifices.

Stopped at the spike line, Nihan peered into enemy territory. Kirehe squinted to see what had caught his attention.

Breezes shifted vines and leaves. Bright colors and inane chatter announced a flock of kukiris. Rain dripped through the canopy, pattering on the plants. Nothing seemed amiss to her.

"What's wrong?"

"Not sure." Nihan's eyes narrowed in his version of a frown.

Kirehe trusted his instincts. He'd never steered her wrong. "Fly. Check from above."

Nihan turned his back on the spikes and loped a few paces. He leaped at a tree, bouncing off its trunk a meter above the ground and startling a flock of kukiris into the air. The next tree, he hit two meters up, and it showered them with water and loose leaves. After the third tree, he had enough height and speed to snap open his wings and gain altitude on his own.

He punched through the canopy, surprising Kirehe. The flying machines ruled above. Though a krata could potentially down one, it always came at the cost of injuries and with the risk of death. Worse, the enemy retaliated for any loss with overwhelming force, even those caused by unbonded kratas.

They stayed above the trees long enough scan the horizon. Green, orange, and red dominated the jungle stretching in every direction. In the distance, Kirehe saw the enormous buildings of Irondoom squatting in a swath of treeless land. Sunshine reflected off dark panels set in the walls. The complex covered territory once held by an Iwan hapa destroyed when the enemy first arrived.

At the apex of his flight, Nihan rolled and dove to return to the safety of the jungle. Kirehe hadn't seen any machines or other concerns. They flew along the dragonline, weaving between trees and around vinefalls.

With nothing to investigate, Kirehe saw no reason to focus on one spot. "Patrol," she whistled to Nihan. He nodded.

As they continued, Kirehe spotted a hunting party with their spears and hide shields. Unlike the dragoncallers, who preferred to run barefoot, the hunters wore boots made of leather and bark to protect their feet. They covered their legs and arms, and wore stiff chest pieces designed to protect their torsos from the glancing blows of their prey's horns, claws, spikes, or frills.

She recognized the mentors with their young hunters, heading for the dragonline. Good. New hunters needed to learn how to find it. If they made the spikes more obvious, the enemy might discover the line and abuse that knowledge to capture unaware hunters or gatherers.

"Cross the line," she told Nihan.

His body turned, and he passed the dragonline to fly inside the buffer zone. Another krata called a greeting. Nihan answered. As they passed in midair, Kirehe waved to the dragoncaller riding the second krata, and Duris returned it.

Not long after, Nihan reached the edge of the territory they patrolled. He flipped and rolled to turn around. They passed Duris and his krata again, as they did at least a few times every day. On the other end of their patrol zone, they saw Taniya and her krata a few times a day.

They flew through sudden rain showers, flocks of kukiris, and patches of bright sunshine, crossing the territory multiple times. As long as hunters or gatherers roamed outside the camps, the dragoncallers patrolled. They often stayed out all day.

Halfway through their fourth full sweep of their patrol zone, Nihan's head snapped to the side. He rolled and turned. Another wingbeat later, Kirehe heard screaming. One more wingbeat brought them close enough for her to hear machine whirr.

"Faster," Kirehe urged Nihan. They needed to save whoever had done something stupid.

CHAPTER 3

MADISON

The white-walled room, lit with diffuse white lights and bearing no decoration or wall consoles, held a single chair. No one sat in the simple, utilitarian seat when a hevit shoved Madison to her knees in front of it. Behind her, more hevits knocked the rest of the crew to the floor. They'd fetched everyone who'd stayed behind on the ship and brought them too. Only she and Jaco had avoided the indignity of gags and bound wrists.

Behind the chair, a panel slid open in the wall to reveal a white corridor full of figures in masks. They wore thick, heavy robes in maroon and black edged with gold. Voluminous folds of velvety fabric swept the floor and obscured their feet. The masks over their faces, white with maroon lines, had no holes for sight or speech, yet the figures glided into the room in two lines with matched precision. The first eight carried sleek black rifles with glowing maroon power cells in long-fingered, gloved hands.

Fans kicked on as the masked figures entered the room, blowing chilled air from the rear door. Madison shivered, not only from the cold. As the masked rifle-bearers reached her, the hevits stepped to the walls in an odd pattern, skipping spaces for no apparent reason. They stopped, their feathers shimmered, and they disappeared.

As she turned her head, Madison caught a strange blur in her periphery and realized they'd left the empty spaces because other hevits already occupied them. How many hevits had they passed on their way to and from Engineering without noticing? Maybe fifty, maybe none—she had no way to know. Trying this again would take thinking about how to find the hevits.

Not that anyone had ever figured it out before. Hevits hadn't become the Lakhan Oligarchy's feared troopers for no reason.

Of course, she'd figured out the layout of Oligarchy ships when no one else had. If anyone could handle the challenge, she could. Assuming she could escape whatever happened next. The cold air didn't give her much hope to work with.

Another ten masked figures followed the rifle-bearers. They arrayed themselves in two perfect arcs around the chair, facing Madison and her crew.

The temperature continued to plunge, numbing the tip of Madison's nose and her fingertips. Her breath puffed in tiny clouds. When she couldn't keep her teeth from chattering anymore, another figure stepped through the rear door.

Thick with muscle and standing over two meters tall, the man approached the chair and sat with his back straight. Both four-fingered hands gripped the armrests. He wore a simple, utilitarian shirt and pants befitting a member of an organized military and bearing no medals or other insignias. Blue undertones to his gray flesh gave him the appearance of a corpse. Thick, white whiskers hung from a short muzzle reminiscent of a dog. His dark eyes scanned the group.

One hevit flickered forward, knelt in front of him, and dropped something in his hand. It returned to its position without a word.

The creature who could only be a genuine lakhan lifted Madison's cybereye and regarded it. "This has been an interesting day." Smooth and rich, his deep voice slithered through the room and into Madison's ears. "A disabled Stardrifter ship at a known jump point at the exact moment a mithrite shipment came through was too good to be true. As soon as we recovered one of your empty escape pods, I realized you had an unexpected motive."

Knowing the hevits could conceal themselves to near invisibility told Madison they'd allowed her to see them. Each one they'd encountered had played a game with them. The crew hadn't taken more than a few steps onto the ship unobserved, if they'd taken any at all.

She should've waited until she saw the flagship. Oolaang would've undone his fake sabotage fast enough to jump away. They could've found a less dangerous ship to board.

"I'm pleased to make your acquaintance, Madison Wayward, niece of the infamous Captain Christopher Wayward. Your boldness has provided entertainment for a short time."

Her cybereye glinted in the light as the lakhan turned it over in his fingers.

"And you are?" Madison asked.

Jaco, kneeling to her left, made a soft noise to express his dismay at her question.

The lakhan tore his attention from the eye to smile at her with a thin veneer of politeness over menace. "Subjugator Cradok."

Madison shrugged. "Never heard of you." She didn't see a way out, so she had no reason to scrape and bow to this tyrant. Without looking, she knew Jaco grimaced at her.

Cradok laughed as if he found that genuinely funny. "Of course not. You Stardrifters are too pathetic and petty to know anything above your station."

"You're right. I don't pay much attention to third-rate bullies who put on grandiose productions to prove how great they are."

"Maddie," Jaco whispered. "Stop it."

Madison never saw the blow coming from her left side. She fell to the floor seeing stars. Jaco rushed forward and tried to shield her from further blows. He took a rifle blow to the gut for it and slumped with a groan. Madison blinked as her one eye refocused and the pain in her face faded to a dull ache.

Cradok clapped three times. The sharp cracks echoed off the walls and ceiling. "My loyal priests don't appreciate your style of bravado."

Calling them priests told Madison the masked people were pharedimi. Their kind served the lakhans as fanatical worshipers. She wobbled to her feet. "Everyone's a critic."

No one had bothered to bind her hands. If she timed it right, she could swipe a pharedim rifle... And get herself and her crew killed because the armed pharedimi and hevits would outnumber her a lot to one.

"Indeed."

"Subjugator, sir," Jaco said as he sat up. "We don't mean you any offense. This is all just a big misunderstanding."

Madison stifled a roll of her eyes. Her eye. She only had one.

"I'm sure it is." Cradok closed his fingers around the cybereye and stood. "That changes nothing. What did you plan to do in Engineering? Disable the engines?" He clasped his hands behind his back and paced forward to stop with his chest mere centimeters from Madison's face.

Refusing to flinch or answer, Madison stared straight ahead. His uniform fit him well, revealing the smooth sculpting of his chest.

"Your courage is predictable, Wayward." He flicked his gaze over the group and pointed to someone behind her. "Kill that one."

Madison whirled. She only needed to see Dani's face to know he'd pointed at her. Dani, with her amazing cheekbones and enchanting eyes, didn't deserve to die any more than anyone else present. "No. Wait." Raising her hands, Madison backed toward Dani. "She doesn't know anything."

"That's what makes her expendable." Cradok flicked his hand at Dani.

Dani whimpered as she shuffled to Madison, unable to speak through her gag. She clutched Madison's pants with her bound hands.

"I was just trying to find it," Madison blurted. With luck, Cradok would believe her and the crew would know she lied. Everyone thinking she'd led them to their doom for no reason... She didn't want that. "I didn't have a plan after that, other than escaping."

Cradok laughed, this time cold and cruel. "As I said, predictable."

Jaco held up his hands. "We'll cooperate."

"Yes, you will."

A hevit shimmered beside Madison and kicked the back of her knee. Before she hit the floor, the hevit wrapped an arm around Dani's neck and cranked her head with a wet crack. Dani fell. When she landed, her dead eyes stared at Madison in shock.

"Why did you do that?" Madison scrambled to her feet, too stunned to think clearly. One moment, Dani had held onto her legs in fear, and the next, she lay dead on the floor. Madison's parents had died out of her sight. She hadn't seen the spark of life leave their eyes. Crew members had lost their lives a few times over the years, but she'd never watched it happen.

"Know this, Wayward." Cradok dropped the cybereye. It bounced once. Without looking, he caught it under his boot before it could roll away. "You have no power here. Your wishes make no difference. I decide whether you live or die." He lifted his foot and slammed his heel onto the eye with a sharp, swift snap. The eye, not designed to withstand such trauma, crunched against the floor.

"This is my ship, and this is my sector. You have trespassed in both." Cradok ground his heel against the eye, crushing it beyond any hope of repair. "For this crime, and others committed prior to this event, I sentence you, Madison Wayward, to a spectacular and entertaining death before an audience. Captain Wayward's niece, on display as animals rip you apart and devour your entrails, is precisely the kind of news I wish to see splashed across the sector. And, for that matter, the galaxy."

Madison blinked. Though she'd asked everyone to accept the possibility they might die, she hadn't believed it would happen. The mission had seemed designed to succeed. Nothing should've stood in their way.

She couldn't breathe.

"The rest of you will join her." Cradok turned his back and waved a hand to dismiss them as no longer worthy of his time. As he headed for the rear door, he added, "There will, however, be only one order for execution. Whether the rest of you live as slaves or die with her makes no difference to me."

Madison's feet moved. She threw a punch at Cradok's back. He whirled faster than she could track and struck her chest with his open palm. Her body flew backward and she landed in a heap, wheezing for breath. Jaco rushed to her and held her down.

"Don't make things worse," he said.

Tears slid down her cheeks.

He strode away. The unarmed pharedimi filed out behind him. Eight rifles pointed at Madison and her crew.

In a daze, Madison let Jaco help her to her feet. The armed pharedimi hustled them past Dani's body and out of the room.

"She has to be wrapped," Madison's stupid mouth blurted. "Before you space a body, it has to be wrapped."

The guard snorted, the sound not muffled by its mask. "Human bodies are dumped into the garbage." Its voice held a light, lyrical quality, making it melodious and pleasant.

Before she could do anything, Jaco seized her arm. "Stop talking. For once in your life, Maddie, shut up."

"You shut up!" She swung at him.

Guards hit them both with rifles. Madison stumbled and lost her footing.

"You can walk, or you can be carried," a guard said. "Make your choice."

Her hands stinging, her face, chest, and back throbbing, and her heart broken for Dani, Madison staggered to her feet. She stumbled into the wall. One of the guards wrapped a gloved hand around her neck and held her upright. They marched her and the crew to an empty room and shoved everyone inside it.

Like every other part of the ship, it had white walls. Madison hit one of them and slid to the floor. She stared at nothing. The moment of Dani's death replayed in her head. Vaguely, she noted Jaco helping

Oolaang remove his bindings and gag. The two of them helped another two. When everyone finished, they made a small pile of gags and bindings in the center of the room.

"Maddie?" Jaco knelt in front of her.

"I can't believe she's gone," Shmar said. "Just like that." He snapped his fingers.

The crew muttered and murmured. Madison ignored them because she couldn't face them.

Jaco touched her knee. "We're alone. We could try to escape."

She laughed. In a flash, it turned to crying. To her own ears, she sounded hysterical. Jaco gathered her into his arms and held her. The rest of the crew huddled in clusters and offered comfort to each other.

When she'd cried herself empty and hollow, she whispered, "We're all going to die." Her mind wouldn't stop seeing Dani's lifeless stare.

Jaco squeezed her and said nothing.

Oolaang stood and shuffled to them. They'd allowed him the small kindness of keeping the goggles that protected his sensitive eyes from bright light, which he still wore. He tucked a hand down the front of his pants. Madison had no idea why he'd do that until he revealed a slim power drill the size of her finger.

She blinked. "You hid a drill in your pants?"

He shrugged. "I had a full tool kit."

"When did you have time to do that?" Jaco asked. Then he held up a hand and shook his head. "No, never mind. It doesn't matter. Try the back wall. There are probably troopers flanking the door."

Madison sat up and nodded her agreement. They could escape. She knew enough about the ship's layout to get them back to Engineering. There, they could complete the mission. Dani wouldn't have died for nothing. "We'll avenge her," she murmured.

Bracing the drill with two hands and himself with his other two, Oolaang pressed the bit against the back wall and activated the drill. Its soft whirring turned to high-pitched squealing. Oolaang jumped and whirled to face the door, hiding the drill behind his back.

Madison cringed and also watched the door.

Nothing happened. No one had heard it.

"Try it in short bursts," Madison said. "So we don't all go deaf, and in case they hear a sustained screech."

Nodding, Oolaang braced again. He drilled through the wall in two-second bursts. Every five bursts, he moved the drill in a circle big enough for his hand. The crew crowded around him, Madison among them. Not only did she want to watch his progress, she also wanted to do her part to muffle the sound and protect him if they heard anything outside.

Ten minutes later, he pried a metal circle off the wall. Thick, solid foam filled the interior. Oolaang used the drill bit to scrape the foam. Dust drifted to the floor.

Hope swelling inside the emptiness of her chest, Madison tried not to watch. No one would ignore that noise on the outer wall. Besides, creating a hole big enough for the smallest of them would take forever.

"I found wires," Oolaang whispered. His hands trembled. "I have no way to know what they're for."

Madison didn't care. Destroying anything on the ship improved their chances of escape. Except life support, of course, but she doubted they ran wires for that through a room like this. "Cut them. All of them."

"Wait," Shmar said. He poked Madison's shoulder. "Blindly following your lead got Dani killed."

"Knock it off," Jaco snapped. "All of us, Dani included, knew this might be a suicide mission."

With Jaco at her back, Madison stood up straighter. "If you want to blame someone for Dani, blame Cradok."

"Then this wouldn't have pokken happened if we hadn't tried to board a pokken flagship!"

Madison sighed and hung her head. "I made a mistake, okay? I didn't think of every single tiny little detail. Now Dani's dead." Raising her head, she met Shmar's angry gaze with defiance. "We won't let her death mean nothing. This is something we can try. It's something we can do.

The alternative is sitting and waiting, and I don't want to do that." She held up a hand, offering it to him. "Are you going to help or get in the way?"

His jaw worked while he chewed her words. Tension trembled through the crew. After a deliberation long enough to make her worry, he slapped his hand into hers. Everyone relaxed enough to feel it in the air. "Fine. Let's try this. But other people get to have ideas."

"I hope other people do have some." She squeezed his hand, then nodded to Oolaang.

The drill whirred. More dust flew. A wire snapped. Nothing happened. Another wire snapped. All the lights in the room died.

In the dark, with the crew crowded together, Madison felt supported, cared for, part of a community. Waiting in the compartment earlier should've given her this feeling, but it hadn't. The anticipation had blocked it.

"There are two more wires," Oolaang said.

"Don't stop now." Madison patted a shoulder lower than hers, which she expected could only belong to Oolaang. Everyone else was taller than her. "One might open the door."

"Maybe we should move to the door, then?" Jaco asked.

"Yes, good idea. You stay with Oolaang." Madison patted another shoulder with no idea who it belonged to. "Everyone else, move to the door. We'll flank it."

The group shuffled to the door together. Madison sent Jaco to the opposite side as her and had everyone count off to keep the numbers even.

"Wire number three," Oolaang said. "There's one more."

They waited.

Nothing happened.

"And wire number four."

The door slid open. Light poured inside the room. Oolaang and his guardian skittered to the side. Madison squinted her one eye, trying to see if any hevits came through. Cradok hadn't struck her as the kind of person who would trust a lock when he had plenty of guards on hand.

"Should we go?" someone whispered.

The ship shuddered and Madison's stomach churned. She covered her mouth to stifle a groan and prevent anything from coming up. Stardrifter FTL travel caused much less nausea, maybe because they had much smaller ships.

"How fast is their FTL?" someone else whispered.

"I guess we'll find out," Madison muttered.

This waiting for nothing grated on her nerves. She lurched through the doorway. When no one attacked her, she waved for everyone to follow. They'd come from the left, she remembered. She ran to the right.

Dashing through the ship this time, Madison didn't stop at corners to peer around them. They needed speed, not stealth. Besides, she couldn't see around the corners without her cybereye.

When she turned the last corner and saw the red door, she thought she might've counted the intersections wrong, because it seemed closer than it should have. Then she ran into a wall with a disturbingly realistic projection of the red door and fell to the floor. The rest of the crew stopped behind her. Barely visible hevits beat and tossed them.

Cradok's laughter echoed off the walls. "I could've just knocked all of you out for the duration of the travel, but I thought I might let you feel hope one more time so I could crush it. This has been highly entertaining, Madison Wayward and company. I'll miss you when you're gone. But not that much."

An unseen force hit Madison's jaw, and she heard nothing else.

CHAPTER 4

KIREHE

Nihan aimed for Irondoom. The jungle flashed past as he swooped between the trees. Kirehe kept an eye out for flying machines. The initial scream had faded fast, and no new ones offered them direction.

Humming, too high and soft for regular humans to hear, announced distant flying machines. Whoever had screamed hadn't attracted one. Yet.

"Help!" Pain pinched a young man's voice. "Is anyone out there? Sanda's hurt and I'm stuck!"

Homing in on the plaintive wails, Nihan turned in a wide arc. They needed to rescue the boy and get him to shut up before the enemy heard him. As if in defiance of Kirehe's wishes, the boy continued to scream for help, his cries growing louder each time.

Kirehe drew her machete and sliced vines they flew past, expecting to need makeshift ropes.

As Nihan slowed to land, he snapped his head toward Irondoom. Kirehe heard it too. Machine hum screamed close.

The boy had attracted a flying machine.

"Shut up!" Kirehe called. She tossed her collected vines at the cleft, hoping at least one would fall into their grasp. "Stay quiet and small or they'll find you! We'll come back. Nihan, distract."

Nihan pumped his wings for speed and altitude. Despite the danger, he headed toward the machine hum. Kirehe clung to his back as low as possible with her machete ready.

"Don't fight. Evade. Take it to the egg pools." The krata breeding ground always had at least a few adult dragons, either sitting on eggs or watching hatchlings. Kirehe knew that, Nihan knew that, and the enemy knew that. Once the enemy realized their destination, they'd break off and return to base.

The angular flying machine stood out against the foliage with its white metal wings and cockpit. Green trim suggested an effort at blending that no one had thought through. From wingtip to wingtip, the machine matched Nihan in size, and it had similar bulk as his body without the head, neck, and tail.

Most importantly, the flyer boasted four laser cannons. Two could fire forward, and two could fire backward. Those lasers didn't burn flesh. Instead, they delivered a stunning blow.

Dead bodies didn't make good sacrifices, after all. Broken bodies, on the other hand, such as those who'd fallen from the back of a dragon, probably worked fine. Duris had once suggested they might want injured sacrifices because dark gods would enjoy pain.

As soon as they saw the flyer, Nihan rolled and flipped to change direction. Laser bolts punched through the jungle. Nihan swerved and wove through trees, making himself a difficult target. More bolts missed by a meter or more as Nihan varied his flapping rhythm.

Kirehe watched to the sides. She took too long to realize the flyer herded them toward Irondoom. Another flyer screamed toward them from the left.

"Go up!"

Nihan pulled up. They shot through the canopy. A third flyer waited too close for them to evade. Snapping in his wings, Nihan shoved his claws forward.

"No!" Kirehe shouted. They didn't want to attack.

They slammed into the flyer's underside. Dragon, rider, and

machine flipped over and sailed in an arc.

Attacking with his jaws, Nihan ripped pieces off the flyer.

"Nihan stop! Evade, not kill!" Horrified, Kirehe imagined more flyers sweeping into the village, destroying everything and killing everyone. If they kept the pilot alive, maybe the enemy wouldn't retaliate.

Her krata tore his claws free, unleashing sparks. Loose parts fell with the disabled flyer.

She pointed at the falling machine. "Catch it!"

"What?" Nihan flapped to maintain his altitude.

"Save the man inside!" Kirehe screamed.

Behind them, the other two flyers emerged from the canopy. Nihan surged downward, chasing the disabled flyer as it plummeted through the trees. Branches cracked under its weight. Laser bolts zapped over Kirehe's head.

Nihan landed on the falling flyer, slamming his claws into its underside, and strained to slow its descent. The flyer's canopy cracked against a large rock. Kirehe heard the machine hum behind them and decided they couldn't afford to sacrifice themselves for the pilot's life.

"Drop it and turn around."

The dragon released the flyer and bolted upward. Lasers blasted, hitting the flyer instead of Nihan. He twisted and faced the two flyers.

Kirehe sensed his uncertainty. "Under."

He dropped to skim the ground as low as he could without his wings slapping the ground. They sliced through vine curtains and startled smaller dragons. Bright colors from kukiris and shorn flowers whirled around them.

Lasers scored the ground, creeping closer with every shot. Nihan pulled in one wing and rolled to use the other for turning. He swept around a tree to turn the other direction. They flipped and twisted.

The flyers swept in wide arcs, unable to turn fast enough to intercept Nihan's acrobatics.

Through the mad flight, Kirehe tried to reorient. She watched for landmarks. Finally, she spotted the cleft with the injured hunter. "We're going the wrong way." With her foot, she nudged to tell him the direction to go.

He swished left. Lasers blasted, forcing him right. He swerved. They sped.

The stupid flyers refused to crash into the trees or each other while keeping up with Nihan. Kirehe drew her machete and tried slashing vines as they slipped through them. Twisting to check her handiwork, she saw they caught on the flyers, but caused no harm and didn't block their dark cockpits

"Egg pools," she reminded Nihan.

He swerved between laser blasts. One bolt slammed into Kirehe's machete and reflected, missing Nihan's wing by centimeters. The steel vibrated. Kirehe lost feeling in her right hand. She dropped the blade and hoped it didn't hit Sanda or the other boy. Even if they had ignored their mentor's warnings and brought enemy flyers.

Stupid boys. They hadn't deserved to leave the cave. When she returned, she intended to give the hunt leader some choice words about those boys. They had yet to earn the dignity of being called men.

She cradled her hand close to her chest and gripped Nihan tighter with her knees. At least her blade had prevented a laser bolt from hitting Nihan. According to other dragoncallers, the kratas could take three or four hits without falling out of the sky. A rider, on the other hand, could take only one.

They played a frustrating game. Nihan aimed for the egg pools. The flyers shot their lasers and forced Nihan to turn away. He wove through trees. They stayed close enough to shoot by taking the easiest path through the jungle.

Stalemate.

Constant acrobatic flying without snacks wore on Nihan. Kirehe could feel his flanks heaving. He let a wingtip crack against a tree too thin to cause damage. If they didn't do something unexpected soon, he'd slow. The flyers would win.

They had to attack. No matter what might happen to the hapa

tomorrow, they had to attack today.

"Time to fight."

"Yes," Nihan growled.

"That one." She tapped her left foot to tell him which flyer to pursue.

He dipped a wing and swung around a tree to the left. Nihan chose to fly directly at the flyer as it flew directly at him. Kirehe stayed low, cursing the loss of her only weapon.

The lasers stopped firing. Checking behind them, Kirehe saw the other flyer giving chase. She'd hoped the two pilots would fire at each other. But no, they proved too smart for that.

Nihan surged upward. The pilots failed to crash their ships. For the moment, though, they had only one pursuer.

The flyers needed a wide arc to turn.

This moment wouldn't last long. Kirehe patted Nihan's back. "Dive to hit!"

Nihan flared his wings, catching enough wind to slow. Then his wings snapped shut and his body rippled downward as if they careened down a steep hill. Claws brandished, he stomped onto the flyer that had failed to slow in time to avoid him.

Dragon, rider, and flyer plummeted. Nihan flared his wings and pumped for altitude. Metal screeched and groaned. His claws tore the cockpit in half, leaving him in the air with the crushed top.

As the flyer crushed trees and smashed against rocks, the pilot shot upward. Fiery jets propelled a seat carrying a bipedal humanoid in the helmet and flight suit. Nihan threw the cockpit canopy at them.

Kirehe wouldn't have done that. She didn't begrudge him the gesture, though.

Canopy and pilot collided. Together, they slammed into a thick tree, with the pilot hitting head first. All of it fell to the ground with a crunch.

"Good job." Kirehe kissed his neck. "Keep moving. One more."

Lasers strafed. Nihan let himself drop. Bolts sizzled past Kirehe and missed Nihan's wings by a hair.

"Tired," Nihan whimpered. He flapped to gain speed.

"I know. Last one. Then we eat." Kirehe needed more than food if the numbness in her hand didn't wear off soon. She'd have to visit TOS Cave to see the healer. His concoctions chased away pain in minutes. They tasted as exciting as boiled rocks. For numbness, he might have to work at a cure, but she trusted he could find one.

If only the healer lived somewhere other than surrounded by obnoxious children with stupid questions, overprotective caretakers, and grumpy elders.

Nihan flapped into a thick patch of vines and leaves. He landed on a wide branch among the foliage and made himself as compact as he could.

Through the leaves and vines, they watched the flyer zoom past. It punched through the canopy and disappeared. They sat in silence broken only by Nihan's heaving breaths.

With Nihan's first muscle twitch, Kirehe patted his back. "Stay still. Wait."

He'd done enough. Despite her injury, she could give him a chance to recover.

The flyer descended in a slow arc, bringing its irritating hum. When it passed beneath them, Kirehe jumped.

"Follow!"

She landed with both feet to the right side of the cockpit. The flyer wobbled. Dropping into a crouch, she scrambled for a handhold. Her fingers found a groove. As the flyer gained speed and angled upward, she leaned low and kicked at the side of the cockpit.

They screamed through the canopy to the clear space above. The flyer leveled out and pointed toward Irondoom.

Whether Kirehe's efforts caused it or not, the cockpit canopy puffed, hissed, and whirred open. The pilot pointed a pistol at her. Kirehe saw no reason to expect the flyer to make sudden movements. She let go of her handhold to chop at the pistol. The weapon flipped out of the pilot's hand and skittered off the edge of the wing.

The pilot squeaked, the sound muffled by their helmet.

Kirehe grabbed the edge of the cockpit and swung her leg. She snapped her knee. Her heel connected with the pilot's helmet. The pilot's head bounced against the cockpit's padding. Seizing the pilot's distraction, Kirehe slammed her heel through the flyer's control panel.

Again, the pilot made a muffled noise, this time of shock. Kirehe yanked out her foot and spun to drive her knee into the pilot's chest. The pilot sagged in their harness. At the same time, the flyer's nose dipped.

"Nihan! Catch me!" Kirehe ran and jumped off the wing.

Nihan exploded from the canopy in a flurry of leaves. She hit his back and clamped her knees around him. He turned aside from the too-close walls of Irondoom.

In the distance, Kirehe noticed a plume of smoke roiling through the trees. Fire rarely posed a serious danger in the jungle, but she needed to make sure none of their crashes caused too much damage.

"Check the smoke." She patted Nihan's neck to get him to turn. "Then food."

"Food first."

"Fire first."

Nihan grumbled in a low, brooding whistle.

Kirehe grinned and hugged his neck as much as she could with one arm still limp. "We'll hunt near the fire."

He nodded and ducked under the trees. They flew slower, with lazy flaps of his wings and much more gliding.

They discovered the smoke where the first flyer had crashed. As Nihan circled it, Kirehe heard a zap, then Nihan shuddered. He clutched his chest. A laser blast from the ground seared a hole through his wing.

"Turn!" Kirehe leaned to try to help him compensate for the injury.

He wobbled and veered to the side.

Another blast hit Nihan's neck and Kirehe's hand. This time, Kirehe saw the pilot of the first craft, helmet off, holding a pistol and firing at them. The pilot had short, orangey hair with subtle stripes of a lighter orange.

Nihan's body dipped. His eyelids drooped.

Though it pained her to do it, Kirehe leaped from his back to a nearby tree. She batted numb hands at the trunk and kicked, trying to wrap her legs around a branch.

Branches snapped under Nihan's weight as he fell.

Kirehe slid down the trunk. Rough bark scraped the exposed flesh of her arms and calves. Her body hit the ground. The earth trembled with the nearby impact of Nihan's bulk.

Scrambling to her feet, Kirehe knew what she had to do. She didn't need her hands to kill that pilot. Once their body lay broken and bleeding on the ground, she could tend to the bright light of her life.

As she tumbled over a rotting log, her right hand woke from numbness with burning agony. Unable to contain the surprise and pain, Kirehe screamed.

Kukiris scattered, disturbed by the noise.

Behind her, someone said something in a language she didn't understand. Intense fire slammed into her back. Kirehe fell over the log to land on the other side in a gasping heap of whimpering misery.

The speaker laughed.

Numbness spread across Kirehe's body as soft footfalls approached. The pilot leaned over the log with a smirk twisting their heart-shaped face. They had slitted eyes like dragons and pale blue skin with no brown undertones.

She would've liked for the log to collapse under the pilot's weight, but it didn't. Kirehe wrenched her foot into the air, trying to connect with the pilot's smug, arrogant eyes, but they moved.

The pilot sneered at her and spoke in their harsh language. Kirehe understood enough. They gloated over her.

"We killed your machines," Kirehe snarled.

Pointing their pistol at Kirehe's face, the pilot blew her a kiss. The blaster fired, and Kirehe couldn't avoid it.

CHAPTER 5

MADISON

Madison woke to damp, crushing heat in bright, glaring light as her body slid down a smooth ramp in the midst of other bodies. She cringed and blinked, her thoughts sluggish. Pain registered in her face, her back, and her chest. Her body landed among others in a pile on uneven, dark rock.

Water blasted from above with enough force to shove everyone downward. People groaned. Madison tried and failed to remember anything. The water tasted bitter. She turned to avoid letting more into her mouth.

"Wake up!" a harsh voice barked.

"Am I dead?" Jaco mumbled.

Jaco. The crew. Madison lifted her head and saw everyone. Except Dani. They'd never see Dani again. Thanks to Cradok. Someday, she'd put her boot on his neck and kill him in the face. For the moment, she needed to gather her wits and figure out their situation.

The water shut off. Drops splatted on Madison's neck. Her drenched coat weighed an extra fifty kilograms.

Boots clacked toward her. "Welcome to the Rikor Six Luxury Resort."

"Thank goodness," Madison said as she wobbled to her hands and knees. The speaker approached from her blind side, but she thought she recognized the melodious tones of a pharedim. Their situation had, therefore, not improved. "I need a vacation."

Force slammed into her gut. She saw the pharedim's boot as she slumped to her side again. His unmasked face unnerved her for some reason she couldn't identify. He had two wide, green eyes, a small, thin nose on a smooth, round face with full, upturned lips, and two ears tapering to sharp yet delicate points. Light blonde hair, parted in the middle of his head, hung in thin, perfect braids.

Everything about him and his dusky pink skin seemed attractive to the point of pretty, including his wiry physique, yet she felt nothing but uncomfortable looking at him. She noticed another pharedim with similar features standing in shadows behind him, illuminated from the front by a soft, blue glow. Both wore the same green and gold uniform with black flourishes.

Two of them against twelve of Captain Wayward's best seemed like good odds.

If she had any idea how to escape. Which she didn't. She couldn't even tell the size of the room or what made the light.

"You will enjoy the accommodations until you die. There are many ways to die here. Some are swifter than others. To extend your life as much as possible, do as you're told, speak only when spoken to, and do not resist."

He paused and gestured to the man in the shadows. "Overseer Neilan is your lord and ruler for the rest of your lives, however short that may be."

Overseer Neilan remained in the shadows. He waved for the speaker to continue.

The speaker clapped his hands twice. More pharedimi strode out of the shadows, each wearing that same green and gold uniform. If they bore rank insignias or other forms of identification, Madison couldn't interpret them. Yet.

One pharedim with striking violet eyes and brown corkscrew curls grabbed Madison's coat and hauled her to her feet. "Move, human."

Madison stumbled in the pharedim's wake.

"Ilai." Overseer Neilan's deep voice rumbled in Madison's chest. "That one doesn't need testing. Put her straight into the execution pit."

"Yes, Overseer." The pharedim with a grip on Madison nodded and changed direction.

Madison met Jaco's gaze. He still seemed groggy. The whole crew needed another ten minutes to wake up. Cradok must've had them drugged.

"What kind of testing?" she asked.

Ilai backhanded Madison across her blind side. "Mouth shut."

Reeling from the blow, Madison rubbed her cheek. "Wait, execu—"

This time, Ilai whirled and drove her knee into Madison's belly. "Be silent or you'll be gagged."

Madison doubled over and threw up bile. Ilai wrapped a hand around Madison's ponytail and kept moving. She coughed and sputtered, struggling to keep her feet and not lose chunks of scalp.

She rubbed her stomach, expecting a fresh bruise there. "Do I die in the pit?"

Ilai growled in frustration and wrenched Madison's ponytail. "Will nothing shut you up?"

Nearby, Jaco laughed, the sound weak and hollow. Someone else sniggered.

Madison spat bile. To her surprise, it had no blood. Her guts hurt. Her everything hurt. "An answer might do the trick."

"No," Overseer Neilan said.

The single word stopped Ilai from hitting Madison again, though she stood ready to deliver a fresh blow.

Overseer Neilan stepped into the light. Like the others of his kind, he was beautiful yet unnerving, with soft teal eyes and short, silky hair. "No one dies on purpose in the execution pit." He approached with grace and gravitas.

The caveat of "on purpose" didn't reassure Madison. Especially not with the possibility of internal injuries.

He stopped in front of her and bent to meet her gaze, his expression inscrutable. "Your death, Madison Wayward, will be spectacular. Our spectacles are planned to the most minute detail, and that takes time. You'll have weeks, perhaps even months, to contemplate your impending end."

Had he delivered this with cool, dispassionate detachment, Madison thought she could've spat some wisecrack into his face. The fervent gleam in his eyes, though, the hint of excitement over the grand entertainment provided by her demise, made her falter. She gulped and tried to rally.

"Do I get a private bath, then?" Her voice only quavered a tiny bit.

Overseer Neilan straightened and waved for Ilai to take her. "Ignore her babbling. We can't have her bleeding to death before her execution."

Madison giggled. "No, that would be bad if I die before my death." She shambled in Ilai's wake, hoping everyone else passed the mysterious testing and earned some other fate.

At least Ilai stopped dragging her by the hair. They passed through a short tunnel of harsh light, leaving Madison wondering what lurked in the darkness. Hevit troopers, torture devices, dead bodies, anything could hide there.

Behind her, someone screamed. Ilai jerked her aside. She tripped and fell into Ilai. The pharedim grunted in disgust and threw her forward, into the pitch black.

She stumbled and slipped, rolled and crumpled. When she stopped, she lay against a wall with her eye to the floor. Metal clanged with the finality of death.

Madison considered staying still for a while. Every piece of her body ached. She could tell her new room had dim light and a slick stone floor, and the warm air held far too much humidity. Water dripped in a steady rhythm.

Footfalls, softer than boots, approached. Someone stopped beside her, radiating heat.

"Are you awake?"

The speaker sounded pleasant and genuine, so Madison lifted her head. She discovered a macrica. Her uncle had a picture of himself with a macrica clan, remica and all. They'd helped him recover after a narrow escape once. This one had the pouch, wide hips, and open-kneed squat of a nucri, the members of the clan responsible for raising children birthed by the remica.

"Sort of. This is the execution pit?"

"Yes."

The walls had the look and feel of rough-hewn rock. Fifteen feet up, metal grates let in dismal light and too much heat. Every surface glistened with dampness. A pool catching drops of water from the ceiling rippled in the center of the wide space. Tiny, brightly colored birds sat on the edge of the pool in a cluster, chirping to each other in tiny, high-pitched voices.

"I'm Rho. I've been waiting here for..." Rho sighed. "I don't know how long. The last batch went to the arena without me. Apparently, the Arena Master prefers even numbers."

"Great. Madison. Maybe you get to die with me, then."

Rho helped her sit up. Madison groaned.

"I gather you were roughed up on your way here."

"You might say that." Madison tried to find a comfortable way to sit. Nothing worked. She gave up and slumped to the floor again.

"May I check your body for serious injuries?" Rho reached to move Madison's coat aside but stopped and waited for her answer.

"Please do. I'd like to know if I'll die before I die." She giggled. It hurt.

Rho smiled and pulled aside Madison's coat, then lifted the thin tank top she wore underneath it. "How colorful."

"Your race has four or five genders, right?"

"Five, yes. Mine is called nucri."

"What pronouns go with that? I mean, if we're going to die

together, I feel like I ought to refer to you properly in my head."

Rho chuckled. "Lakhan Basic has no way to properly translate many words from my language. Use 'they' and 'their.' It's closest." They laid a hand on Madison's belly and applied gentle pressure. "Am I causing sharp pain or not?"

Madison groaned. "Not. It's kind of all over."

"I'm fairly certain that's good. Human anatomy is, I admit, somewhat strange to me. Your heart is in an odd place."

The door opened, and someone shoved Oolaang inside. They'd taken his goggles, leaving his large eyes bare. He stumbled and slipped, falling onto his hands and knees. Behind him, the door clanged shut again.

Trying to get up and help Oolaang hurt too much. Madison groaned again and stayed on her back. Rho moved instead. They offered Oolaang a hand and helped him stand.

Guilt pressed on Madison's shoulders. The crew should've all earned the right to live and ply their skills. "I'm so sorry, Oolaang. I thought for sure they'd want a mechanic."

He shuffled across the slick floor to hunch beside her. "They only tested me for fighting. I don't think they care about anything else."

"That's stupid." It didn't sound fair, either.

Oolaang took her hand and squeezed it. "We all knew following you might end in death. This isn't your fault. You were right, after all."

Yes, she was right. To achieve real success, she needed a way to neutralize the hevits. Everyone needed that, though. No one had any options. Super-fast, super-stealthy, and super-dedicated to the Oligarchy cause, the hevits always won. Scanning for heat didn't even work against them.

"Damned hevit troopers," Madison grumbled.

Rho sighed and shook their head. "They're the reason I'm here. I tried to steal an egg."

Madison blinked. "What for? There are much easier ways to get breakfast."

"I've studied them as much as anyone could, and I think I could raise one to be loyal to me. They're too perfectly obedient. If I'm right, they have a racial trait of imprinting on whoever takes the mother role for them. That person teaches them how to be a good hevit, and they follow the example for the rest of their lives."

While Madison couldn't deny the allure of pet hevits, even without the cybernetic enhancements, the process of acquiring them didn't help in the near term. She'd have to survive her execution to help Rho provide the Stardrifters with hevit soldiers. Minor details.

More of the crew stumbled into the chamber. Every single person fell. Madison suspected they let the floor stay wet on purpose. Slipping and falling meant not turning and charging the door.

Rho shuffled between them, helping whoever needed it. Counting and scanning faces, Madison watched as eight people made their choices regarding her. All chose to huddle in a separate clump, far enough from Madison and Oolaang to mutter and grumble to themselves.

She'd hoped they might feel the same as Oolaang but couldn't begrudge them heaping blame on her shoulders. With luck, at least Jaco and Shmar had proven capable enough at fighting for the Overseer to spare their lives.

"An odd number again," Rho muttered as she returned to Madison's side. "I don't think any of them like you."

"I'm not surprised." Madison closed her eye, hoping some of the aches across her body would fade.

More bodies stumbled and slipped, then the door clanged again.

"It's Jaco and Shmar," Oolaang murmured as Rho left to tend the two men. "I guess they weren't good enough either."

"What do they even do here that they test for fighting?" Madison left her eye closed. She didn't want to watch Jaco abandon her.

"Have you never heard of Rikor Six?" Oolaang asked.

"No."

"The biggest attraction is the gladiator arena. They even have a place where you can pay to have sex with the gladiators."

"Way to go, Maddie," Jaco said. "Let your mouth get you all banged up."

Tension eased in her neck. She smiled up at him and noticed a fresh black eye. "These people are too melodramatic."

"Still an odd number," Rho grumbled. "Knowing one person might be spared again is almost worse torture than knowing we all get to die."

Jaco touched the skin under Madison's empty eye socket with a light, gentle brush. "There might be one more. They brought in a girl. I heard one of them say she was native."

Madison waggled her brow. The effort hurt, but not enough to make her stop. "Oh yeah? Pretty?"

He snorted. "At a time like this, that's what's on your mind?"

"When is it ever not?" She grinned at him.

A body flew out of the queer, persistent darkness engulfing the door. She hit the floor and slid across it, her arms and legs jerking with spasms. The door clanged before she stopped sliding.

"That's her," Jaco said.

Madison heaved herself onto her elbows to get a good look. The new girl wore thin, simple clothes, the top having no sleeves and a gap wide enough to leave her midriff exposed. She had thick muscles across her whole body and the most amazing abs. Short, dark hair complemented delightfully brown skin. Calluses and dirt on her bare feet suggested the woman never wore shoes or boots. If she lived on this world, the heat probably made barefoot life more practical.

Fascinating tattoos accented parts of the woman's body. Spiky shapes like horns or claws in red and black curved over her right eyebrow and around her eye. More slid down the side of her face like a tail pointing toward her ear. The one on her belly formed a jagged fan with the point aimed at her belly button from the right side and the wide arc splayed outward. Black X's circled her wrist with red outlines. Overlapping diamond shapes reminiscent of scales spiraled around her left arm from her shoulder to her elbow.

"Nihan!" the woman shouted. She had a strange accent with an amazing lilt. Her wide-open eyes, gold-flecked and gorgeous, stared without comprehension as if she'd lost her sight. She kept twitching.

"I don't know what a nihan is," Madison murmured, "but I want to be it."

Rho touched the woman's arm. "Can you hear me?"

The woman's body convulsed, and she screamed.

"She has amazing lungs."

Jaco rolled his eyes. "You're hurt, idiot. Rest now, lust later."

"I can do both at once. Here, help me turn so I can stare at the most amazing thing I've ever seen." Madison batted her eye at Jaco. "It'll help me come up with a plan to get us out of this mess."

"Sure it will." Jaco shook his head and helped her move so she could watch the vision of loveliness.

This gorgeous woman's suffering made Madison curse herself for goading Ilai. Without all her bruises, she could sit and fuss over the woman instead of letting Rho do it.

"Oolaang, tell me more about Rikor Six."

"I don't know much more. In the shop where I worked before joining the crew, we had a qusamadi ship come once, and they talked a lot about how much they looked forward to coming here. They were especially interested in watching the local beasts rip apart prisoners, which sounds like what Cradok expected to happen to you."

"Qusamadi are such pokkentoffs," Jaco muttered.

Oolaang shrugged. "It makes them good arms dealers and slave traders."

Rho dragged the woman by her armpits to bring her closer to Madison. The woman babbled, whistled, and chirped. Her mouth moved with no sound coming out, then she chirped more. Twitching followed that, then another scream.

The flock of birds at the pool of water jumped into the air as a group and flitted to the metal grates. Despite their fluff, they fit through the open squares.

"Goodness." Rho sighed. "I think she was hit by a stunner. When the feeling returns, it's quite painful."

Madison reached a hand toward the woman's. With a sigh, Jaco helped her clutch the woman's hand. She squeezed, hoping to send a message of solidarity over the pain. The woman blinked and stared at the ceiling.

"If they test for fighting ability, then they're looking for new gladiators, right?"

"I know they took Tau for that purpose." Rho leaned against the wall and clutched their hands around their pouch. "A prasilor from my family. You might call them warriors or guardians. When the soldiers captured me, their lakhan leader took revenge on my family and killed our remica. A prasilor without a remica..." They sighed. "Tau survived the attack and was taken prisoner. No one else from our family clutch survived."

Madison heard an unspoken comment in Rho's tone, a wish they could have all died together. "Lakhans and pharedimi and hevits and qusamadi all suck. They can all die in a giant fire."

"Lakhans are immortal," Rho said.

"Maybe," Oolaang said.

The woman squeezed Madison's hand, taking her attention from Oolaang relating Captain Wayward's favorite story about the death of a lakhan. She met the woman's gaze, and it seemed her sight had returned.

Halting, pain-laced words spilled from the woman's mouth. Madison didn't understand any of it. Except she kind of did. The old texts her uncle loved to pore over used a language called Terinanal. Neither he nor anyone else Madison knew had a pronunciation guide for Terinanal, so they sounded it out. If she shifted some of the vowel sounds, the woman's speech seemed similar.

Weird.

After pondering the words, Madison thought the woman had asked if her body was dying.

"No. It's waking up." She hoped she said it right.

The woman squinted and frowned at her. Before she could say anything else, spasms rocked her body and she screamed again.

Communication, it seemed, would take a while, but at least Madison had a place to start.

CHAPTER 6

KIREHE

Only one place Kirehe knew could harbor so much dank despair—Irondoom. Sanda and the other hunter boy had caused this. If they survived the enemy's retaliation for her destruction of three flyers, she would make sure they learned one day what their stupidity had caused.

Control of her body crept back in fits and starts. Each time she suffered a bout of spasms and sharp, burning agony, she recovered some small amount of feeling someplace. One time, she could move a finger. The next, her tongue no longer failed her.

The moment she could, she asked a nearby flock of kukiris to find Skila. No one had ever escaped the sacrifices in Irondoom before, but that didn't mean she wouldn't try. Skila could find Nihan. Nihan could find Lipa. Lipa could bring enough raptors to shake the foundations and get her free.

This person holding her hand and the other sacrifices could come with her. She didn't know what to think of the strange machine parts the one woman had instead of an eye, brow ridge, and part of her cheek. From the way she twisted to see with the normal eye, the machine parts had no functional purpose, other than the obvious one of protecting her brain.

Another wave of fire bowed her body, ripping another scream

from her throat. The woman with the machine not-eye kept a tight grip on her hand, which helped. When it finished, Kirehe gasped for breath and felt weaker yet more in control.

"You're from here?" the woman with the machine parts asked. Her accent sounded odd, like nothing Kirehe had heard before. At least she could understand this one person, though. The enemy used a foreign language that grated on her ears.

"No. Out there." Kirehe raised a feeble hand to point but had no idea which direction to indicate. "Tosnorth village."

"I meant the planet."

"Then yes. I'm from this planet. You're not?"

"No." The woman with the machine parts smiled. "My name is Madison. This is Jaco, Oolaang, and Rho."

"Kirehe." Fire swept her body again. She screamed.

"Kiki!" Skila plummeted from the metal grate in the wall to land on her chest. "Followed! Meanies. Swatting. Flock."

The flock of kukiris she'd sent in search of Skila returned to the unpleasant chamber. They swooped through the air, snatching bugs allowed to wander freely in their short absence.

Kirehe couldn't lift her hand high enough to reach Skila and pet her. "Good. Can you find Nihan?"

Skila walked up her body to nuzzle her cheek. "Nihan hurt. Taken. Big nets. Machines. Skila follow!"

Nihan taken meant Nihan lost. If she'd let him hunt first, they wouldn't have met that pilot. To think they'd killed three flyers only to suffer defeat at the hands of an enemy pilot on foot. Her poor Nihan.

She remembered hugging him with her small arms when he'd first hatched. They'd learned to hunt and swim together. Without him… No. She wouldn't give up on him. If she had survived to be captured, then so had he. With Skila's help, she'd find and free him, even if she couldn't escape herself.

"Are you…talking to that bird?"

Kirehe blinked at Madison, and she saw the group of four staring at her. The man's mouth hung open. "Skila is a kukiri."

Madison squinted for a moment, then shook her head. "I don't understand those words, but are you talking to it?"

Yet another person to spread idiot rumors about her made Kirehe glare at the ceiling. "Skila, you did good." She wanted to send a message to Tosnorth, but nothing they could do would help until she could help herself. If they could even do anything useful. After all, no one else had ever escaped Irondoom. Why would they sacrifice anyone to try to make her the first? "Stay with this flock for now."

The kukiri chirped her happiness and scampered across the floor in tiny, bounding leaps. Despite everything, the tiny dragon's delight made her smile again.

"Yes, I can communicate with the kukiris. I'm a dragoncaller."

"I don't understand that word either."

Kirehe's leg burned. She screamed. Rho helped her drink stale, metallic water. Better to have poor quality liquid than no liquid.

"I can speak to the dragons."

"Dragons." Madison raised an eyebrow. She turned to the others and used the enemy's language to speak to them. They responded in the same tongue.

Annoyed with herself for allowing the enemy to trick her, Kirehe tried to sit up. She tossed Madison's hand aside. As she fumbled and flailed, another wave of fire overtook her. Rho raised their hands and made soothing noises, trying to stop Kirehe from sitting up.

"Stop," Madison said. "You need to lie still."

Kirehe spat at her. "I don't care what you say! I'm not stupid. You're the enemy." She rolled onto her belly and wriggled enough to squirm a short distance.

"Whoa! Wait. I'm not your enemy. We're all sentenced to die here." Madison crawled alongside her, pain pinching her features.

"You speak their evil tongue." Kirehe kept wriggling, powering through another episode of fire and grinding her jaws together to keep the scream inside.

"Oh." Madison reached over and patted Kirehe's arm. "No, it's not their language. I mean, it is, but everybody speaks Lakhan Basic. We all have to be able to communicate with each other. That's why we learn it. So we can understand them. I could teach you, if you give me a chance."

Curling her lip in disgust, Kirehe stopped struggling. "I want nothing to do with their filthy words."

Madison opened and shut her mouth.

The man said something and smirked.

They spoke to each other. To Kirehe, it sounded like mating season banter.

When they'd finished, with Jaco rolling his eyes and Madison having the last word, Madison turned to Kirehe. "I appreciate that opinion, but it would help you understand what they're saying around you."

"I don't care what they're saying."

"What if you could use it to escape?"

Kirehe's knee exploded with agony. She screamed. This routine irritated her enough to consider Madison's point. If she knew the basics of their language, she might have a better chance of fooling them or learning things without them realizing.

"I suppose."

"Rho wants to know how many times they shot you so they can guess how much longer you have to suffer."

She thought back to the moments before she'd passed out. The pilot had shot her once in the chest and once in the face. "Twice, as far as I know. Plus the two times they grazed me."

Madison's brow climbed. The other three also seemed surprised when she related this. "Wow. You're pretty tough."

Kirehe shrugged as much as her shoulders allowed. "I'm a dragoncaller." Duris could've taken as many hits, if not more. Other dragoncallers could probably do the same. Other members of her hapa might suffer more against the laser weapons. She thought the elder hunters, in the decade before they returned to TOS Cave to spend their end days with help, could withstand laser assaults at their level of skill and endurance.

"Oh, that's a compound word. Dragon and caller. So you call dragons. And, apparently, kick ass. If I had an idea for an escape plan, would you help us carry it out?" Madison offered her hand again.

Having that contact had provided some measure of comfort when the pain hit. Kirehe took her hand. "I intend to escape. If you'd like to help with your understanding of the enemy and their words, I welcome it."

"Excellent." Madison held on while another episode tore across Kirehe's body. She flinched at the scream but didn't let go.

Kirehe appreciated Madison's steadiness. "How long does the one called Rho think this will last? I wish to rest, and my body won't let me."

"A few more hours, probably. Do you know anything about what goes on here? In the whole complex, I mean. Not just down here."

"The enemy captures my people and sacrifices us to their evil gods for more power. We don't know what they do with the maras and kratas they capture. No one has ever escaped."

"Maras and kratas? What are those?"

If Madison and the others came from different planets, she supposed they may never have heard of dragons. Instead of ignoring the question, she offered a full description of both kinds of dragon. "The kukiris are also dragons. Very small ones." She pointed at the flock near the water hole. "They come in many different colors."

"Those are dragons?"

"Tiny dragons with tiny brains."

Madison grinned. "Which you know because you can talk to them."

"Yes."

"This is the best execution pit ever." Madison turned and chattered to the others.

While they spoke, Kirehe suffered through another episode. Madison kept her grip firm. Watching Madison, she noticed the others gave her a subtle kind of deference. She served as her pack's alpha.

The other group of people stayed far away. Though all these people except Rho wore similar clothing, they didn't like each other. Some rift of distrust or betrayal ran between them.

They reminded her of maras. Packs often grew with births to ten or twelve before splitting. Sometimes they split amicably, with no bad blood. Other times, a rival refused to accept an alpha's dominance anymore despite their continued superiority. The pack split out of hate. Nothing good came of them meeting again.

She could tell who the other group had selected as their replacement alpha. He had the same broad-shouldered build as the hapa's hunters. Kirehe doubted these two packs would clash physically, but they never would agree on anything. If they somehow did, bitterness would poison it.

Another burning spasm ripped across Kirehe's body. When it stopped, she tried rolling onto her side. One leg still refused to cooperate, and her chest didn't feel right. Her arms had returned to her control, though. As she made more of an effort to sit up, Rho rushed to her side. The three of them besides Madison helped her lean against the wall.

"If you can talk to those," Madison waved toward the kukiris while still lying on the floor, "can you ask them questions about the complex?"

"I can ask. What do you want to know?"

Madison's eye gleamed with excitement. "Anything that might help us survive or avoid our execution. How they work, the layout, who's in charge, that sort of thing. I can make a plan, but I need information. And there's no way to know how long we have until our execution."

"They may not have much to tell, but I'll see what I can learn." She whistled to get the flock's attention. "Skila, come here. Bring your new friends."

The kukiris fluttered from across the room to land on her lap. Skila perched on her shoulder and purred. Kirehe rubbed under her chin.

"I need your help to know more about Irondoom."

The flock inundated her with information delivered in short bursts. As they took turns to tell her what they knew, Kirehe tried to guess what extra questions might help Madison. Like all kukiris, their attentions wavered quickly. She clamped down on a spasm episode to avoid scaring them, and didn't chide them for wandering in search of food.

Her people had no idea what really happened at Irondoom. Their ideas came close, but she now knew they'd accepted guesses as truth.

When the last one jumped off her leg to chase a bug, she waited for another spasm to pass before speaking again.

"In this place, people fight other people while others watch. The fighting people live above us, in a cooler section where the kukiris find less prey. Many people practice for the fighting, and they are given weapons. Most of the time, these people don't kill each other.

"The watching people come and go. They stay in rooms where the kukiris are not welcome and can't find prey. Some parts of the complex are very cold, and the kukiris don't go there. There are two cooking places, one where the kukiris are welcome, and one where they are not.

"The complex has a pack of maras they keep locked up and underfed." According to the kukiris, the poor things never saw true sunlight and never smelled fresh air. They never ran in the jungle or hunted real prey. They deserved freedom as much as Kirehe. "This pack sometimes is put in the fighting place to attack and eat people."

She'd asked about Nihan, but none of the kukiris had seen a live krata recently. Skila had no new information to add.

"Huh." Madison closed her eye and seemed to fall asleep. Her chest rose and fell, and she said nothing for several minutes. Then she sucked in a breath like she'd startled herself awake with a nightmare.

"I'm guessing they haven't tested you for fighting yet since you couldn't even move when you got here. That means they have yet to do it. I'm going to ask you to do something weird."

Kirehe clenched her jaw against another spasm. Her eyelids drooped and she wanted to sleep. "What is it?"

"I think the test is to see whether you'd make a good fighter or not. Since you can take more than one stunner and keep going, I think you're probably the type would make a good fighter. So I'm going to ask you to pretend like you're not. Pretend like you're incompetent or clumsy. Untrained. Weaker than you look. And don't let them see you talking to the dragons."

The request made no sense. If the fighting people didn't kill each other, Kirehe wanted to become one of them. She'd have time to plan and discover Irondoom's weaknesses. Skila and the kukiris could help her.

"Why would I do that?"

"Because I think you could help us all survive the execution. And I'd really like to do that. Especially if I can do it with you."

"All of you? Even them?" Kirehe pointed at the other pack. "They hate you."

Madison turned her head to see them and sighed. "They're angry because I failed them, and scared because we're all sentenced to die. I'm not happy about that either. But yes, even them."

"How did you fail them?" If Madison expected Kirehe to trust her enough to take a chance with her life, Kirehe wanted to know a lot more about her.

For several moments, Madison continued to watch the other pack. She closed her eye. Kirehe whimpered at another spasm. When it passed, she thought Madison had fallen asleep again.

"Beyond your world, the Lakhan Oligarchy rules everything. They control dozens of worlds. Humans like us are mostly slave labor. Oolaang's race are mostly slaves too. Either that or paid so little we all might as well be slaves. Some of us are free, living on spaceships in a loose group that doesn't have a chance of challenging the Oligarchy. The people who run it are called lakhans. That's their race. They can't be killed, they're strong and smart, and we can't defeat them.

"Our people survive because we scatter. We don't stay to fight. We do everything we can to take what we need and not more than that. Which is hard, because we're not allowed to own anything we can't take and hide someplace. All the worlds where we can be free are desolate places no one else wants. The biggest villages we have are spaceships, and we don't have contact with other ships very often."

Life offworld sounded terrible. In a way, though, it sounded the same as life on the planet. The enemy forced her people to stay outside a specific part of their world. Anyone crossing that line, like Kirehe, became a sacrifice. Or, she now knew, a slave.

Kirehe frowned but didn't interrupt.

"I think I've figured out something that will help our people fight against the Oligarchy. I convinced all of them," she gestured to encompass all those in the room, "to help me prove it. And we did, but we got caught. Because I didn't expect some of the things we encountered. I don't know that I ever could have. But now I know about those things, so I can figure something out. If we can just survive and escape this world, I know I've got information that will mean hope to our people."

She opened her eye and met Kirehe's gaze. "To do that, I need your help. The way you can help us for the moment is to pretend you don't know how to fight. Please."

Kirehe didn't think Madison often asked for help. "Is there any chance that what you're doing will help my people too?"

"The end goal is to defeat the Oligarchy, and that's who runs this place, so yes. Not right away, I mean. They're entrenched. They control everything and have plenty of people benefitting from their rule. But if everyone does a little bit, I know we can win someday. And that would mean your people can have this place and do whatever you want with it."

Imagining flying with no limits and no humming made Kirehe smile through her exhaustion. She wanted to skim the trees on Nihan's back, not having to dodge anything, not worrying about the flyers. No spike lines would mean no patrols. They could live without borders or fear.

"Yes. I'll do it. I don't understand how that'll help, but knowing why is enough."

"Thank you." Madison smiled at her. "I promise you won't do any of this alone. Aside from the testing, I mean. That's all on you."

Finally able to summon a chuckle, Kirehe nodded. "I think the laser blast sickness is wearing off." She curled onto her side and closed her eyes.

Sleep came swiftly.

CHAPTER 7

MADISON

Watching Kirehe fall asleep gave Madison a moment of happiness. Kirehe had everything—looks, brains, muscles… dragons. She didn't seem interested, but Madison could bask in the glow of this amazing person without needing a physical relationship.

Having such amazing perfection so close and yet out of reach would eat at her heart, but she'd survived worse.

"Ugh, I wish I could just fall asleep." She stared at the ceiling, trying to muddle on the problem of replacing her eye.

"What's the plan?" Jaco asked. "Because I can tell you have one." He laid beside her, hands behind his head as a crude cushion.

"Kirehe is going to save us all. For now, anyway." She checked the other group. They'd probably elected Shmar as their leader by now. Before they'd left, she should've seen how much of a problem he'd turn into.

The other group huddled together. Shmar glared at her. He had every right to hate her. She deserved it. To save his life, though, she needed to convince him to trust her one more time. If she could get him, she got the whole group.

Shmar crossed his arms and kept glaring. Some of the crew tried to sleep. Others looked anywhere except at Madison.

She returned to staring at the ceiling. The rough surface angled with a slight incline toward the pool, causing water to slide across it and drip there. Thank goodness for the little dragon-birds. Their chirps and whistles kept the plunk of water drops from becoming maddening.

Beside her, Jaco rolled to his side, watching Shmar. Madison held up a hand. "Leave it alone."

"He's still glaring at you."

"Let him glare." She didn't care. Shmar sat on her blind side.

"He shouldn't. This wasn't your fault."

Madison sighed. "It doesn't matter. If he wants to glare, that's his problem."

Jaco slumped. "He's going to get us all killed because he hates you now."

"Maybe. Maybe he only gets himself killed."

He shifted, the cloth of his soggy jacket rustling on the rock. "And the rest of the crew because they're going to listen to him instead of you."

"I can't control what they decide to do." She hated saying that. It sounded like giving up.

"Like hell you can't." He poked her shoulder. "Get up and talk to them."

Madison shook her head. "Can't get up. Hurts too much. They can wait until I get some rest."

"You shouldn't need to do it."

She patted his arm. "You're a good friend, Jaco. Knock it off. I don't need a guard dog."

He grumbled without words. Madison closed her eye and tried to relax. Guilt bunched the muscles of her shoulders and tightened her neck. She should've expected the hevits. Cradok must've told them to make themselves visible. After the short time dealing with him, she thought that sounded like something he'd do.

Somehow, Cradok had guessed everything about the plan except her goal. Maybe cameras had watched the access bridge, or maybe he'd figured it out after capturing an escape pod. For their next attempt—

Jaco nudged her. "It's not going to wait."

She opened her eye to find Jaco leaning toward her as if to throw his body in the path of danger to protect her. When she turned her head, she saw Shmar standing over her.

Shmar held his fists at his sides. His glare hadn't lessened. "This is your fault. We're going to pokken die because of you and your pokken plan."

Madison didn't think he'd hit her. At least, she hadn't until that moment. The menace creeping over every inch of him gave her reason to doubt his ability to restrain himself. "Yep. I forced everyone to climb into that ship. I'm the worst kind of tyrant. No one had any choice at all. And I was completely opaque about the risks."

Jaco stood and held out a hand to ward off Shmar. "Back off."

"You led us into a trap!" Shmar smacked Jaco's hand aside. "And you're just as bad. She could hand you over to save herself, and you'd go with a stupid pokken smile on your face!"

Refusing to flinch or wriggle away, Madison smirked. "He's right. Your smile does get pretty stupid when you're scared. Very confusing."

Both men rolled their eyes. For one brief, shining moment, Madison hoped they'd bond over their shared reaction.

Jaco shoved Shmar with both hands against his chest. All the hope died. "I'm not surprised you don't understand loyalty."

Shmar threw a punch at Jaco's head. Madison curled out of the way and protected her head. The two men scuffled. Thanks to Jaco's interest in Madison's health, the fight moved to the side.

Stardrifters prized shooting over fistfighting, so their inability to cause each other serious harm didn't surprise Madison. Mostly, they shoved and threw punches that didn't connect. Foot stomps missed, shoulder slams hit. The two men grunted and growled. They fell to the floor and rolled around, scrabbling for dominance.

Madison stopped watching. No wonder neither had passed the fighting test. Gladiators would have to keep the crowd watching. These two bored her. She only cared about the outcome because she didn't want Jaco to lose.

Blurred figures burst through the darkness of the door and separated the scuffling pair. Electricity crackled around each man, and they spasmed in separate puddles of misery.

"No fighting," a gruff voice barked.

The blurs disappeared and the door clanged shut.

Madison giggled. "That's right, boys. If you don't know how to fight, you can't fight. Only professionals are allowed to engage in fisticuffs for the glory of the crowd!"

Jaco and Shmar both lay on the ground, panting and glaring at each other.

Rho sighed. "Now we'll listen to them scream while they recover from stunning. I hope Kirehe can get enough sleep to recover."

Now that she knew someone listened outside the door, Madison had no intention of revealing her plan in Lakhan Basic. As such, she didn't say that she thought it might help Kirehe perform poorly.

She also now knew they left the door open while hevits rushed in to break up a fight. Which she found interesting. Given a little more information, she thought she could try a prison break.

"Oolaang, how long has this arena place been here?"

"Oh, I don't know. At least a century. Probably longer. I remember once watching a compilation of fight highlights for a gladiator right after he retired. The bar had a whole bunch of them from previous retired gladiators, going back several decades. If I remember right, the bartender told someone they rotated the catalog of compilations every so often, so there have to be compilations going back a long time. So, actually, I suppose it's probably at least a few centuries."

"Gladiators retire? That doesn't seem so bad to be one, then." Freeing a slave who no longer served their purpose sounded weird, but she supposed even the lakhans had some sense of decency buried under their frigid, evil exteriors.

Oolaang coughed. "Retirement is what they call it when a gladiator gets to fight a death match against the Arena Master. The Arena Master is a lakhan, Viriok."

"Ah." That sounded more like how the lakhans operated. If something ceased to do its job, they killed it. That the death sometimes came with glory made no difference. The Arena Master had a job to do, and that job sounded like it included making as much of a spectacle of anything and everything as possible.

Madison frowned, wondering how much effort they'd put into securing their execution prisoners after having at least a century to observe and react to the behaviors of the damned.

They didn't leave an open door unguarded to handle a fight between prisoners slated for execution. Overseer Neilan had far too much experience to allow that to happen. Even if he had a reasonable lifespan, Viriok would've set up procedures long ago. Madison didn't know much about the pharedimi, but she did know they followed lakhan rules like zealots adhering to edicts hand-delivered by their god.

Escaping this hellhole would take more cunning than slipping through a door unnoticed. Thinking it might work would only lead to more physical punishment. For anyone who followed her, they might suffer the same immediate fate as Dani had.

She watched Rho collect Jaco, who couldn't move, and bring him to lie beside her. Two other crewmen picked up Shmar and dragged him to their side of the chamber.

Stupid hevits. They should've let the two men reach a resolution. By breaking up the fight without a clear victor, they'd ensured nothing changed. Two angry men glared across a widening chasm, growling their threats. Everyone else had made a decision.

If Madison hadn't run off her mouth and goaded that pharedim to beat the kut out of her, she could've faced Shmar herself. Jaco had compunctions about kneeing another man in the balls, but Madison didn't. The fight could've ended before it began.

Boys.

Good thing she had Kirehe to pin her hopes on.

Speaking of the amazing, gorgeous native, one of the one dragon-birds fluttered to Kirehe and landed in her open hand. It fluffed its feathers and settled. The critter's tiny tail wrapped around its tiny body to touch its tinier nose.

Madison had never seen anything so adorable. She wanted to crawl closer and snuggle beside them. If she thought for one moment that Kirehe would allow it, she'd do so. Asking her to throw a fight had felt like pushing things far enough for a first meeting.

Her plan would work. They'd either escape in the chaos and confusion, or things would change enough that she'd have more time to figure out a new plan. Or her plan would backfire, and Madison would die a messy death like Cradok wanted.

She had a solid plan and liked her odds.

"I'm coming for you, Cradok," she muttered under her breath. She'd get there.

CHAPTER 8

KIREHE

This time of year, the sun always shone on Irondoom. When Kirehe woke, Skila purred in her hand. She raised the kukiri to her face to rub cheeks with her. The tip of Skila's tail tickled her chin.

"Stay with the flock," she kept her chirps quiet. Even if Madison hadn't asked her to keep her ability quiet, she saw the wisdom of giving the enemy no reason to keep the dragons away from her. "I'll tell you if it's safe to come close."

"Danger?"

"Danger for me. Not for you."

Skila hugged two of Kirehe's fingers. "Safe."

"Soon." Kirehe kissed the kukiri and tossed her. She watched Skila flap and gain control of her flight. Skila darted for the metal grate and wriggled through.

If only Kirehe could escape so easily.

Everyone else in the chamber lay on the floor, resting or sleeping. Kirehe crept to the pool and drank as much of the dead-tasting water as she could stand. She heard machines humming, too quiet to have noticed through the spasms and kukiri chatter. The sound came from the small area of darkness along one wall.

Kirehe crossed the room and reached into the thick shadow. Her hand hit a round bar. Feeling along it, she discovered a grate similar to the ones on the walls, probably serving as a door. Curling her fingers around the bars and closing her eyes to focus, she listened to determine where she'd find the machines.

Two machines, each with a tiny distinction between them, like the difference between various similar kukiri voices, flanked the metal grate. More echoed off the walls, fainter and harder to distinguish.

Voices in the distance drew closer. She heard boots clack on the floor. They stopped close by. One of the smooth-voice enemy spoke. The door shuddered with a tiny click, then it swung open, carrying her through the darkness and into the bright light on the other side.

The smooth-voiced one raised delicate, arched brows at her. Kirehe tensed to fight. Then she remembered her promise to Madison.

Don't fight.

She trusted the girl's plan, so she would pretend she had no ability to fight. She leaped at the smooth-voiced one and forced herself to trip over nothing. Instead of attacking, she fell to the floor and failed to roll with it. Her elbows and knees banged on the rock. She wouldn't get bruises from such inconsequential contact, but it stung.

The smooth-voiced one laughed and gloated over her.

Before rising to her hands and knees, she darted furtive glances at the sources of the machine hum. Neither spot held anything she could see, though she knew the machines didn't sit inside the walls. They hovered in front of the walls.

Surrendering to the smooth-voiced one, she hung her head and shuffled up the lighted path as directed. Behind her, the door clanged shut. The smooth-voiced one chattered at her, possibly unaware Kirehe didn't understand the language.

Several paces down the corridor, the smooth-voiced one shoved her into a different pool of darkness. She let herself fall and tumble across the floor until she stopped in a wide pool of less harsh light. Four more machines hummed out of reach, in the darkness surrounding the light.

These people had a serious fondness for using darkness as a form of control.

Two of the smooth-voiced ones stepped into the light. They didn't hum. So far, none of them did. The machines were something else.

One held a staff. The other held a shorter stick in one hand, similar in length to Kirehe's machete. She hoped someone found her machete. Even if she never used it again, the hapa could give it to someone else.

A voice in the darkness said something short and sharp.

The two smooth-voiced ones advanced on her, brandishing their weapons.

Kirehe shifted her weight, preparing to dodge and counterattack. Except she needed to fail. They couldn't detect her training. She stopped herself from moving to keep both in sight. Instead, she remembered her early lessons. When she'd first begun training, she hadn't known how to stay aware of her surroundings and situation.

She turned her head back and forth, purposely failing to keep track of both enemies. One whacked her with their staff.

Her body wanted to wrap an arm around the staff as it struck and take it away. She didn't let it, turning the aborted movement into a clumsy jerk. The other stick swung for her leg. An automatic kick to the side began. By force of will, she leaned off balance and fell as she snapped out her leg.

Failing on purpose took more work than beating these people with their own sticks.

Already sweating, Kirehe took her time rolling to her hands and knees. She hoped she appeared to lack the endurance needed for such battle.

The voice in the darkness spoke again.

Both enemies let her clamber to her feet before approaching again. This made sense if they wanted to get the measure of her. Whenever she'd started with a new teacher, they'd assessed her in much the same way. In those cases, she'd wanted to prove her skill and had bounced back as fast as possible.

She feigned weakness where one stick had hit her. She let them hit her. She tripped and stumbled on purpose. She gasped for breath despite not needing to.

Even if they saw something worth training, a real teacher knew nothing could fix clumsiness. Muscles with no endurance shouldn't seem desirable either.

For good measure, she stopped trying to attack early. Her focus turned to flinching from a beating and covering her head.

The voice in the darkness called out. Both her opponents stopped and withdrew from the light. Her escort returned and pointed. Kirehe faked a limp. They took hold of her arm and hauled her through the darkness to the corridor again.

As she shambled up the light tunnel, she mulled over what she'd learned from the two assessors. The smooth-voiced people had some fighting skills, but she could've beaten them both if she'd tried. Their style emphasized single combat, which gave her an advantage when facing two of them. In a real fight, they'd foul each other's attacks.

If they didn't have a trained team available to assess new fighters for their entertainments, she doubted they had many trained teams.

The machines intrigued her. Kirehe wanted to know what made the noises. As they traveled the short distance, she decided to use her feigned clumsiness to her advantage.

Her escort spoke with disgust and disappointment as they shoved her toward the door. Once in the darkness, Kirehe grunted and feigned tripping to the side. She hit a body covered in something soft like feathers or fur.

Creatures made the machine hum.

Her target retaliated with a swift knee strike. Kirehe partially blocked it and tumbled through the door. She scrambled into the light, appearing afraid of the unseen creature.

The door clanged shut.

Kirehe backed to the wall in case they kept watching. Her escort laughed, the sound fading as they walked away.

"Excellent," Madison whispered.

Sinking to the floor beside her new friend, Kirehe grinned. "I haven't fought so poorly since my tenth year. What did they say?"

Madison's eye lit up with amusement. "They said exactly what I wanted to hear. Most importantly, you'll be part of our execution event."

"And this is good?"

"Yes." Madison giggled. "They're planning to feed us to beasts."

Kirehe wrinkled her nose. "That doesn't sound good."

"Are you sure about that? Didn't the little dragon-birds tell you what kind of beasts they keep here?"

First, Kirehe furrowed her brow as she pondered what Madison meant. The kukiris had told her about maras and nothing else. They were kept for…

…eating people. Which sounded a lot like an execution. She wouldn't have called them "beasts." To her, that word meant creatures too dumb to train. Otherwise, she would've realized this immediately.

"You believe we'll face mara dragons in the execution event."

"Which you can talk to, right?"

"Yes." Though the time had passed for a chance to weigh the risks of this plan, Kirehe decided to explain them anyway. "Talk to, not control. I haven't trained with these. And they're underfed, which means their hunger will rule them. Maras are smarter than kukiris, but still animals. If the barbarians here have trained them to attack and eat people, I may not be able to save everyone."

Madison's humor faded. "Do what you can. I'm not expecting a miracle. No one is." She nodded toward the other pack. "They aren't even expecting a chance anymore."

"If everyone stays behind me and uses me as a shield, I can try to keep them from attacking anyone. I make no promises, though. I am one person, not five."

"I understand. Getting the others to believe and trust me will take some effort."

Kirehe checked the other pack. They slept in a group, most with their backs to her. They had no fighting instincts, or they would sleep facing their enemies. Perhaps they still trusted Madison to a certain degree. "I could speak to them."

"They won't understand you. It's pretty uncommon among our people to know this language. And I can't tell them what you're going to do because I don't want any of the pharedimi or hevits to overhear it. I really don't know where they're listening."

"It does seem clear they have no or little knowledge of my language. I believe they would've used it with me during the assessment if they did." She stared at the pool of darkness. "What happens when we succeed at not being eaten?" Though she considered this plan risky, she had no doubt she could protect herself and at least a few others. Madison seemed likely to follow directions, and she thought the four-armed man, the pouch-person, and the vain boy would do whatever she said. At least they would survive.

"I'm not sure." Madison sighed. "I don't know enough to plan that far. Which bothers me, but not as much as the idea of dying. I'm a big fan of continuing to live."

Kirehe snorted. "As are we all."

"My best guess is that it depends a lot on how much of a show we put on. So if you can do anything flashy, you should do it."

"Fighting isn't supposed to be flashy. The point is to defeat your enemy with as little effort as possible. Swift, efficient, decisive."

Madison opened her mouth, then shut it without speaking. She squinted and pursed her lips. The expression suggested she needed to think. Kirehe waited. They had plenty of time.

"Do whatever you need to. Survival is more important than being flashy, right? One thing at a time."

"Agreed." Kirehe patted Madison's shoulder, taking care to use a gentle touch. The girl didn't need more pain. "For now, you need to try to repair the breach of trust with them." She nodded to the other pack.

Madison grimaced. "I think your part in this is easier."

Kirehe grinned. "So do I."

CHAPTER 9

MADISON

Rest had both helped and made things worse. Madison groaned as she sat up, her body bruised and battered yet no longer aching so hard she couldn't move. As she leaned against the wall beside Kirehe, green blocks the size of two fingers flew into the room, one after another.

She counted as the blocks formed a loose pile. After number fourteen, the door clanged shut. Fourteen coincided with the number of occupants in the room.

Before she could ask, Kirehe stood and collected two. She sniffed a block on her way back to Madison. Sitting, she licked one. The other, she tossed into Madison's hands.

"I think it's food." Kirehe nibbled on the corner and grimaced. "It's not good, but it's food." She bit off half the block and chewed it.

Madison curled her lip at her block. "I'm not sure I'd call it food."

Kirehe swallowed. "No, not really. But if you eat it quickly, the taste doesn't linger." She stuffed the rest of the block into her mouth.

When Madison didn't follow suit within half a minute, Kirehe took Madison's hand and shoved it at her mouth.

"Your body needs food. Take what you can get."

Since the gorgeous girl did it, Madison didn't resist. She shoved half the block into her mouth and discovered a flat, bland flavor similar to plastic. It left no aftertaste, at least, and dissolved fast in her mouth. "I suppose it's better than nothing."

"Some kind of food is always better than no food."

Madison nodded. "Would you pick up blocks for these three? I don't want them to get left out if the other group decides to get greedy or be spiteful."

She did not at all ask that because it allowed her to watch Kirehe get up, saunter to the pile, bend over, and return. Nope, not the least bit intentional on her part.

"You're looking at me funny." Kirehe set the bars in a neat line between the other three.

"Hm?" Madison batted her eye at Kirehe. "I have no idea what you mean."

Kirehe wrinkled her nose. "Is there something wrong with your eye? I can help you flush it at the pool."

Stifling a sigh that Kirehe should prove so resistant to her charms, Madison shook her head and stopped trying. For the moment. "No, I'm fine. Thanks."

Shmar lumbered to the pile and squatted beside them. He counted the remaining blocks. Twice. Then he scooped them all into one hand and stood.

Kirehe stared at her, daring her to engage with Shmar.

Fine. She could let him hurt her. "Really, Shmar? You really think I'd steal food from you guys?"

Instead of saying anything, Shmar took the food blocks to his side and set them where everybody would see them. Then he spun and jabbed a finger at Kirehe. "I don't know her. Or that one." He pointed at Rho.

"And since they're sitting with me, they must be bad." Madison scowled at him. Maybe she hadn't shown great judgment recently, but he should still have trusted her willingness to trust two people in the same situation as them.

Shmar crossed his arms. "I'm dead because of you."

"Don't be an ass. You're not dead yet."

"No." He held up a hand to stop her. "I don't care what crazy plan you have cooked up, because the last two are the reason why we're all dead."

Madison huffed. "It was really just the one. That second one, I'm pretty sure that didn't change anything."

"If we hadn't followed you the second time, we might have escaped."

She laughed at him. "That's the stupidest thing you've ever said."

He scowled with so much anger that Madison curbed her laughter. "You don't know they would've caught us. He expected you to do what you did."

"How would you have gotten the ship out of there? Magic? Beating up pharedimi?" She snorted and scoffed at him. "You couldn't even pass the fighting test here."

"And you have no idea what the test was like," he snapped.

She raised her chin. "I know what they were looking for. Potential. Which you clearly don't have, since you only know how to shoot a blaster."

He stomped his foot while taking a step toward her. His arms slashed through the air. "You're not always right!"

Kirehe laid a hand on her arm. "I think regaining his trust is supposed to make him quieter, not louder."

"Boy, do you not know anything about men." For Shmar's benefit, Madison didn't smirk. She did, however, get a flutter in her chest and a happy tingle on her arm.

"There you go," Shmar growled. "Choosing a stranger over your crew."

Madison lurched to her feet. The effort knocked the wind out of her. She wheezed as she shouted at him. "That's right!" She jabbed a thumb at her chest. "My crew! Not yours. You've never led so much as an escape pod to anything resembling victory, so don't you stand there and tell me how much better you'd do. Did I make mistakes? Yes! I made mistakes. Dani is dead because I didn't think of something that I should have. That doesn't make me a traitor or unfit, or whatever else you've decided I am."

His scowl stayed in place, but he didn't respond.

"Captain Wayward makes mistakes too."

"His mistakes don't cost lives." Shmar sounded less cranky, which seemed like an improvement.

She frowned. "I've seen him make mistakes that got people killed. Those lives lost ate him up inside for a long time. If you think I'm not upset about Dani, you're wrong. And if you think I'm not wracking my brain to come up with options for us, you're worse than wrong. You're dumb."

"I'm not dumb." He straightened to his full height and glowered down at her. "And I don't care about whatever pokken plan you've got this time. We're going to die. I'm not going to let you give me some pokken swell of hope over a crazy pokken idea that probably won't work because you'll never stop forgetting one little pokken detail. Or making one pokken mistake. You're no Captain Wayward. You're just his niece."

Madison didn't want him to have the last word. She didn't want anything he said to be true. Kirehe hadn't promised she could save everyone. Even if she could, that didn't mean the pharedimi or Viriok would spare them for their cleverness or creativity. She hoped they would earn a reprieve as a result, but couldn't offer any guarantees.

"You're just a pokken gunner," Jaco snapped.

"Jaco," Madison murmured. "Shut up."

Shmar curled his lip at Jaco. "And you're just a pokken cabin boy begging for scraps at the big kid table." He jutted his chin at Madison.

"That's head cabin boy to you," Madison said with a roll of her eye. She stopped Jaco from charging at Shmar with a hand on his chest. "Knock it off. We're done here, okay? I give up. Go be cranky with the rest of the crew and brood about dying until whenever they get around to killing us. Let me know if you get bored with that, then we'll talk. Until then, we'll stay over here, and you can stay over there."

Shmar whirled and stalked to his group, all of whom had

awakened during their shouting match. Madison saw Oolaang and Rho awake also. Their food blocks sat untouched between them.

Madison stepped close to Jaco and nudged him backward. "Stop trying to fight with him."

"Stop goading him."

"Stop rushing to my defense."

"Stop being yourself."

She huffed. "Fine. That thing is food. Bolt it so you don't taste it."

"That went well," Kirehe said.

"Don't you start too." Madison shoved Jaco, forcing him to take one step back, then gave up and let go. She skirted around him to lean against the wall and slid down it to sit beside Kirehe again.

Jaco glared at Shmar. Shmar glared at Jaco. Oolaang stood and moved in front of Jaco. He could see over Oolaang's head, of course, but couldn't storm through him.

"We're all scared and upset," Oolaang said. "Leave him be. Leave them all be. Give them time to handle things. Either they'll see that Madison did the best she could and made us no promises, or they won't. You can't change that. Especially not by acting like Maddie's attack dog."

Though he could've stayed there and waited for Jaco to settle down, Oolaang didn't. He shuffled to Madison's side and sat, then he took the food block and bit off a piece.

"No one has ever escaped from Rikor Six," Oolaang said. "I know that much."

"We'll be the first," Madison said. If she wished hard enough, it would come true. Taking it one step at a time would help. With Kirehe on their side, they had the first one handled. After that, she could only hope fourteen souls earned the distinction of leaving Rikor Six under their own power.

Fourteen became her mantra.

CHAPTER 10

KIREHE

Fifteen days passed. Kirehe could tell by the cycle of the kukiri flock. They arrived early in the morning and left a few hours later. Skila made a point of greeting her each day. She looked forward to that moment and treasured it. For the rest of each day, she learned a series of words in the enemy language from Madison and exercised as much as she could.

Watching Jaco and Madison interact, she decided they shared a deep, close friendship. They acted nothing like any of the lovers Kirehe had observed, either human or dragon. She, of course, had never found anyone as pleasant or interesting as a dragon, so she had no personal basis to judge by.

The other pack intrigued her. Shmar seemed too proud to relent. Other members of his pack argued with him, yet none proved strong enough to either challenge him or break from him. Their alpha had cowed them, which meant he had the potential of a good alpha. Protecting them from the maras would prove his worth.

She doubted he'd succeed.

Once everyone woke, one of the smooth-voiced ones called into the chamber. Kirehe understood enough. Madison had made sure to teach her the word for execution. They shuffled out of the room in a dismal line with their heads down. Oolaang shaded his eyes with two hands. Kirehe did her best to fit among them. She didn't feel as defeated as they appeared but tried to affect the same mannerisms.

Even Madison seemed beaten. The heat, so she'd said, wore on her, as did the damp air. Jaco and Oolaang also complained about the temperature. In spaceships, they didn't have so much heat, according to Madison. They lived in cold places, which sounded terrible.

The miserable line followed the corridor of light. Kirehe could hear the soft machine hum from the fluffy creatures hiding in the darkness. Madison had called them "hevits." The name didn't fit. They deserved a sneaky, stealthy name, like ninjas.

As they marched to their doom, Kirehe heard noise in the distance. It grew closer with every step. She couldn't decipher it. The sound reminded her of nothing she'd heard before. If the entire Tosnorth village coughed at the same time, and kept doing so without pausing, it might match the strange sound.

They turned a corner and climbed a set of steps. Light spilled through a metal grate door at the end of the corridor. The noise continued to grow. On the other side of the door, white stone like that of the building's outer frame made Kirehe think they might escape through the roof. She wished Skila had come with her. The kukiri could've taken a message to any nearby kratas.

Except even the wild kratas avoided Irondoom. A kukiri calling for help wouldn't summon a single one. The kratas would either ignore her or laugh. Any dragoncallers she found would report Kirehe as lost, mourn her, and move on.

No help would come from the outside.

"Stop," their smooth-voiced escort ordered. They said something else.

Everyone turned to stare at Madison. She heaved a sigh and trudged to the front of the line.

The escort leaned close to Madison and spoke words Kirehe couldn't hear, much less understand.

Madison snorted. She asked something about dinner.

Their escort stepped away, murmuring a threat of some kind.

Along with some derisive words, Madison laughed.

The grate lifted. Madison stepped through it. Intense light flared over her. Noise exploded as if someone had unleashed a horde of angry kratas. Jaco followed her. They kept going. Madison strode deeper into the new cavern with her head high.

Kirehe stepped through the door. Two meter high, white stone walls in a huge, unbroken circle surrounded a strange floor the color of dried blood. The material seemed granular, yet it sprang enough to put a bounce in Kirehe's step. Above the wall, clear material like thick plastic separated a throng of people from them. More people than she'd ever seen in one place cheered, screamed, and pumped their fists in the air.

That explained the noise.

Not a single person in the crowd appeared human. She saw many of the same type as that pilot who'd shot her. Others had flat faces, eyes on stalks, or other oddities. This place, her homeworld, served aliens instead of its own people.

When she looked up, Kirehe discovered a dome, which told her they stood inside the largest of Irondoom's buildings. The others had flat roofs. One section of the tiered spectator area, perhaps forty meters in the air, had a square platform with a throne-like chair. White vapor roiled around the gray-skinned alien sitting in that chair. People in strange masks and thick clothing of the same green and gold as the smooth-voice ones stood beside and behind him.

Across from the grate they stepped through, another grate, much larger than the two-man door they'd used, remained closed. Even Kirehe could figure out what would rush through that gate.

Madison kept walking until she stood in the center of the vast arena. The rest of the prisoners clustered. Predictably, the two packs formed separate groups, though a few in the rival pack hovered in the space between, too terrified to make a true choice.

Turning to take in the sights and determine the best course of action, Kirehe kept going. On purpose, following the plan of appearing harmless, she bumped into Madison from behind. The crowd roared with laughter.

Madison chewed on her lip. Jaco swung his arms like that would force out the fear. Oolaang stationed himself behind Kirehe and hid his face. The small man's eyes, so she'd learned, couldn't handle bright light. Rho kept a hand on Oolaang's shoulder.

"Steady," Rho said. They raised their chin and spoke with determined dignity.

"Whatever you do," Kirehe said, "stay together and make sure I remain between you and all the maras."

Madison repeated this for the others. Members of the other pack heard her. Whether they would heed her, Kirehe couldn't say. Fear wriggled across their bodies and faces with wild abandon.

The gray-skinned alien stood at the edge of his platform, his green and gold cape shimmering in the spotlight trained on him. His voice rumbled and echoed from every angle. From the first moment he opened his mouth, the unruly crowd quieted and listened.

If nothing else, Kirehe could admit that ability to command attention deserved respect. She wouldn't underestimate this enemy.

As he spoke, machines buzzed into the arena. Five small white balls, each the size of a kukiri, flew a meter or two above Kirehe's head. One hovered over Madison. The rest swerved and swooped above the remaining prisoners.

Many among the crowd raised a hand to their face with a blue glow. Overhead, the low edge of the dome showed several copies of a close image of Madison from above. As she watched, Kirehe realized the ball machines took pictures and transmitted them to the spots on the walls.

The sacred texts in TFT Cave included descriptions of such things. Kirehe had never understood the sections about video until this moment.

She understood some of the gray-skinned master's words but paid more attention to how he spoke than what he said. He used grand gestures and vocal inflections. His entire body participated. The crowd responded to him. Half a minute into his speech, he pointed at Madison and said her name.

Madison raised a single finger for the cameras. For some reason, a titter rippled through the crowd.

Kirehe sniffed the air. Besides the stink of fear and death, she caught a breath of mara dragon. The creature's musk tasted sick. It needed help. She would help it in whatever way she could. If it let her.

While the gray-skinned master kept talking, Kirehe shifted, one step at a time, until she stood between Madison and the large gate. The time for subterfuge had ended. She wished she could have a staff or stick to extend her reach. What she had, she would work with.

"Stay close," Jaco told the other pack.

She stopped paying attention to them and the speaker. Her focus narrowed to the maras. Nothing else mattered. Those in the arena with her would either let her protect them or not. They bore responsibility for their actions. No matter what anyone said or did, she would not accept blame for their deaths.

The gray-skinned master stopped talking. He clapped twice, the sound resonating in Kirehe's chest. In front of her, the gate cranked open, bit by bit. Her heart sped in anticipation. But not fear. Kirehe didn't fear maras. She never had and never would. They could smell fear in the air.

To them, it tasted sickly-sweet, like the hard-shell fruit.

In the wild, maras moved cautiously when approaching prey, wary of startling it. These maras thundered into the arena, running fast enough to overtake Kirehe in moments.

The crowd screamed their excitement, drowning all noise.

Kirehe spread her arms and whistled, "Stop!" With this command, she stomped her foot and bared her teeth. If they couldn't hear her, she had a big problem.

The maras slowed to a walk, approaching her. Crowd noise dimmed.

"Hungry," the lead mara whined, her jaws open and claws

brandished.

Behind the lead, the rest of the pack shifted. A good pack would stop and listen. This pack couldn't stand still and wouldn't focus on Kirehe. Their eyes darted, focusing on the prisoners behind her.

"Not food." Kirehe whistled at them, her voice higher in pitch than humans could hear. "Friends. Many friends."

One of the prisoners warbled their fear.

With the lead mara's attention hanging by a thread, Kirehe couldn't do anything about the other prisoners' actions.

"Where to find food?" The lead mara stepped closer.

Her pack shifted closer.

Kirehe waved her hands, trying to attract their attention. "Not here."

"Hungry now. Smell food."

The lead mara jerked her body, performing a startle maneuver maras used to flush prey into the waiting claws of packmates. Kirehe had never seen one do it without packmates in place to catch the prey. She hadn't expected it but didn't flinch.

These maras had a sickness of mind more than body.

Behind Kirehe, the prisoners all reacted to the startle-fake. Even Madison squeaked. The pack, including the lead mara, launched around Kirehe, flowing like a stream around a boulder.

Kirehe gathered as many as she could behind her and swung them around to keep herself between them and the pack. Those behind her whimpered and sighed as they watched the carnage.

Most of the prisoners had run. Kirehe glanced back to see Madison, Jaco, Oolaang, Rho, and Shmar huddling behind her, averting their gazes. The rest had succumbed to their terror and now faced the consequences.

Kirehe watched because she needed to see how they worked if she wanted to undo the demented training these maras had undergone. And she needed to know if they would respect an alpha.

The maras had no trouble catching all those who fled. People in the stands cheered as they pounced on men and women, ripping claws through their bodies. Blood painted the floor. Body parts flew. Screams dwindled until Kirehe could hear nothing over the crowd.

In the midst of all this death, Kirehe saw a light of hope. The pack didn't perform clean, instant kills, which matched wild mara behavior. Instead, they disabled each target and moved on. They deferred to the lead mara, which also boded well. She performed the kill and ripped out her preferred organ to eat it.

Despite their hunger, the pack waited for her to finish.

"Can't you stop them?" Madison whimpered.

If she had access to the Tosnorth cave healer, she might've tried to prevent the last few deaths. Without such swift and skilled intervention, those people would bleed to death within minutes with or without her help. "There's no point."

When the lead mara devoured the last man's liver, the pack pounced on the corpses and descended into a flurry of desperate ravaging. They choked down parts that wild maras would leave for scavengers. Their frantic efforts splashed blood everywhere, including all over their own scales and feathers. Body parts and cloth flew around them. The scene reminded Kirehe of a gory pillow ripping open.

Wild maras ate with care. They made no mess. What blood they spilled landed on the ground and plants, not themselves. The lead mara often made her pack wait after eating the liver, testing their loyalty and restraint. These wouldn't have listened even if their lead tried.

The frenzy calmed. The maras slowed their assaults on the corpses.

"Stay here," Kirehe said.

"Are you kidding?" Madison whimpered. "I'm staying with you."

"I'm going to challenge the alpha for dominance. If you want to participate in that, you can, but I suspect you won't fare well."

Madison burbled a nervous laugh and patted Kirehe's shoulder. "Uh, yeah. You go ahead and do that. We'll wait here. Watch. Provide performance critique afterward. That sort of thing."

Kirehe nodded, trusting Madison to keep her pack under control. She strode to the maras with a confident swagger. The stench of their kills roiled her stomach, but she didn't dare let them see that.

The crowd quieted, which helped her.

She stopped close enough to be sure they could hear her and raised her fists. As she had avoided during her assessment, she lifted her heels off the ground and bent her knees. "I am your alpha," she growled. "You will obey me."

As one, the maras raised their bloody snouts to stare at her. The pack shifted their attention to the lead, as Kirehe expected.

"I am your alpha," the lead mara said. "You will obey me."

"You're not strong enough to control me." Kirehe added an obnoxious hiss, the kind used by young rivals too stupid to know when they challenged too high. She had to goad this mara into fighting her because the rest of this pack wouldn't respect her without a decisive victory. They'd shown as much in their actions and behavior.

To her surprise, the lead mara echoed the hiss.

The lead mara raised her claws, opened her jaws, and ran at Kirehe. Crowd noise surged. Kirehe danced to the side and punched down, delivering a blow to the top of the mara's head. Her fist cracked against the mara's eye ridge, causing little harm. The mara's claws missed Kirehe by a wide margin.

Kirehe let momentum carry her into a roll. She landed on her feet behind the mara and jumped over a tail slap.

Crowd noise faded into the background. Kirehe watched the mara's shoulders, haunches, and head. She trusted the rest of the mara pack and Madison's pack to stay clear, at least until this fight ended.

"I am your alpha. You will obey me." Kirehe stomped her foot to make sure she had the lead's attention and anger.

"I am the alpha!" The lead spun and slashed.

Kirehe blocked both claw attacks with one sweep of her arm. She used the other hand to slam the mara's head aside. Pivoting on one foot, she snapped her leg and kicked the mara's neck.

Like Lipa, once the mara lost her focus and any semblance of an advantage, she lost the fight. Kirehe stepped close and swept the mara's leg while shoving her with a shoulder. The poor thing fell on her side and flailed.

Kirehe slid back and let her thrash. She glanced at the rest of the pack. They watched in silence. To her surprise, a hush had fallen over the entire arena.

In the lead mara's position, Lipa would have yielded. Lipa liked to rebel and take chances, but she didn't need to beat Kirehe. She only wanted to try, to put her neck out and see what happened.

This mara scrambled to her feet and flared her claws again. "I will not obey you!"

With a lift of her chin, Kirehe held out her hand and waved for the mara to attack, knowing it would infuriate the poor thing.

Everyone gasped except Kirehe. She stood her ground while the mara charged her, screaming wordless defiance and rage.

The moment before the mara crashed into her, Kirehe stepped to the right. She snapped her arm to the left to block an attack and jammed her shoulder into the mara's neck. Taking the mara's forelimb, she used the creature's own momentum to flip the mara's bulk over her back. The mara landed on the ground and slid across the stone.

Kirehe made a point to turn and reset her stance as if she'd done nothing of great import or difficulty, as if she hadn't trained for years to gain the skill and strength to toss a mara dragon. In her periphery, she noticed Shmar leaning like he intended to run. She held up a hand to keep him and the others still.

Large movements would distract the maras. Until their alpha conceded to Kirehe, they could behave unpredictably and she had no control over them.

The lead mara struggled to her feet again. She shook her head and snapped her jaws a few times, her sharp teeth clacking together in the eerie silence. Her snout snapped to point at Kirehe. "I am the alpha."

"No. Obey me."

In an unexpected show of petulance, the lead mara stomped her foot and screamed at Kirehe.

This mara wouldn't give up until Kirehe knocked her unconscious. So be it.

Before the mara stopped roaring, Kirehe charged her. At the last moment, as the mara recoiled, she leaped and thrust out her foot. Her heel slammed into the mara's flank. The mara stumbled to the ground. Kirehe landed on her other side and delivered a backward kick. She spun and slammed her fist into the mara's head, hitting the back of her neck below the skull.

The mara squawked in pain. Kirehe hated to hurt her, but she needed the mara to submit. Between her feet, knees, and fists, she pummeled the mara until the poor thing slumped, unable to rise.

Around her, the crowd erupted into thundering cheers. The rest of the mara pack flinched at the noise as they trotted to Kirehe. Each bowed their heads to her, one by one, calling her the alpha. She patted their necks and scratched behind their frills. They moved close, smearing blood all over her body.

Finally, the maras acted like normal.

CHAPTER 11

MADISON

Watching Kirehe beat up a fanged, clawed monster made Madison's heart beat fifty zillion times a minute. She wanted to kiss that woman so hard it hurt. If she'd learned anything from this display, though, she knew she would never, ever touch Kirehe without her permission.

"If she's not interested in you, I'm next in line," Jaco murmured.

Madison jabbed her elbow into his side. If Kirehe didn't like women, she thought she might die from the unfairness. Then Jaco could do whatever he wanted. Including getting his ass kicked by the hottest thing Madison had ever seen.

Tearing her gaze from the amazing sight of Kirehe hugging and scritching a bunch of dragons, she noticed Arena Master Viriok watching all of them. He stood on the edge of his platform, too far away to read his expression. One of the masked pharedim bobbed at his elbow. He shook his head and said something, then waved off the pharedim.

"My guests, what an excellent surprise for you all!" Viriok opened his arms wide.

The crowd cheered.

Madison's mouth ran dry. If she'd guessed wrong about how the place worked, this plan had accomplished nothing except a delay. She'd take a delay so long as it lasted more than five minutes.

"We promised you death, and we have delivered. Fourteen walked in and only six will walk out. Is that enough blood to slake your thirst?"

Eight lives lost. Madison wished they'd listened to her. She glanced at Shmar, who stood with his hands covering his face. If only he'd listened. If only she'd tried harder. If only they'd had enough privacy for her to explain.

As if to explain what Viriok asked, a dozen pharedimi with blaster rifles jogged through the smaller door. They ran to the group and lined up to form a firing squad more than sufficient to hit everyone twice over.

The crowd chanted, "Live! Live! Live!"

Madison chose to appreciate this. She stopped herself from doing anything stupid, like blowing kisses or waving. One wrong move and they might change their minds.

"I hear you!" Viriok raised his arms in triumph. "These special souls are granted a reprieve from death." He paused, creating a dramatic effect. "For now."

All the pharedimi lowered their weapons. One on the end waved for everyone to follow them. "Let's go, people. Get moving."

"I want to go with the maras," Kirehe said. "Ask them if I can go with the pack."

Madison waved for her to come along. "This isn't a good time. Come now, ask later."

Kirehe sighed. She crouched over the fallen mara and kissed its cheek, then bumped her head against each member of the pack. They shared whistles and chirps.

The pharedimi didn't interrupt Kirehe. They also didn't let anyone else stand around and wait for her. One jabbed a rifle against Madison's back and forced her to walk while four stayed to collect Kirehe.

As they left, more pharedimi poured from the larger door with electrified sticks. Madison had a feeling Kirehe wouldn't approve of pharedim animal handling methods. She waved for Kirehe to get moving.

Kirehe saw her and let the armed pharedimi lead her to the door. Madison had no doubt she allowed it. If she wanted to, Kirehe could probably disarm them all before any managed to fire a single shot.

Maybe not. Still, Kirehe was amazing, and Madison wanted to tell her.

"After that incredible treat, we have another." Viriok's voice echoed less once they stepped through the door and into the light corridor again.

Their escorts stopped them, waiting for Kirehe. Madison watched as hover vehicles zoomed from the larger door to clean up the mess. The mara pack picked up their downed packmate and carried its weight between them, which surprised Madison. They followed their armed pharedim keepers without a fuss, which surprised her even more.

"Direct your attention to the screens, my guests, to prepare for the next event." Viriok stopped talking, and Madison tuned out the arena.

Two heavily-muscled people strode up the light corridor with one pharedim escort. The human woman wore several pieces of shiny golden armor over various parts of her body. Where the metal didn't cover, she wore skin-tight fabric the same color as her medium-brown flesh. In some places, tufts of bright green fur provided a garish accent. A thick, leather-wrapped sword hilt stuck over her left shoulder.

The human man beside her wore a similar costume and sported a dark beard. A small, thin scar traced a line across his right temple, from his eye to his ear. He carried a thick staff instead of a sword.

Madison expected the guards to shuffle everyone elsewhere, but they didn't. Kirehe joined them, and still they waited.

Both newcomers ignored all of them. They stopped two steps before the doorway and waited with grim expressions. The man patted the woman's shoulder and murmured something too low for Madison to hear. In response, the woman said nothing and nodded. Both wore makeup designed to give them the appearance of animals.

Lights in the arena dimmed. The woman strode through the door. The man followed her. Their escort shut the door.

One escort for two people meant Overseer Neilan trusted them not to try anything. She suspected both had served in the arena for a long time. In her wildest dreams, she couldn't imagine any authority here ever trusting her that much. Now that she knew it could happen, though, the wheels in her head turned.

"Stay quiet," one of the pharedim guards said. "Anyone who makes a sound gets a beating. You're waiting here until I say otherwise."

For once, Madison followed orders. Keeping her mouth shut, she took a step toward the door. No one stopped her from watching through the metal grate.

Darkness engulfed the arena floor. A few meters above it, dim light bathed the stands. Madison couldn't see the video still playing, but she noticed when its light faded. A moment later, the lights on the stands also faded.

"Please give Erryl a warm welcome," Viriok purred into the pitch darkness.

A spotlight flared into life with the man at the center. He looked up at Viriok and raised a hand in salute. The crowd cheered for him.

"And his opponent, everyone's favorite, Anya."

A second spotlight flared around the woman. The crowd cheered more for her. She drew her sword and pointed it at Viriok.

"What's this?" Viriok sounded surprised. "Anya, you wish to challenge me?"

The woman nodded.

"What say you, my guests? Has Anya earned this distinction? Is she worthy?"

When the spotlight on the man faded before the crowd's roar of excitement began, Madison realized the event had been scripted. Anya's challenge hadn't surprised him.

She wanted to ask questions. After spending two weeks recovering from her last beating, she preferred not to get another one.

"Very well. I accept your challenge, Anya."

The male gladiator reached the door. It opened for him. He stopped to watch with Madison.

"Fifteen years," he murmured to Madison. "Respect."

Madison nodded. After only fifteen days, the idea of fifteen years stuck in the pits under the arena sounded like the worst kind of hell.

Cold air blasted through the door, filling the arena. Viriok landed on the floor on one knee, with one fist on the ground and the other holding a gleaming metal spear aloft. He'd jumped from his platform, apparently. He also had a much more impressive flair for the dramatic than Cradok.

Viriok stood, no longer wearing his cape. He slammed the butt of his spear against the ground.

"Behold," a female pharedim voice boomed. "The Arena Master will now fight Gladiator Anya. If she wins, she earns her freedom."

"And if she loses?" Madison whispered to Erryl.

Erryl glanced at her, then shook his head as if he considered her a fool. "This is her retirement."

Suddenly, the situation made sense. Oolaang had told her about this. Anya had passed her prime. Viriok no longer found her useful, except as a glorious victim of his ego.

The lights rose on the arena floor, but not in the stands. Anya and Viriok circled each other as if the entire match had a script. Kirehe leaned against Madison to watch with her. No one else seemed interested. Madison didn't blame them. They'd lost eight more friends in the blink of an eye.

Viriok made no aggressive moves. Anya finally turned and crossed the distance at a run. The crowd gasped and squealed. Her blade clanged against his spear. Together, they danced, their blades flashing in the light.

"Why isn't he fighting?" Kirehe whispered.

Madison had no answer. To her, he fought well. She passed the question to Erryl.

"To get good footage for the cameras."

"Really?" Madison asked.

"Yes, really. She'll be remembered." Erryl sounded like he considered that a great honor.

When Madison relayed the answer to Kirehe, she raised her brow.

"That sounds stupid."

Madison shrugged. She didn't get it either. On second thought, she did. Oolaang had mentioned the compilation videos. Viriok cared about appearances and grandiose spectacle. Killing off a gladiator he could trust who had earned audience favor cost him something. Turning it into a glorious battle instead of a perfunctory execution allowed him to squeeze the last magnificent drops out of someone's life.

Viriok operated on a level of evil Madison could appreciate as thorough.

At the point when Anya tired, Viriok swept in and murdered her with a display of speed, strength, and prowess Madison found breathtaking. The blow Cradok had delivered to Madison's chest had given her a bone-deep bruise. She suspected Viriok could do better with less effort. Even Kirehe wouldn't stand a chance against him.

Viriok planted his boot on Anya's body. He yanked out his spear and plunged it through her neck, giving her a swift, merciful death.

"Behold Anya," the pharedim announcer voice said. "She will be remembered as one of the greats among our constellation of stars. May her memory inspire others to follow in her footsteps."

The arena lights shut off, and the crowd erupted into wild cheering and applause.

Erryl shoved Madison and Kirehe aside and stood away from the door. It opened as the lights came on in the arena stands again. Viriok stepped through the door, and it shut behind him.

"The arena's program has concluded for today. Thank you for coming. Other attractions have opened their doors and await you." Madison stopped listening to the announcer as she listed a variety of diversions.

"Madison Wayward." Viriok sounded much less scary without the amplification projecting his voice across the arena. Standing this close to him still terrified Madison. After seeing him in action, she had no interest in provoking him. Much. "Your execution has been postponed. The rest of you will have your skills reviewed."

He turned to Kirehe. "What is your name?"

Kirehe knew those words. Madison had taught her. "Kirehe."

Viriok nodded. "Where is Overseer Neilan?"

"Here, Your Benevolence." Overseer Neilan hurried into view, puffing as if he'd run to arrive on time.

"Why was this one in the execution match?"

Overseer Neilan bowed in obedience. "She performed poorly in assessment, Your Benevolence. As one of the local savages, she may not have understood the point."

Viriok smirked. "I think she played you for the fool, Neilan."

Overseer Neilan's mouth twitched with dismay. "That is also possible, Your Benevolence."

Viriok rapped the butt of his staff on the floor. "Take Kirehe to the gladiator pit. Return these others to the execution pit. I want them assessed for useful skills and added to the slave rosters by the end of the week. We'll reschedule the Wayward execution. Make it a month to attract as many as possible by then. Come up with a good idea for a showy death for her by herself. No more surprises."

"Yes, Your Benevolence."

"I have useful skills," Madison said. She smiled wide enough to catch a glint of light with her teeth.

Viriok turned to regard her. "Yes. One of them is crushing Stardrifter morale by dying messily in my arena. That's the one I plan to utilize."

Madison cleared her throat because Viriok turned to leave. "Just throwing this out there, but I speak the local language."

He stalked into the darkness. "I don't care."

Overseer Neilan finally straightened. "You heard Lord Viriok. Get them where they need to go."

Pharedim guards hustled Kirehe in one direction and everyone else in another.

Kirehe yanked her arm out of a guard's grasp. "Madison! What's happening?"

"Trust me! I'll figure something out!" Madison had no idea why she said that. What, exactly, would she figure out? How to convince Viriok to kill her with his bare hands? The fastest way to aggravate Overseer Neilan?

Jaco took her arm and tugged her in the direction the guards wanted them to go.

Kirehe balled her hands into fists and refused to move. "Tell me what's going on," she growled.

"Tell her something so no one gets shot," Jaco murmured.

"Go with them," Madison said. Watching the guards back off Kirehe gave her an idea. It almost had enough meat to qualify as a plan. "For now. Be difficult, but not impossible. Snap at them and don't do anything they want unless they point a weapon at you."

Kirehe relaxed her stance. "I would've done that anyway."

A guard shoved Madison forward. She stumbled and let Jaco guide her. "I know. That's what makes you amazing!"

The guards herded the survivors into the darkness, and they stumbled into the execution pit as a clump. Madison fell under Shmar's weight and groaned. Rho toppled onto him. Oolaang squeaked as he narrowly escaped a pummeling under Jaco's weight.

They wriggled and squirmed to disentangle from each other. Madison sat against the wall where she'd spent two weeks teaching Kirehe to speak the language. Shmar lay on the floor where he'd spent two weeks ignoring her and muttering with a bunch of people who'd died less than half an hour earlier. Jaco trudged to the pool and washed his face and hands with crappy water. Oolaang and Rho stayed on the floor where they'd fallen, both staring at nothing.

In fairness, Madison wanted to stare at nothing and not think too. She hoped her new plan didn't leave her much time for that.

CHAPTER 12

KIREHE

Along the way to the new place, Kirehe puzzled over the last thing Madison had said. Why did Madison consider her amazing? For not liking this confinement?

The man walked with her and spoke to her. She understood a few of the words, like his name. By the time they reached a new metal grate door, this one without a barrier of darkness, he'd given up on trying to ask her questions. He shrugged and left her behind as he entered a new room. The guards used enough pointing with their rifles that she understood she needed to follow him.

Unlike the execution pit, this new place had cooler air and a sterile smell. Green, gold, and white decorated everything. Thin chairs and tables occupied half of the space, many of them holding people. Along the wall behind them, a row of shelves carried platters with an array of foods trundling from one end to the other as if on rollers. At one end, the platters arrived through a small opening. At the other, the platters disappeared through another small opening.

Tubes marked with signs stuck out of the wall beside the rolling food, then stacked cups and plates, and containers full of utensils. Beside that, two large bins sat on a wheeled cart.

Strange, inscrutable devices occupied the other half of the room. For the moment, everyone present gave their attention to a large screen dominating one wall. The video showed images of Anya performing spectacular maneuvers and defeating a variety of opponents.

Those present must have known her, and they chose this method to honor her pointless death.

Most of the people appeared human. The rest had a similar bipedal build with varying differences. One person had angular muscles, making their body appear squarish. Another, like Oolaang, had four arms. Unlike Oolaang, this person loomed over everyone else with massive bulk, and two of their arms were short and spindly. Everyone wore similar plain, functional clothing in green with yellow trim, like a bland version of the uniforms worn by the smooth-voiced ones.

Four doorways led to other rooms or corridors. Her smooth-voiced escort nudged her to the left. She considered smacking him, but Madison had said to play along somewhat. Enough to avoid true harm delivered for being too difficult.

Through the doorway her escort indicated, she found a row of white doors set in the white walls, which seemed stupid. Each had two symbols.

Her escort took her to a particular door and opened it for her. Inside, the room had no light of its own. Kirehe had no interest in a dark room.

She turned to leave. The escort pointed inside and said something. Kirehe pointed at the doorway. He poked her in the shoulder. She slapped him across the face.

"No," she snarled.

The escort glared at her for a moment, then raised his arms in exasperation and stalked out of the hallway, muttering.

Kirehe let him go. She waited half a minute in case he returned with an explanation, then she ventured back to the large room.

She headed for the food. After two weeks of food blocks, she could eat almost anything. Plate in hand, she watched the food trundle past for a short time before picking up a utensil and using it to spear red things. Bolstered by this small victory, she speared and scooped small portions of everything that would fit on her plate. Since she had nothing to say to anyone and no interest in the video, she sat at an empty table with her back to the screen and tried each thing in turn.

A man slid into a chair at her table with a cup of purple liquid. He talked at her with a pleasant smile. She said nothing and continued to test the food. This stringy one had a strange flavor, like burnt risi. The white goo tasted good but settled in her stomach like a brick.

The man knocked a knuckle on the table. She looked up to see him with his brow raised, expecting an answer to something.

"Kirehe," she said, and pointed to her chest. Then she tried the reddish-blue meat-like substance. It squeaked against her teeth, which bothered her, though it tasted fine.

"What?"

"My name is Kirehe." She thought she pronounced all the words correctly.

He stared at her. She ate more of the meat-stuff. He drank from his cup.

"Bryor."

Madison had taught her a phrase for a reply to that. She couldn't recall the order for the words. "Meet you good me." That didn't sound right, but she couldn't remember for sure.

Frowning, he said something else, then he left.

Left to her food, she watched Bryor slide into another chair at a table with other men. While he spoke, he pointed at Kirehe. Erryl, the man she'd met after the execution match, squinted at Kirehe. They talked for a minute or two, then Erryl stood.

"Overseer!" Erryl stalked to the metal grate door and shouted through it.

Kirehe stopped paying attention to him. She quite liked some of the foods. Others had strange flavors she found obnoxious or gross. Once she'd eaten as much as she cared to, Kirehe dropped off her plate and utensils, fetched a cup of white liquid that tasted fine, and wandered.

By then, the video had stopped playing. Instead, the screen

showed a view outside. These people knew no decency at all. Taunting them with an image of the outside when they knew they couldn't have it struck her as unnecessarily cruel.

She had no use for a fake view of her home.

Three of the doorways led to halls like the one with that room, except for one. That other doorway led to two large rooms. One had an entire wall made of mirror. Kirehe had only seen small, irregular mirrors before, and only in TFT Cave. This mirror spanned one meter in height and at least ten in width. The room otherwise held nothing.

After a few minutes of watching herself make faces in the mirror, the room lost its novelty. She checked the other room. Two stools sat against one wall beside stacks of sticks. Aside from the people, it held nothing else.

Six women and four men sparred in pairs with sticks like those in the stacks. She could tell they sparred for training because they traded blows in an equitable fashion and didn't try to harm each other.

Kirehe sat on a stool and watched them. One woman used a strange style Kirehe didn't understand, and she wanted to decode it. The woman's feet shifted in strange ways, and she used odd movements to feint. Though her partner used a different style, she didn't confuse him with her movements. They'd probably trained together before.

Once she noticed the man's different style, she realized they each used different movements, different attacks, different blocks, and different stances. So many different ways to fight! She had no idea people devised so many options for the purpose of attacking and killing.

Watching their rhythms soothed her mind. She hadn't enjoyed watching all those people die. They meant nothing to her, yet it felt like a personal offense to have people die under mara dragon claws. Not that she accepted any blame. They should have stayed behind her. But the maras shouldn't have killed them.

Dragoncallers trained maras to protect all the Iwa people. They might need to kill sentient foes, but they would never eat people. Risi dragons tasted much better, as did many other species. The maras and

Nihan had told her as much. Sometimes, they found fresh human corpses and ate them by mistake, so they knew the difference.

These people had committed a crime by driving them to kill and eat sentients.

"Hi." One of the women approached her with a strained smile. She said other things.

Kirehe let her talk, then introduced herself.

The woman's smile faltered. "Taria." She asked a question.

Raising her hands, Kirehe shook her head.

The woman huffed and stormed out of the room. "Overseer!"

Apparently, Kirehe made everyone want to talk to the overseer. She shrugged at the rest of the occupants of the room and left. If no one could understand her, she'd have to put more effort into learning the language. She did want to escape, after all. Madison hadn't come with her, so she needed to figure out things for herself, at least for now.

At least she'd temporarily saved a few lives by failing the assessment. Otherwise, today hadn't accomplished much more than upgrading her food choices.

CHAPTER 13

MADISON

The execution pit hadn't felt so empty before. Madison sat on the floor, staring at her hands. She'd think of something. Any minute now, a brilliant idea would pop into her head and solve at least one of her problems. Even if it only solved the crushing weight of guilt over the loss of so many members of the crew, she'd count it a victory.

"They're dead because of you," Shmar grumbled.

Jaco huffed. "They're dead because they panicked. If anyone's to blame for that, it's you."

"Shut up," Madison said. "They're dead. Arguing about it won't change that. Nothing you can say will bring them back."

Shmar covered his face. His shoulders shook. Rho squatted beside him and patted his shoulder. They made soothing noises without using words.

Oolaang sat and stared in a dejected lump with no sign he saw or heard anything.

Madison thought of their names. She rubbed her eye, hoping it would blot out the images of dragons chasing them down and killing them. She couldn't stop seeing those things slashing across spines or legs to disable.

Crowd noise had drowned out their voices. She didn't have to listen to their helpless cries echoing in her head because a throng of soulless, evil people had rejoiced in their deaths.

Since grasping the concept of her position in the galaxy as an outlaw under Oligarchy rule, she'd come to understand that the pharedimi served because they wanted to. Those who served the Oligarchy did so because they made that choice. She knew that.

Until she saw all those people reveling in the violent deaths of sentient beings, she hadn't truly internalized what that meant. They liked the Oligarchy. The tyrannical policies benefited them. Anyone who didn't conform deserved to die, and they wanted to watch.

To them, those in the arena didn't count as people. Viriok owned them all. They were possessions. Toys. Everyone who chose to owe him fealty felt the same. In no way would any of them ever consider Madison a full sentient being worthy of dignity or respect.

People she'd known and cared about for years had died in a moment of pain and terror because a vast sea of people considered them toys.

Once upon a time, she'd thought the lakhans were the worst part about the Lakhan Oligarchy. But the lakhans only managed it. The pharedimi, the hevits, the qusamadi, and the other races who feasted on lakhan table scraps were no better. In many ways, they were worse. They propped up the tyrants and kept them in power.

At least the dead no longer had to face such overwhelming odds. The dead had no worries or fears.

"Madison, what's your new plan?" Jaco sat beside her and draped an arm over her shoulders.

She shook her head and rested her chin on her knees. "I don't have one."

"But you have an idea, right?"

"No." She pictured a dragon ripping out Jaco's spine. Her best friend's death would crush her. Bantering with him had always kept her spirits high whenever things seemed low. At the moment, she didn't have the energy for it.

He paused for a long, empty moment. "Are you sure?"

"There are guards everywhere. The grates are too small to get through. Kirehe is gone. Everyone else is dead. This place is a fortress. We're surrounded by hundreds of people who want to cheer while we die. All of you get to live glamorous lives as slaves while I'm going to die as soon as they set up another spectacle for just me. What kind of plan do you think I should have?" Until she reached the end, she didn't realize she'd let her voice rise to a frustrated, angry shout.

The chamber echoed with ringing silence.

Jaco leaned close and held her. His chest moved like he intended to say something, but he didn't. Words wouldn't solve any problems anyway.

If she refused to eat the food blocks, would they let her starve to death? Then she'd die without pomp or spectacle, which seemed like the only revenge left to take.

Jaco's warmth made her sweat more than the sweltering air, but she took the comfort he offered, even if it didn't help.

Some time later, she startled awake at the sound of her name barked across the room.

"Madison Wayward," the pharedim snapped, probably for the second or third time. "Wake up, you twit."

"Suck void," she grumbled.

"Come to the door. Overseer Neilan wants to speak with you."

Madison sat up and glared at the darkness. What would he do if she refused? Kill her? "No. He can come to me."

The voice didn't answer. Instead, she caught the edge of a blur. Something, probably a hevit, grabbed her and tossed her into the darkness. She flailed and landed in a heap with bright light glaring into her face.

"No, Wayward, you will come to the door." Ilai, the pharedim who'd originally hauled her to the execution pit crouched at her head so Madison saw her face upside-down. "You can either walk to see the overseer, or you can be carried. Which do you prefer? Before you decide, I should mention the carrying option includes a beating."

"Gosh, a beating is so scary when I know I'm going to die soon."

Ilai offered her a tight little smirk that somehow curled both sides of her mouth at the same time while still evoking her disdain.

Madison blinked as she realized why she found their appearance so unnerving. Their faces had perfect symmetry. Humans never did. She knew that from reading random books on her uncle's ship. Most races had overall symmetry without perfection as a result of some evolutionary issues with adapting to habitat, or something like that. Two eyes separated by a nose was normal. Those two eyes at exactly the same distance from the midline sharing the exact same midpoint, size, and shape was not normal.

"Carry her. Don't bother with the beating. She might try to goad you into causing internal injuries." Ilai stood and gestured toward Madison.

"Curses, you've figured out my diabolical plan—dying before I'm supposed to." The fact Ilai had figured out something she'd considered bothered her. Did these people know everything? Could they read her mind?

No, if they could, they would've figured out her plan with Kirehe. Like she'd thought before, Viriok had run this place long enough to have encountered a lot of possibilities. Outthinking him would take more than simple, easy-to-execute plans.

Strong arms lifted her and flopped her over a shoulder she couldn't see as anything other than a vague blur. She could feel it, though. Soft fur or tiny feathers covered its wiry body. Two wings stuck out of its shoulder blades, not big enough to do more than assist with aiming while falling.

The hevit carried her a short distance before dumping her on a floor. She scrambled to her feet in time to see the door clang shut in a small cage. Outside the cage, Overseer Neilan sat in a swivel chair surrounded on three sides by consoles. He faced her through the gap, illuminated by a soft blue glow from the screens around him.

Also through the bars, Madison could see a closed door separate from the bars the hevit had dumped her through. Which made sense. Overseer Neilan needed his own door for his office, separate from the cage.

"Madison Wayward." Overseer Neilan steepled his fingers, giving him the look of a two-bit movie villain.

"Everyone really likes saying my whole name here." Seeing no way out and unwilling to sit to give him the higher ground, she leaned against the bars behind her.

Overseer Neilan's face flickered with annoyance. "You said in the hall that you can communicate with Kirehe."

Madison's pulse lurched to high speed. She hadn't expected Kirehe to succeed at causing annoyance, especially not this fast. "Yes, I can speak her language."

Overseer Neilan nodded. He fixed her with a smug grin. "You will teach this language to one of my people."

She laughed. "You can take a long walk out a short airlock."

His grin faltered. "Excuse me?"

"Not happening. If you want my help with anything, I want a stay of execution. And I'm not going to teach anyone anything because I'm not stupid enough to think you'll enforce the stay one second longer than it takes your people to learn to communicate with her."

Overseer Neilan scowled. "Very well. Return her to the execution pit. We'll manage without her help. If you change your mind, Wayward, we're always listening." He waved a hand.

Madison walked back to her cell with Ilai for an escort. Her mind raced. Everything rested on Kirehe's shoulders at this point. The amazing, gorgeous native girl could save everyone. Returning to her seat beside Jaco, Madison tried to think of some way she could get a message to Kirehe.

The dragon-bird flock slipped through the grate for their daily sit at the water hole. Madison recognized the one Kirehe called Skila. Though she couldn't talk to the birds like Kirehe, maybe she could find a way to get that one to take a message.

Could Kirehe read? Madison had no idea. Most of their two weeks together had passed with a lot of lethargy and trying to wrap Kirehe's tongue around the phonemes of Lakhan Basic.

At some point, she wanted to wrap Kirehe's tongue around other things, but she preferred privacy for that. She also still had yet to determine Kirehe's preferences. She hadn't acted interested, but she also hadn't acted interested in Jaco or anyone else.

She wrestled herself back on topic with a force of will. And refused to think about wrestling.

A message for Kirehe carried by a tiny dragon-bird needed to be small, lightweight, and easily understood. This message would convey that Madison wanted Kirehe to cause more trouble and to ask for Madison. The second part seemed more important than the first. After all, Kirehe had said she'd refuse to cooperate without prompting.

The message itself…

Since she didn't know if Kirehe could read, it didn't matter that she had no access to writing implements or mediums. What would make Kirehe think of Madison? A lock of her hair might work, but she had nothing sharp to cut it.

She patted her body, trying to think of a way to remind Kirehe of her. Without the laces of her boots, they'd fall off her feet, so she dismissed that idea. Her coat, lying on the floor for use as a pillow, had buttons along with the buckles. Using her teeth, she popped a button off the coat and focused on the next step in her plan.

The dragon-birds chirped to each other, making plenty of noise. She'd seen Rho scare them into scattering by approaching. She'd also seen Kirehe not scare them with her approach.

Taking small, slow steps, she moved toward the flock. As she neared, they turned and chattered at her. Madison lowered her body until she laid on the floor and held up the button. Keeping her gaze fixed on Skila, she waited.

"I need you to take this to Kirehe. Please."

The flock shifted away from her. Skila didn't. Kirehe's pet dragon-bird tilted its head and watched her. Madison pushed the button toward Skila.

It chirped at her. She wished she had some clue what it said. On the chance it didn't trust her, she set the button on the floor and backed away.

"Kirehe."

Skila chirped. It hopped off the edge of the pool and walked on all four limbs to the button. Quieting, it circled and sniffed the button. Skila sat on its haunches and picked up the button in its foreclaws. It put the button in its mouth and tried to gnaw on it.

Great. Madison's button would wind up wowing birds with brains the size of a pea as an amazing artifact acquired at great personal cost by the brave, daring Skila. Perfect. She'd defaced her coat for no reason. Not that she needed it on this forsaken sauna of a planet.

Skila chirped again, then leaped into the air with the button.

Thanks to the heat, Madison lacked the energy to pace. She sat beside Jaco again, stewing with the desire to cause something to happen. Even if her button message worked, she wanted to put more effort into her new plan. Doing something beat doing nothing, except she had nothing to do.

For a while, she and Jaco played stupid word games or hand games like roshambo. They'd learned to entertain each other in confined quarters during long stretches in space when neither felt like reading. Captain Wayward didn't want kids—or adults—running around his ship like lunatics more than one hour out of every standard Stardrifter day.

Half an hour after they started, Oolaang joined them. Then Shmar scuttled close and gave the dumb games half-hearted effort. Rho came with him and learned how to play each game.

Eventually, they goaded Shmar into a weak laugh.

CHAPTER 14

KIREHE

People contorted their bodies to use the strange contraptions in the large room. They grunted and strained against the devices as if using them required effort. Kirehe had no idea why anyone would do this. No one seemed to enjoy using them. Some people lifted and lowered things for no apparent reason, also not enjoying it.

Their behavior baffled her.

The temperature also bothered her. At first, the cool, dry air had refreshed her. The longer she stayed in it, the colder she felt. She shivered and jogged through the entire area, searching for warmth. Once she noticed the area had no insects, she wondered if they used the cold to keep them out. With no insects, the kukiris would never come.

She was more alone than she'd thought.

"Kirehe!" The moment she returned to the large room, a smooth-voiced one—Madison had referred to them as "pharedimi"—called her name.

Since she had nothing better to do, she crossed the room to reach him. "I want to see the maras."

He wouldn't understand her. She knew that. They all talked to her despite knowing she wouldn't understand, so why shouldn't she do the same?

The pharedim held up a hand. A blue glow sprang into life over it with a tiny picture of a strange, rectangular object. He said a short word.

She stared at him.

He frowned and twitched a finger. The picture changed to one of the flat, round lifting things. Again, he spoke a single word.

Convinced he had no use, she walked away from him. Behind her, she heard voices. Someone yelled. She returned to the mirror room to watch herself practice unarmed blocks and attacks. Adjusting to the backward image would, she decided, take time. At least the practice kept her moving and warmed her body.

Before she wanted to stop, the pharedim barged into the room with a small, handheld screen. She sighed and finished the movement he'd interrupted.

He held up the screen so she could see it. The picture showed that same rectangular thing. An obviously fake person walked to the rectangle, laid on it, and closed their eyes. The pharedim spoke a few words this time. For some reason, he seemed to feel this all made sense.

She stared at him. These people had strange ideas about everything. "I want to see the maras. Take me to the maras now."

The pharedim sighed and tried the second image again, of a lifting thing. This time, a fake person picked up the lifting thing like the people in the large room. They raised and lowered it. While pointing at Kirehe and then the doorway, he spoke some words.

If he wanted her to lift things for no reason, he would learn about disappointment. She snatched the screen from his hand and poked it like he had. He huffed and crossed his arms. The picture changed to a chair, then a table.

She caught something he said as he complained. "Slow down."

Madison had taught her those words early, so she'd know when she spoke too fast for her to understand. Hoping to irritate him, she poked the screen faster. Pictures changed at high speed, showing her food items, weapons, armor pieces, and other things she had no names for.

When she reached a picture of a mara, she stopped. The creature crouched with its frills standing high and claws open, displaying anger.

She pointed to it. "I want to see the maras."

The pharedim who hadn't bothered to tell her his name took the tablet from her outstretched hand. He tried to repeat what she'd said, mangling the sounds into nonsense.

Because nothing bad had happened before, she slapped him. This time, she put much more effort into her swing. Her hand hit with a crack.

He staggered backward, dropped the screen, and covered his cheek with a hand. Whatever he said, it sounded like a threat.

Kirehe shifted her weight so she could fight. Machine hum entered the room. She saw the blur of a hevit in the soft light, then it shivered into view. The hevit stood two steps inside the room, watching her. This pharedim had the power to call a hevit guard to rescue him, and one arrived fast enough for Kirehe to suspect they lurked inside the soft-edged prison. Noise from the food, the video, and the contorting people had masked their hum from her.

Sizing up the hevit, she considered fighting it to see what would happen. Knowing the enemy and their methods might help form her escape plan.

The pharedim growled something else, which sounded like a command.

Kirehe took a step toward the hevit, threat implied across every line of her body. She watched the hevit as it tensed for battle.

"Wait." The pharedim held up a hand to stop Kirehe. He sounded incredulous as he spewed words at her.

She wanted to try it. Madison feared them and considered them unbeatable. Kirehe didn't believe in unbeatable.

Raising his hands in exasperation again, the pharedim stalked out of the room. The hevit shivered until it blurred from Kirehe's sight and followed him.

The lack of follow-through intrigued Kirehe. Did they not realize she would push and push until she discovered the breaking point? Or did they fear her? No, not possible. More experienced dragoncallers could fight much better than she. Without any dragons, she could only do so much.

She relaxed and returned to her practice, pondering the motivation for making a threat without delivering. If they wanted to confuse her, it worked.

When she finished, she collected more food. In the large room, the lights had dimmed enough to notice, giving the feel of evening twilight. The number of people in the large room had decreased by more than half. Those who remained sat in small clusters, talking with drinks. Kirehe avoided them. They ignored her.

The dim lighting and her second full belly after near-starvation for two weeks took their toll. She stood and wondered where people slept. So far, she hadn't seen a single hammock. Maybe she'd made a mistake in avoiding that dark room when she'd first arrived. To reach that room, her escort had taken her through that door.

Retracing her steps earlier led her to a white door. She thought the symbols matched the ones the escort had tried to show her. In case she remembered wrong, she opened the door slowly and listened. Someone snored inside.

If they meant for her to share a room with a stranger, she meant to hit the pharedim with a fist next time, not an open palm.

She returned to the mirror room, which remained empty, intending to sleep there. In the distance, though, she heard Skila calling her. Standing the doorway, she turned and chirped.

"Here, in a cool place!"

"Coming! Toy!"

Kirehe wondered what Skila had found and waited for her. The tiny dragon fluttered up the hallway carrying something dark blue. She held out her hand, and Skila landed.

Skila raised a button as if she'd found the most wondrous treasure imaginable. "Madad gived!"

Madison had given Skila a button. Kirehe took it and turned it over in her fingers. She recognized it from Madison's coat. She liked her coat enough to complain about it a great deal. Removing a button seemed a strange gesture.

"You don't need to hide anymore. You can stay with me as much as you want. Would you like me to keep your toy until we can find a good place to store it?"

"Kiki keep." Skila nodded and purred.

Kirehe tucked the button into her waistband. It would leave an imprint on her skin there. "I'm going to sleep. Skila watch."

Skila tensed for serious work. "Skila watch."

Amused by Skila, Kirehe smiled and settled against the wall to sleep. She woke later to Skila warbling by her ear. The pharedim had returned with his handheld tablet again.

Kirehe rolled to her feet with Skila on her shoulder. The pharedim stopped and blinked at the kukiri.

Skila hissed at him.

"What do you want?" Kirehe crossed her arms and looked down at him despite his standing six or seven centimeters taller. Then, because this twit hadn't bothered to introduce himself, she tapped her chest. "Kirehe."

He paused. "Soallen."

"Meet you good me."

Soallen sighed and held out his screen. The picture showed a sword. He mimed swinging a blade.

Kirehe suspected he wanted her to use the sticks like those men and women she'd watched. She thought of the button. Instead of cooperating to do something she wanted to do, she smacked the screen out of his hand. He watched it fly across the room with a pained grimace and cringed when it hit the floor.

"Madison."

"What?"

"Madison. Now."

Soallen huffed as he retrieved the screen and checked it. He said Madison's name with a lot of other words that sounded like a possible explanation for why he wouldn't bring Madison.

"He won't bring Madad," she told Skila.

Skila unleashed a stream of potent insults at Soallen, all centered around his probable inability to prove he could provide enough food to find a mate. Kukiris took such matters seriously.

"Madison." Kirehe jabbed a finger at him. "No Madison, no do." She smacked the screen out of his hand again.

Soallen bobbled and lost control of the screen. He scooped it off the floor and stormed out.

"They'll bring Madad."

"Like Madad."

"Me too." She hoped they didn't wait long.

CHAPTER 15

MADISON

Once again, Ilai woke Madison by barking her name. A few more hours, maybe even a day, had passed. Despite the tedium of that time, Madison kept hoping Skila had done its job, and that it would work. The others had watched her give the button to the bird, and even Shmar seemed somewhat hopeful. He sat with the rest of them, at least. Oolaang had begun talking again.

"Madison Wayward, wake up and come to the door."

"I suppose I'll cooperate this time." Madison stood and stretched. She took her time without lagging. Keeping herself pain-free held enough allure to make a small effort toward compliance, especially when she had no reason to resist.

Ilai chuckled. "How refreshing."

Madison walked through the darkness and into the corridor of light. "I don't want to get all predictable on you. Gotta keep you on your toes. This way, yeah?" She strode up the corridor to the overseer's office without waiting for her escort.

Ilai hurried to keep up with her. "I didn't say where to go."

"Gosh, how would I ever guess that I'm supposed to follow this tunnel of light? I don't know if I can wrap my tiny, pathetic human brain around something you're all trying so hard to keep us from figuring out."

"Just get into the cage," Ilai snapped.

Madison complied. Overseer Neilan either had good news or bad news, and she didn't see a reason to cause a problem over hearing it. From the mild frown on Overseer Neilan's face, she guessed he had good news. From her perspective, not his.

"Madison Wayward. His Supreme Benevolence Viriok has agreed to indefinitely postpone your execution. In return, you will act as a go-between with the gladiator Kirehe. It will be your duty to ensure her willing participation in all required activities, including training and arena events. Should she refuse to perform any required function, the postponement will end and you will die in the arena, in a manner of Viriok's choosing. Do you accept these terms?"

Either the button had worked, or Kirehe had done enough on her own. Madison didn't bother stifling a grin of victory. "Are you going to tell me upfront which activities are required?"

"This will be made clear, yes."

She almost jumped at the offer. All that in return for not dying sounded great. One more thing mattered to her, though. "I want something else added in. Viriok said to assess the rest of the prisoners and give them jobs. I want them to stay with Kirehe and me. We get to live in a group, and they do something useful nearby. You still do what Viriok wants."

Overseer Neilan curled his lip. He turned to one of his consoles and tapped keys. "I'm willing to make this happen. There will be no further concessions made."

Survival? Check. Protect the others? Check. Stay with Kirehe? Check.

Escape this hellhole? Work in progress.

"I accept your terms, Overseer Neilan."

"Take her to Gladiator Housing."

Madison left the cage under her own power and with a bounce in her step. Ilai steered her into a different tunnel of light. Though she could've complained about the others not coming with her, she believed Overseer Neilan would keep his word. They might not join her for a few days, but they'd get there.

Ahead, she saw a door into a dimmer, softer world than the execution pit. A pharedim stepped into the way, blocking Ilai from throwing her into that new area.

"Here she is, Soallen. All yours." Ilai let go of Madison's arm and disappeared into the darkness.

"You guys really do like this whole spooky thing with the darkness."

"Shut up, human. Kirehe is now your responsibility. You will share room forty-two with her. The room has her schedule, and she will follow it. I trust you can read?"

"Yes, Smarmallen, the human slave can read."

He slapped her.

She rubbed her cheek and worked her jaw to make sure he hadn't broken anything.

"You're not a gladiator," he snapped. "They are afforded certain privileges. You are not. This is special dispensation because Kirehe shows great promise to prove highly profitable. You show no such promise."

Aside from a potential bruise, nothing seemed wrong with her face. Madison stuck her hands in her pockets. "Overseer Neilan is better at this. You should try watching him sometime."

Soallen turned his back on her and pushed the door open. "Get inside."

Madison, unable to keep a grin off her face, strode into the fun, happy room. A handful of human men and women sat on couches, talking. Each bulged with muscles and moved with the effortless grace of an experienced, capable warrior.

The door shut behind her. She checked and discovered Soallen hadn't accompanied her inside. First, she had to find Kirehe. From the interest thrown at her by this tiny number of people in a huge room, she needed a protector inside this prison. Any of these people could beat the kut out of her with one hand tied behind their back, even when she had two eyes.

She had a strong feeling the prison held a lot more than seven gladiators. With an obvious blind side, she doubted she'd last more than two seconds among the whole population.

"Hi. I'm looking for the native girl with short, dark hair? She doesn't speak Lakhan Basic?"

Everyone pointed at one door.

"Are you the translator we demanded?" one of the women asked.

"Yep, that's me. I'm here to make sure she gets with the program and stays with it."

This satisfied the group. Madison hurried to the doorway in question. In another room, she found Kirehe lying on the floor, asleep, with Skila on her chest.

The dragon-bird jumped to attention and chirped like crazy. Kirehe's eyes snapped open and she rolled to her feet in a smooth, cat-like motion. In that first few moments, she tracked Madison without recognition, ready to destroy her. Then the brilliant, glorious hunter woke up and relaxed.

Kirehe's smile lit up the whole room. She dug in the waistband of her pants and held up the result. "I got your button."

Unable to contain her relief and joy, Madison jumped and hugged her. In her embrace, Kirehe stiffened, so she kept it quick and gave Kirehe space. The mighty dragon warrior didn't like the physical stuff so much. Rather, she didn't like it with people. Kirehe had practically draped herself all over those dragons in the arena.

"I'm supposed to make sure you do the stuff you're supposed to, probably starting with sleeping in your room instead of whatever this room is for." Madison took Kirehe's hand and tugged for her to follow.

Kirehe didn't resist or reject her hand. "These people are very clever morons."

Madison giggled and led Kirehe to the central room. She peered through a doorway and checked the numbers on the doors. Nope, wrong section. "I'm hoping they're actually very daft geniuses. Cleverness is harder to beat than smarts."

They crossed the room under the watchful gaze of the gladiators still sitting together. Madison did her best to appear somewhat stern and exasperated, as anyone dealing with Kirehe probably should. On her next try, she found the hall with the right numbers and took Kirehe to forty-two.

"Soallen showed me this room. It's still dark."

Madison stepped inside. Soft white light blossomed in the room, emanating from thin strips along the edge between the walls and the ceiling.

"Oh."

Grinning, Madison tugged Kirehe into the room. She shut the door. For one glorious moment, they had complete privacy. Madison spared a thought for all the wonderful things they could do behind a closed door with two beds, each big enough for two tall people.

"What's that?" Kirehe pointed at the bed. "He kept showing me pictures of that, and I don't know why."

Glorious moment gone. She tried to think of how to explain and couldn't come up with a word for "bed." Maybe they didn't have one. "You sleep on it."

Kirehe furrowed her brow, making her forehead crinkle. Her nose wrinkled too. "I sleep in a hammock."

Madison wanted to kiss her adorable nose. "Yeah, we have those on the ship because they take up less space." She sat on the edge of the bed and beckoned Kirehe closer. The mattress had a fair amount of squish. "This is better. Try it."

With a shrug, Kirehe sat beside her. She jumped to her feet as if the bed had pinched her and crouched, ready to attack it. "Why does it act like a mire bog?"

Unable to stop herself, Madison laughed. "Have you really never experienced one of these? A soft thing?"

"In TOS Cave, the elders use pillows to sit and everyone sleeps on mats. Hammocks are too hard to string inside."

Madison unlaced her boots and noticed a second door in the wall, and also a sliding door. The idea of a soft, squishy bed had entranced her too much to notice or care about anything else. In addition, a digital clock on the wall showed the time with red numbers. "I want to hear all about this TOS Cave, but not right now. Right now, I want to find out what's inside those other doors."

Kirehe turned and approached the sliding door like she thought venomous snakes might leap out at any moment. She rapped a fist against the door.

"What, you don't have doors either?" Madison dropped her boots and breezed past Kirehe. She shoved the sliding door open and found what she'd expected—an empty closet. Before Kirehe could try to assault the other door, she stepped to the side and opened it.

A bathroom. Gladiators got private bathrooms. As Madison stepped inside, she sighed from sheer joy. A huge tub with a showerhead dominated the room.

She glanced back and saw Kirehe eyeing the room with a frown. "Please tell me you know how to use a toilet."

Kirehe huffed at her. "Of course I know how to use a toilet. I've just never seen one this…white. Even the ones in TFT Cave are metal." She poked the toilet bowl with a toe. "Is this plastic? It doesn't feel like plastic."

"Wait." Madison squinted at Kirehe. "You've never seen a bed, you don't speak Lakhan Basic, and you live in the jungle of an undeveloped world, but you know what plastic is?"

"We have many artifacts from the founding times." Kirehe shrugged. "My village, Tosnorth, has all plastic bowls for food. Other plastic things have failed over time, and some are kept in TFT Cave for preservation, but the bowls remain."

Madison knew humans hadn't sprung out of spaceships. Somewhere in the galaxy, or maybe a different galaxy, humans had evolved on a planet and pushed into the stars. And no one cared about that planet anymore because they had no information about it. About two millennia ago, give or take, they'd left it behind and taken to the stars.

Most people assumed a catastrophic event had sent them fleeing, like the star expanding or an impending asteroid impact.

No one in their right mind would leave a perfectly good, functional planet for the Lakhan Oligarchy.

"How long ago were the founding times?"

Kirehe shrugged. "The elders always say 'long ago' and leave it at that."

"Do your people keep track of years?"

"Yes. I know I'm seventeen years old. The days grow shorter and longer, so we can tell where we are in our annual orbit around our system's star. In a relative sense, anyway. Our ancestors left warnings to not leave the planet again unless we faced a planetary disaster, so we haven't pursued the study of our star system."

Madison had thought Kirehe's people nothing more than primitive humans stuck on a backwater world with no real knowledge of anything Madison would consider useful. Her view of them shattered, she decided to stop asking questions until she'd had a chance to digest this information and determine if it helped them escape in any way.

"You know what? I'm pretty tired. I also haven't bathed in forever. I'm going to wash off some grime and then get some sleep."

Kirehe nodded. "Will you show me how this bathing thing works?"

"Absolutely." Madison tried not to act like a gleeful idiot as she turned on the water, showed Kirehe how to adjust the temperature, then stripped and enjoyed the privilege of bathing in the same tub as the amazing jungle princess dragon warrior of Rikor Six.

With no touching. Because Kirehe didn't want that.

Yet.

CHAPTER 16

KIREHE

The soft bed seemed wrong. Kirehe slept on it, but she didn't like it. Her body ached in strange places when she woke. Madison seemed happy with the cushioning. Skila rooted under the blankets and tore up a pillow.

By the time she and Madison emerged from their room, the large area had filled with people again. Many used the contortion devices and lifting things. Others ate. Madison needed no help to figure out how to get food.

The food selections had changed, though it remained weighted toward meat. Skila left in search of her own meal while Kirehe and Madison sat at a table and ate together.

People watched them. Some glanced in their direction and looked away once or twice a minute. Others openly stared. Bryor invited himself to sit with them and spoke with Madison. She seemed unimpressed with him, and this seemed to bother him.

When he left, Madison said, "He's an ass with a really high opinion of himself."

Kirehe nodded, unsurprised. "What did he want?"

"For me to tell you some stupid kut about knowing your place." Madison shrugged. "This prison has to have some kind of social order. We just have to figure out how to navigate it. Shouldn't take long. Those people over there are in charge." She pointed to a cluster of four humans, two men and two women, at one table. "I've got that much already. Everyone else is somewhere between you, as the new kid, and them."

Beyond the obvious, human pack dynamics mystified Kirehe. She understood how dragons worked. Not people. People too often behaved unpredictably. They had more complex needs than food, water, and mating.

"I found your schedule, by the way." Madison produced a handheld screen and set it on the table.

Kirehe resisted the urge to throw it across the room. "I have a schedule?"

"Yes. And if you don't do all this stuff, you get into trouble and I get killed. At least try everything. If you really hate something, I'll talk to Soallen or whoever to make a change."

"Fine." Kirehe curled her lip in disgust, but if she had to do these things, she'd do them. "When can I see the maras?"

Madison tapped the screen. "That's not on here."

"I want to see the maras." She thumped her hand on the table. That pack needed her to undo the terrible things these idiots had done to them.

"Okay, but it's not on here." Madison raised her hands in surrender. "I'll have to ask about it. Cooperating with this list will help you get what you want faster."

Kirehe jabbed the table with a finger. "I don't want to do what they want. That's surrendering. They won't win."

"It's not surrender." Madison gestured to indicate the room. "This is better than the execution pit, right?"

The question felt like a trap. Kirehe eyed Madison, wondering what trick she played. "Yes?"

"If you don't cooperate, at least one of us goes back there. If you do cooperate, they might let down their guard or reveal a piece of information we can use. We're not here to get comfortable. We're here to discover the next opportunity so we can make the next plan. Each step takes us closer to getting out of this place. Okay?"

Madison's arguments made sense. Kirehe pointed at the stupid screen. "I'll do what this thing says. But I want to see the maras as soon as possible."

"I get it. I have to figure out who to ask and how, and then it'll happen."

Kirehe supposed she had to accept that as good enough. "What do I need to do today?"

"The first thing on the list is getting measured. They probably want to make you costumes and stuff." Madison tapped on the screen. "That's in the room where I found you this morning. Scheduled for ten minutes from now. Maybe I can get a few extra changes of clothes too."

As they stood, Kirehe noticed a man approaching with the swagger of a confident predator. He glared at her, making his intent clear.

Kirehe handed her plates to Madison. "Take these to the bin while I handle trouble."

Madison gulped and turned away, nodding.

At least she didn't have to worry about Madison's ego. The girl seemed to know her weaknesses and accepted help overcoming them.

Stepping away from the table, Kirehe shifted her weight to appear off-guard. She kept the man in her periphery, pretending to watch Madison, so he'd think he could take her by surprise.

Bryor, Kirehe noticed, watched her. Others also watched as if they'd had advance notice. The man telegraphed his first punch so hard Kirehe had more than enough time to slide back.

She smacked his wrist aside and kicked his gut. He hopped back. Though he appeared ready to fight, he hunched his shoulders and grimaced. Kirehe watched him bounce on the balls of his feet like she preferred to do. With every passing moment, he recovered from the kick.

He said something to taunt her. She didn't react. Murmurs ran through the room.

After several tense seconds, he dropped his guard and opened his mouth to laugh. She slid forward and snapped a kick at his knee, following it with a punch to the face, and elbow to his side.

The man stumbled backward, taken by surprise.

She stepped in, grabbed his arm and shoulder, and swept his foot. To make sure he stayed down, she punched him in the groin.

Her attacker squealed like a stuck risi and curled around his privates.

The room erupted into shouting. Kirehe noticed only a handful shouted at her. Most jabbed fingers at other people in the room. One woman approached with a wide grin and raised her hand to Kirehe.

Kirehe raised her hand in an echo of the gesture and the other woman slapped her palm with a laugh. The gesture seemed to express approval.

Among all these people, Kirehe noticed a girl among them who gazed at Kirehe with an unsettling expression. She'd never seen it before and didn't understand it. The girl seemed to like Kirehe, at least. Nothing about the expression spoke of anger or hate. She saw something more like wonder in the girl's eyes.

Madison slipped to her side and guided her out of the room, rescuing her from a strange, confusing situation. "You just proved you're not a fluke," Madison murmured as they escaped. "And I've just figured out who's on which team. I don't think you'll have to do that again."

"Good." Kirehe let her lead until they reached the mirror room. She liked this room because she could stand at the mirror and amuse herself while still watching the door. The novelty of her reflection would wear off eventually, but not soon.

Madison leaned against the wall and watched her with a curious little smile. Kirehe couldn't decide how she felt about the way Madison kept looking at her. Her expression always brightened when she saw Kirehe.

Most of all, she remembered Madison holding her hand while those spasms had wracked her body. She hadn't flinched or let go, and she'd provided an anchor when Kirehe had needed one.

Without Madison's request to fail her assessment, Kirehe would have become a gladiator anyway, but she might not have met the maras. From their behavior, Kirehe knew they only used the maras for executions. Her fights wouldn't have put her into contact with the pack.

Skila might never have found her either, because this area had no bugs to eat. Sitting in that dank hole for two weeks had allowed them to meet again. If Nihan had survived, she had no doubt Madison would prove capable of bringing him to her.

Choosing to trust Madison this far had severed Kirehe well. Madison's efforts centered around Madison's survival, but she'd tried to save the rest of those people. Her failure on their part hadn't changed the fact she'd tried.

Kirehe decided she liked Madison a great deal.

Two pharedimi entered the room, each carrying a small case. Soft machine hum accompanied them. Kirehe saw the blur of two hevits before they shifted their color so Madison and Kirehe could see them as a hulking threat. Their presence declared the danger of attacking either of these two pharedimi.

"These people are here to measure you," Madison said. "Come let them do it."

Kirehe obeyed. She jogged to Madison and let the two people do what they wished. They used handheld devices with green lights to scan her body. At Madison's direction, she raised and lowered her arms, bent over double, squatted, and raised each leg as high as she could.

When they'd finished that, Madison asked, "Do you know how to fight with weapons? Besides dragons, I mean."

"Dragons are not weapons. They're creatures."

"Yes, I know." Madison gestured for her to answer the real question. "It's a saying. Weapons?"

"I can use weapons, yes. I prefer a blade like so." She described her lost machete as precisely as she could. "Also, the weapon Viriok used to kill Anya is one I like."

Madison nodded and explained to the pharedimi.

Skila returned from her wandering and landed on Kirehe's

shoulder. One of the pharedim exclaimed in wonder. He reached to touch Skila. Skila snapped her tiny jaws and hissed a warning. The pharedim jumped back and jabbered at Madison.

After a short conversation, Madison turned to Kirehe. "They want some pictures of Skila so they can use the same colors on your costume. So you match."

Kirehe chuckled. "They want to fawn over you, Skila." She lifted the kukiri off her shoulder and displayed her in her hands. "Preen for them."

One pharedim cooed over Skila's proud posing while the other scanned her. Kirehe glanced at Madison and had a feeling the girl noticed their delight with kukiris. She probably already had ideas for at least one way to abuse it later.

Finally, they left, taking the hevits with them.

"That was interesting," Madison said. "I recall Oolaang mentioning that people could pay for sex with the gladiators."

Kirehe blanched.

Madison held up her hands. "You don't have to do anything. Apparently, in addition to measuring you for costuming, they also use that information to find a lookalike slave who gets to, er, perform that duty. Also, they said we'd get some regular clothes like everyone else has within a day or two. Those come in standard sizes, so they didn't need to measure me."

"They force slaves to have sex with the kind of people who cheer at the sight of gory death?" Kirehe crossed her arms in discomfort, wondering if they would ever discover the bottom of this pit of depravity.

"After watching my friends ripped apart, I'm not sure anything here can surprise me." Madison rubbed her arm and shifted her weight. "My goal is to get us out of here. If I can collapse the whole operation on the way, then I'll do that. If not, I'll be sick about it, but getting us free is my priority."

Kirehe nodded. She understood. Someone had to escape this place to speak of its horrors to others. If no one knew, they had no reason to oppose it. "We."

"What?"

"You're not doing this alone." Kirehe rested a hand on Madison's shoulder. "Stop thinking as if you are. We will collapse this operation if we can, not you."

Madison smiled and her real eye lit with gratitude. "Thanks. I knew I could count on you, but it's nice to hear it out loud."

"You've helped me, and I've helped you. You like me, and I like you. This makes us friends. Friends stand back-to-back against enemies and protect each other." Kirehe raised a hand for Madison to clasp.

Did some of the light fade from Madison's expression, or had she imagined that?

Taking her hand, Madison nodded. "We'll get through this together. Next up is letting them assess your fighting skill again. This time, beat the kut out of them."

Kirehe would worry about decoding Madison's feelings later. For now, she got to hit at least one pharedim without consequence. "I can hardly wait."

CHAPTER 17

MADISON

After leaving Kirehe with Soallen for her assessment in the practice chamber, which he assured her would take some time, Madison returned to the large room. She saw no sign of the idiot who'd challenged Kirehe, and everyone had calmed after the short fight.

At what point would the hevits step in to stop a fight between gladiators? She wanted to know the answer without having to find out the hard way.

As she approached the conveyor belt carrying food platters in hope of finding a dessert to linger over, someone shoved her from her blind side.

"Madison Wayward," her attacker growled.

Madison fell to the floor and scrambled to get back to her feet. "Hey, I'm infamous. That's exciting."

A qusamadi stood with her fists on her hips. This one had black hair with a patch of white in the front center to go with her slitted black eyes. "I see you've been taken down a notch or two."

"Yep, they finally caught me," Madison said as she straightened. She glanced to each side, checking for a gang and didn't find anyone else threatening her. "Recently. Not as long ago as they caught you, though."

"Eat lasers," the qusamadi girl snarled. Her hands clenched into fists, her short claws biting into her palms.

Madison pretended to think about it. "Not really to my taste. If that's what you like, though, go for it. I'm not going to judge anyone over how they have fun. So who are you?"

The qusamadi stabbed the air with a finger pointed at Madison. "Don't pretend you don't know. It's your fault I'm here."

"Not pretending." Madison shrugged, knowing she shouldn't taunt the clawed person and doing it anyway. Maybe she could learn the hevit response time. Hopefully, that knowledge would come without pain. "You're nobody to me."

The girl's eyes narrowed. She simmered almost enough for steam to spout from her pointed ears. "Natalyais. My name is Natalyais Isokovria."

Madison had heard the name Isokovria before. The family built weapons and ships for the Oligarchy. Like all qusamadi operations, they practiced crass, blatant nepotism and didn't care who knew about it.

"Oooohhhh. You're the— Wait." She shrugged. "Nope. Never heard of you. Did you do something spectacular to wind up here? Or was it just ordinary stupidity?"

Natalyais shoved her with two hands to the chest. Madison slipped and fell to the floor.

Erryl, who Madison had determined served as one of the leaders in this prison, stepped between them. "Natalyais, save it for the arena."

"She's not a gladiator! She won't go into the arena." Natalyais shoved against him.

The man stood firm, like a giant, immovable rock, with his arms crossed over his chest. "Do we attack the defenseless servants?"

Madison kept her mouth shut as she clambered to her feet.

"No," Natalyais grumbled.

"Is there any glory to be had outside the arena?"

Natalyais growled in her throat. "No."

"Make sure you remember that." Erryl remained standing between Natalyais and Madison.

With a final growl of frustrated anger, Natalyais whirled and stalked away.

Madison opened her mouth to thank Erryl for his intervention.

He glared down at her. "Stay out of sight when your girl isn't around, slave. You're not one of us." Then he stalked away.

"Fun, happy place we're in," Madison muttered. She didn't want to meet any other gladiators with inexplicable grudges, so she scuttled to Kirehe's room. Less than a minute after she shut the door, someone opened it.

Ilai strode in with no regard for privacy. "Oh, good. I thought I might have to deal with the savage."

"What do you want?"

"You have a visitor. Come with me."

"A visitor?" Madison stared at her. "The other prisoners are supposed to live here with us, not visit."

Ilai huffed and stabbed a finger toward the floor like she called a dog to heel. "Slave, shut up and follow me. Now."

"Everyone is kinda cranky today. Is there something in the water?" Madison stuffed her hands in her pockets and followed Ilai.

Saying nothing, Ilai set a swift pace to the end of the hallway. Instead of using the doorway, she placed her hand on the wall. A section slid open.

The gladiator housing area had secret doors. Madison wondered what the scanner checked. If they could cut off Ilai's hand to activate a secret door, she had something to work with. Then again, given how much freedom everyone had inside the prison, Viriok had probably thought of that.

Ilai pointed for Madison to step into a small, empty room.

"You know if you kill me, she won't cooperate, right?"

"Move, slave," Ilai snapped.

Madison sighed and stepped through the open doorway. The door slid shut behind her. She stood in a metal box large enough for the biggest guy she'd seen in the prison to stand without moving. This seemed pointless until the floor lifted, taking her upward.

Ilai had brought her to an elevator. The platform took her to a different floor with several plush couches and armchairs upholstered in green and gold. One vreesliik man stood at a table, pouring amber liquid from a decanter to a tumbler.

The vreesliik people all had a triangular head covered with scales. Their eyes, dark with white centers, sat at the top, like a frog. They had four thick, bulging fingers on short, muscular arms, with a long torso and stubby legs. This one wore draping, sumptuous, velvety cloth that shifted from deep purple to light blue when he moved.

Not sure what to expect, Madison decided to try one of the chairs. They looked comfortable.

She walked into a wall she couldn't see at the edge of the elevator platform. The surface flickered with the impact.

They used a force field for this one purpose. Everywhere else, they used metal bars. Weird.

"Hello," the vreesliik said. He glanced at Madison and moved his jaws for a moment. "I asked to see that savage girl. Who are you?"

Madison blinked, adjusted her calculations, and plowed forward with the best guess she had. "Her manager. She's a true savage, and can't even speak a proper language. I can communicate with her, though. She knows a rudimentary human tongue I learned in my youth."

"Ah. It wouldn't do me much good to talk to her, then. And I suppose you're more likely to have some modicum of manners." He picked up his glass and sat in one of the chairs. "I wanted to thank her for making me an obscene amount of money. I couldn't resist the sucker's bet of someone not dying, and chose both her and you for fun. Long odds gave me a very handsome payout, all thanks to her."

Of course these vile people bet on what order everyone died. "I'll make sure she's aware of your gratitude."

"As a show of appreciation, I'd like to back her as a patron."

Madison's mind spun with possibilities. "Please forgive my ignorance. As I'm sure you know, I haven't been here long. What does that mean, exactly?"

"It means she fights for me, Zorileck. Which isn't your concern. But it also means that, so long as she wins, I'll pay for small comforts, luxuries, that sort of thing. There are rules and boundaries about what I can give, of course. So long as it's allowed, it's hers. If she keeps winning."

The arrangement sounded stupid. He gained nothing from it that mattered. Some perception of reflected glory, but nothing else.

Madison had no problem taking advantage of his vanity. "That's very generous of you." She considered a short list of things that seemed harmless. "Something she would appreciate a great deal is a regular shipment of live crickets."

He laughed. "Done. Anything else?"

Skila would die with joy. "A thick, fuzzy blanket would be nice. She's used to a warmer climate than they provide in here. In your preferred color, of course. And a hammock to sleep in."

"Her needs are truly simple." He slurped his drink. "I knew this would be a good choice. Those monsters are going to be amazing in the arena with her. She does have control over them, doesn't she?"

Kirehe wanted more time with the dragons. Zorileck had just handed her an opportunity to try to make that happen without much effort. "Her control is tenuous right now. It would be stronger if she had time to train with them."

Zorileck nodded. "She should have that, then. The rest of it can be sent shortly." He sloshed down the rest of his drink and tossed the glass aside. It bounced on the cushioned floor. "If she has any other requests, I'll be listed as her patron shortly. Asking for other things should be simple. I'll expect you to take my meetings promptly in the future."

Madison wanted to tell him to stuff his promptness somewhere creative. She bowed to him. "I will certainly come as soon as I'm informed by the pharedimi of your desire. And I look forward to serving you as well as Kirehe."

"Yes, a modicum of manners." Zorileck walked away, making Madison wonder what he considered "manners."

Slaves gave deference and respect, of course. They didn't receive any.

As soon as he left the room, the platform lowered. The elevator reached the bottom, and the door opened. Madison stepped out, and the door shut behind her. Since the danger hadn't abated in the five minutes she'd spent with Zorileck, and Ilai hadn't waited for her, she scuttled back to the room.

As soon as Zorileck fulfilled his promises, life would get better. As soon as Madison found the list of restrictions, she'd find a way to work around it.

She had a new plan.

CHAPTER 18

KIREHE

Within three days, Kirehe had a hammock, a supply of bugs for Skila, and a wonderful purple blanket. Jaco, Shmar, Rho, and Oolaang joined them in her room, making it cramped and stifling enough to keep Kirehe sticking to her schedule.

For the first time, Soallen brought Kirehe to the dank, miserable cages where they kept the maras. Each mara stayed in a separate tiny cave with bars across the entrance. Kirehe stood in the center of a dim stone ring with the caves on one end. The maras couldn't even see each other from their holes.

In the wild, mara packs did everything together. They slept, ate, lounged, and ran as a pack, not as individuals.

"Let them out." These words, she'd anticipated needing and asked Madison to teach her.

Soallen stood beside her, holding a red stick humming like a machine. He pressed a button on the stick and it crackled with electricity. The stick, she realized was not for her. They used these things to keep the maras at bay.

She shooed him with both hands, trying to get him to leave. "Out. Me. Them. Together. You out."

He pursed his lips like he meant to argue, then shrugged and left. As always, the door clanged behind her, trapping her in yet another place.

At least she could spend time with maras.

The cage doors slid open. Kirehe expected them to challenge her dominance again. To her surprise, they all approached with their heads down, even the lead mara. They huddled around her as if she could rescue them from this terrible place.

Kirehe hugged the lead mara's neck. The pack had deep wounds in need of healing, not fighting.

"I am Kirehe. What are your names?"

Turning her hands to scritching behind the lead mara's frill, she watched them stare at her like the question made no sense. Kirehe suspected these maras had all hatched in captivity. Even if the enemy had scooped up young maras, they would've at least known the name of their alpha, and recognized they should have similar names.

"How do you call each other?" She hugged the next mara.

"Call? Name?" The lead mara cocked her head.

Fine. These maras needed names. Kirehe could provide. She patted the lead mara's snout. "You are Chana. When I call Chana, I mean you."

"Chana." The lead mara repeated the name several times.

"You are Wooni." Kirehe hugged each mara and scritched them, then gave them a name. The other three, she called Heetay, Fobi, and Rila. For the next hour, she ran them through silly games to help them learn their names.

Between Chana, Fobi, and Rila, the three females of the pack, Kirehe couldn't figure out why Chana had taken the lead. None of the three seemed stronger, smarter, or faster than the other two. She couldn't say for sure, but she thought these maras might have hatched from the same clutch of eggs at least two years earlier. They all had similar frills, similar scale and feather patterns, and the same shape to their nose and eye ridges.

Soallen's voice came from a spot on the wall. "Time's up."

Kirehe wished she could scowl at his face. "No. More time."

After a short pause, Madison's voice replaced Soallen's. He must've anticipated her refusal and collected Madison to deal with her. "Soallen says the dragons have to get back into their cages, and you have to go to the next thing. The schedule says grandstanding in the mirror room."

Draping her arms over the maras as if she could save them from danger, Kirehe shook her head. "They're not going back into those cages. They need to stay together. This is a pack, a group. They need to stay in a group."

After a much longer pause, Madison said, "Soallen says it's not safe for the handlers to feed them if they're not in the cages."

"Soallen is a moron."

"Yes, but he's the moron in charge."

"I'll feed them. No more zapping sticks. One cage, together."

"Even if he goes for that, which I'll ask, he's not going to be able to agree to it right this minute. They don't have a place like that to put them. You have to get them back in the cages for now. Then you can scream at him all you want about anything you want. Small steps, Kirehe, not giant leaps. Remember how long it took to get everyone out of the execution pit? They're afraid of the dragons, and they don't trust you because we're prisoners here. Slaves."

Kirehe sighed. She turned to the maras and hated herself. "You have to go back into the cages now."

They didn't whine or argue. They slunk to their cages like she'd beaten them into submission.

More than she hated herself for inflicting this pain on them, she hated the pharedimi. Her rage for them smoldered in her belly. When the time came, when she had the right chance, she'd rip off their heads and cut out their spines.

Her head hung, she returned to the gate and shuffled out. As soon as she cleared the door and it shut, Madison stepped into view and draped an arm around her shoulders.

"Soallen wants to know what benefit they'll get from housing the dragons in a single cage."

"Soallen can jump off a cliff for all I care."

Madison sighed. "Yes. But again, he's in charge of you and your training. We need to come up with a reason he'll find compelling." When Kirehe continued to stew instead of answering, Madison said, "We'll get the others to help think about it."

"I hate them. I hate everything about them. They all need to die."

"Yep, me too. They're awful. I'd like to see a plague sweep through here and kill all the people who run the show and come to watch it. Since that won't happen, we have to take our time and wiggle through what they'll let us do. I've got some ideas, and I'm working on getting what we need to put an escape plan into motion. It'll just take time. Getting a new place for the dragons will also take time."

At least she'd given the maras some hope. And names. Kirehe knew she'd improved their lives enough for them to believe she'd return and take care of them.

They walked through the corridor of light to return to the gladiator area. As always, hevits hummed in the darkness.

Once again, she had the thought to provoke one to see what would happen. "What would happen if I attack one of these hevits?" This corridor of light seemed stupid since she could hear at least five of them, but she still wondered.

Madison raised her brow and blinked. "The rest would come help it beat you half to death. Why would you want to?"

"I'm curious how good they really are."

The pause and once-over Madison gave her spoke volumes about questioning her sanity. "Let's…not find out. Yet."

Kirehe chuckled. "You fear them."

"They're invisible," Madison let go of Kirehe's shoulders to count off reasons on her fingers. "Also silent, fanatical, can kill me without trying, and answer to Viriok. Yes. I fear them."

"They're not silent or invisible, only hard to detect." Kirehe took Madison's hand. Madison liked that, and Kirehe didn't mind.

"Maybe to super-amazing jungle princess dragon warriors, but I can't hear or see them if they don't want me to." Madison squeezed her hand, which Kirehe interpreted as a need for comfort.

Something flickered in Madison's expression that Kirehe didn't understand. Though she sounded like she made a joke, Kirehe wondered if some new thing bothered her.

"I'm a jungle princess dragon warrior now?" She watched Madison's face as they crossed into Gladiator Housing again, trying to decode what she saw.

"Aren't you?" Madison's smile seemed strained. Again, something else flickered across her face. The nature of it eluded Kirehe.

"I don't think we have princesses. The rest seems correct, though." Kirehe decided to give up and ask. "Is something wrong?"

"You mean other than the whole slave thing? No, of course not." Madison let go of her hand and backed toward their sleeping room. "Go ahead. I'll see you later."

Kirehe watched Madison turn and jog out of the large common room, almost fleeing for the sleeping room.

If Madison refused to discuss something, Kirehe didn't believe she could force it. Whatever upset her would either solve itself or cause enough distress to make her speak. Perhaps something had reminded her of one of the dead. She hadn't mourned that Kirehe had seen, and the enemy hadn't given them any options for closure.

Her people burned their dead. Anyone who wished took a piece of bone afterward and used it as a focal point to remember. Madison's pack retained nothing from their dead, not even a button from a coat or a lace from a boot. Those people had ceased to exist outside of their memories.

Time eroded good memories. Pain etched the worst ones into stone.

Kirehe shrugged and picked up a piece of fruit on her way to the mirror room. To her surprise, she discovered Overseer Neilan himself in the room, with another gladiator already present. Machine hum pointed to several hevits in the room.

The overseer took no chances with his personal safety.

A third gladiator joined them. Overseer Neilan spent an hour showing the three of them how to gesture and make facial expressions for a large crowd. Kirehe understood enough of what he said to grasp the purpose of these lessons.

They wanted the crowd to cheer for them and against their opponent. To do so, they had to make the crowd feel involved and like they had some control over the outcome. It required ridiculous, grandiose gestures big enough for people to see from a great distance.

If the crowd loved them, they earned Viriok's notice. His notice earned them more privileges and rewards. Fewer restrictions would govern what Kirehe's sponsor could give her. Madison could enact whatever strange plans she chose.

She dutifully practiced every movement the overseer commanded. When he dismissed them, Kirehe felt spent, having used muscles in strange ways. She collected a plate of food, standing beside a man who nodded to her like she belonged. A woman waved for her to join the small group at their table, so she did.

Beyond their names, Kirehe caught bits and pieces of the conversation. By now, everyone knew she didn't speak the language. No one pressed her to contribute. They seemed content to have her sit with them as if her presence conferred status.

Several gladiators flowed around the table, something Kirehe had already learned to expect. Everyone wanted to see her. No one tried to touch her after the fight a few days earlier, at least. She had proven herself capable of defending herself in personal fights under these circumstances.

Whether she could perform in the arena, she had yet to prove. And these people knew it. She could tell by the way they scrutinized her as they passed. Some seemed pleasant, at least. Most did not.

A young girl, one who scuttled around the edges of everything and couldn't stop watching Kirehe, lurked and watched Kirehe eat. She'd done this without fail since that fight. So far, Kirehe hadn't noticed any other children in the prison, so this one stood out even as she tried so hard to blend in.

Kirehe flashed the table group a smile and took her plates to the bin. She filled a cup with juice and took a path out of the area to pass near to the girl. Trying not to call attention to either herself or the girl, she said, "Follow," when she walked by.

As she'd hoped, the girl flitted from spot to spot, tailing her to her room. Kirehe opened the door and gestured for the girl to enter.

The scrawny girl gulped and slunk inside like she expected a beating.

"Who's this?" Madison asked, frowning at the girl.

The others all tended to their daily chores elsewhere. Jaco and Shmar worked in the laundry, moving bundles of clothing. Rho tended injured gladiators in the infirmary. Oolaang fixed machine things.

Madison lounged on the bed. At Kirehe's request, the pharedimi had removed one bed and replaced the other with hammocks. Rho preferred the squishy box. The rest of them liked the swinging rope bundles, and Zorileck had provided nice, smooth ones.

"She keeps following me." Kirehe shrugged. "I don't know why. Find out?"

Her expression clearing, Madison slid to the edge of the bed and patted beside herself for the girl to sit with her. She used soothing words, and spoke as if to a frightened animal.

The girl hopped onto the edge of the bed, still hunched and fearful.

Kirehe decided she didn't need to make Madison's job harder. She excused herself to the bathroom. Once she'd used it, she stared at herself in the mirror, practicing some of the silly things the overseer had suggested.

Escaping this place required playing along. Kirehe would play along the best she could. Madison had a plan.

CHAPTER 19

MADISON

Kirehe had brought the best gift imaginable. The kid obviously worshiped Kirehe as a hero for some reason, which meant they had a new ally. Madison smiled at her, grateful Kirehe had taken her distracting self out of the room.

"My name is Madison. How about you?"

"Lylla." She sat on the edge of the bed, staring at the bathroom door. Madison couldn't decide how old Lylla might be. She was maybe five feet tall and had a thin, wispy body Kirehe could probably break in half by glaring at too hard.

"Nice to meet you, Lylla. You seem kind of young to be a gladiator."

Lylla tore her gaze from the door to sigh with her whole body and hang her head. "I was born here."

"Really?" Despite the free mingling of gladiators regardless of gender, Madison had thought they'd prevent that somehow to keep their gladiators in top condition.

"My mom was Anya."

"Oh. I'm sorry." Madison offered her arm to Lylla.

The girl slid close and sheltered under Madison's arm, pressing close. "I think the pharedimi forgot about me. I mean, I was just kind of Mom's kid. I helped people, and Mom was popular and amazing, so they let me stay with her. Then they retired her. Erryl moved into our suite and said I could only stay if I…did stuff for him that I don't want to do. So I don't really have a place to stay right now."

Madison growled in the back of her throat. After her run-in with Natalyais and Erryl, she believed Lylla. "You can stay with us. But we need you to do something too."

Lylla gulped and nodded.

"We need you to give us information about how things work down here. I've got the basic idea, but you know all these people already. And maybe more of the layout."

Blinking, Lylla pulled away. "That's it?"

"Yep." Madison grinned at her. "Information is power, kid. I want it. You can share the bed with Rho, or we can get you a hammock of your own. Rho is really nice, though. You'll like them."

"Them? Isn't Rho a boy or girl?"

Madison shook her head. "Some people aren't either. It's a thing that happens. We call Rho they or them because that's what they want to be called."

Lylla frowned. "It sounds kind of awkward."

"You know what's more awkward? Someone using a word to describe you that doesn't fit. Like, if I decided to call you a boy because I didn't feel like calling you a girl."

For several heartbeats, Lylla sat in thought. Then she nodded. "Okay. I don't really understand, but I can use the words they want."

"Then you can stay with us." Madison hugged her close again. "Now, I know Erryl is a top dog in here, and there are a few others. Tell me more about that."

"There are four teams. Kirehe is in the Corvik team. Erryl is the team leader since Mom retired."

Madison held up a hand. "She's dead, Lylla. Viriok murdered her because he thought she was getting too old to make money anymore. That's not glorious or wonderful. It's barbaric and wrong. They give us all these nice things so we behave, but it's still a prison and we're still all slaves. When we're not useful anymore, they kill us because we're property. Never forget that."

Lylla nodded. Tears rolled down her cheeks. Madison held her while she cried. Kirehe emerged from their bathroom, and Madison waved for her to leave. Later, they could help Lylla overcome her hero worship complex. For now, the kid needed to feel things. Besides, Kirehe had an appointment with the maras soon. She'd keep that without Madison goading her into it.

With her arms wrapped around this miserable girl, Madison thought about the dead. Dani's death had shaken her. Cradok had murdered her because he could. He'd done it to affect everyone else, to terrorize them. Because one dead prisoner didn't matter when he had twelve more.

Viriok had killed Anya for a reason, but he could've shuffled her into some other job and let her live. Instead, he killed her to keep the rest of the gladiators in line. Everyone bought this pile of kut about glory and being remembered because the alternative meant an empty, meaningless death. Viriok had, in essence, killed Anya to terrorize everyone else, just like Cradok. Because he had dozens more ready to step into her place.

Lakhans were a blight on the universe. An arrogant, evil blight.

Lylla sniffled and hugged Madison as her tears subsided. "The other teams are Ackrion, Bretikor, and Degrikar. Nobody knows what those names mean. I figure they're the original gladiators or something, but I can't find anything that says so. Each team has a leader, and they get extra rewards for lots of different things. They've got patrons, and they get rewarded based on which team has the most wins.

"They also all get demerits whenever something bad happens. Like, that fight between Kirehe and Wally earned all the leaders a demerit. Since the hevits didn't have to get involved, it wasn't a big deal. And stuff like that happens all the time, so nobody cares. Natalyais attacking you, though, only earned Erryl a demerit because it only involved members of his own team. It would've been worse if she'd hurt you."

Madison thought about the scuffle. Erryl had stepped in after it started but before Natalyais could give her worse than a bruise. And he'd talked about glory, not about treating Madison better.

"Do they share the rewards?"

Lylla barked a laugh. "No. They share the demerits, though. Keep an eye out and you'll notice it. They do it at the end of every cycle, when the team stats are reset. That's what the countdown on the wall screens in the common room is for."

"I hadn't noticed it. But then, I already got the message that I'm not supposed to spend time out there."

"You can watch the matches with everyone and they won't bother you so long as you stay in the back. Everybody watches the matches. They all want to win, so they watch to get ideas for how to beat the guys on the other teams. Some of those people even bet on each other with their patron gifts."

Madison grimaced. "Gross."

Lylla shrugged. "It's a good way to get on someone's good side. Or to get something you're restricted from without the pharedimi having any control over it. They watch everything, you know. Even in these rooms. But they don't pay attention to everything. I know they don't because Mom and I tested it plenty of times. I'm pretty sure it's a few people and some computers watching a zillion camera feeds. Big movements and excitement catch their attention. Two people sitting in a room like this is boring. Especially when neither is a gladiator."

"Good to know." Madison had suspected the pharedimi watched them. She thought Overseer Neilan spent time personally scanning the camera feeds. She hadn't guessed they had cameras everywhere, or that someone actively monitored them all.

She had a thought, and wanted to ask, but wondered if the automated monitoring would pick up on her asking about implants or other control devices.

"Um, do you know if they stuck…things…with signals into our bodies?"

"Yep. They did. They always know where we are. I think it's here? I'm not sure." Lylla tapped the back of her neck, then acted like she had an itch there. "This one time, I went with Mom to watch her fight and got bored, so I wandered off to explore. Nobody noticed. I found a door in the dark of that corridor, and got halfway down a hidden tunnel before someone hauled me out. They waved a wand behind my head to figure out who I was."

Madison didn't remember losing consciousness long enough to have something implanted in her neck. She also didn't remember anyone jabbing her there. Neither meant they hadn't done it. She just didn't remember it.

"Do you think they can see in the dark?"

"No, they can't. But the lights come on whenever you move more than shifting in your sleep, so it doesn't really matter."

Madison had an engineer living in the room. If they provided him enough cover, he could figure out how to get around the motion sensors for the lights. Then they'd have some options for working in the dark.

"Do you think you could find that tunnel again?"

"Of course. I always know where I am. Right now, we're two meters below ground and fifty meters from the arena. The hallway is sixty-three meters to the arena, though, because it starts over there and turns a corner. And the arena itself is at ground level. There's a gentle slope in the corridor, so minor you don't really notice it."

She blinked at Lylla. The girl had some kind of sense for direction and depth, which could prove useful in an escape. Among Stardrifters, she'd heard of weirder abilities, though she didn't have one herself, and neither did Oolaang, Jaco, or Shmar. She'd have to consider what questions to ask the girl and how to deploy her for best effect.

Lylla pointed to the clock on the wall. "Today's matches will start in a few minutes. It's a good time to people-watch. You can get an idea of what they expect Kirehe to do in the arena. She should watch too. After how crazy she drove the crowd at your execution, they won't let her wait long before her first match."

Ilai threw open the door. Jaco and Shmar shambled in, each carrying a sack, as they did every day. Today's burdens seemed larger than usual.

"They have Kirehe's first costume. Her first fight is tomorrow. It's on her schedule. Make sure she's ready on time." Ilai definitely saw Lylla. She didn't seem to care.

Madison nodded to make Ilai go away. The pharedim glanced from one person to the next, then left. Jaco and Shmar dumped their bundles on the floor, mumbled incomprehensible things, and climbed into their hammocks.

If Madison hoped to use either of them for anything, she needed to find a way to get their shifts shortened. Overseer Neilan probably had them pushed to exhaustion on purpose, to keep them out of trouble. The request needed some teeth or sweetening. She'd have to think about it.

"Ilai thinks I'm up to something, so let's go check out the matches." Madison took Lylla's hand and urged her to come along. "Maybe she'll waste some of her time watching me instead of getting things done."

Lylla grinned. "Mom did things just to annoy them too. Not often, but once in a while."

They hurried to the common room. Gladiators sat in clusters, facing the screens. Lylla directed Madison to a spot between their hallway entry and a stack of weights. Someone would have to make an effort to harass either of them. Since they'd have their backs to the wall, Madison and Lylla would see anyone coming in time to flee back to the room.

Together, they sat on the floor as the screens changed from a view of the outside world to the glitter of the arena.

They saw the arena from above. Spotlights roved the crowd. Lights flashed among them. From the camera vantage point, they saw Viriok step to the edge of his platform and raise his arms in greeting. Light glimmered off the gold of his clothing and cape.

"Welcome to today's contests and entertainments!"

The crowd roared.

Viriok spun fast enough to make his cape twirl and catch the light. He sat in his throne and waved for someone to do something.

Beside him, a masked pharedim raised their arms. "Our glorious guests, welcome Tyron!"

Madison recognized this female pharedim's voice as the one who'd announced Anya's retirement match. "Why do they wear masks? Soallen, Ilai, and Overseer Neilan don't."

She didn't have to shout because the crowd gave Tyron a lukewarm, uninspired cheer. The gladiators in the room made no noise at all. As far as Madison could tell, they studied the video feed rather than watching it.

"The Arena Master likes it colder than they do," Lylla murmured. "The masks and robes keep them warm. And make them look creepy. That one is Oylesa, the high priest. She's the head pharedim on Rikor Six. Overseer Neilan is afraid of her."

"Facing Tyron, we welcome a new challenger! Introducing Hallor the Mad."

"The first match is always where they put the newest gladiators," Lylla said. "Kirehe will go first tomorrow."

Madison thought the crowd seemed disappointed by Hallor, though they cheered more for him than Tyron. "Is Tyron new?"

"No. He's been here for a while." Lylla pointed at one of the top women. She sat with Erryl and one other top woman. Madison didn't see the fourth.

"He's part of her team," Lylla continued. "Degrikar. They usually win the most matches because they put in the most effort. Everyone trains together, and they share notes about the other teams. Corvick always tries, but they put all the weirdos and freaks in it. Mom wound up there because of me."

"Why doesn't the crowd like him, then? I mean, does he play as a villain or something?"

Lylla pointed to the screen. "Watch."

Madison shut up and watched. The screen split to give them a view of each man. The angle shifted as they moved toward each other.

Hallor screamed at Tyron with his body flexed and tense. Tyron sneered and stood ready to defend. As the match progressed, Madison found Hallor five times more entertaining. He raised his arms to involve the audience, he screamed, and he rushed Tyron.

Tyron…stood there and waited.

In a real fight, Madison thought Tyron had the better plan. He didn't waste energy on anything extra. While Hallor preened and postured, Tyron watched him.

"Come on, Tyron," someone grumbled. "Do something."

Madison agreed. Tyron was boring. If everyone fought like that, no one would come to the arena. That behavior sounded like a great protest, but everyone would have to do it. With this varied crew, used to luxuries and rewards for grand performances, no one would agree to participate. Even Kirehe would do anything to get more for her dragons.

In the end, Tyron won because he didn't tire himself early. The crowd didn't appreciate the simple punch to the face he used to take down Hallor.

The gladiators heaved various sighs, as if they'd expected this and found it distasteful.

"Don't look at me," his team leader groused. "I've told him. Over and over. He won't listen."

"He won't get many more chances," Erryl said.

"The savage is going to kick his ass," another woman said.

"If she gets to fight him," someone else said.

The arena darkened without Oylesa recognizing Tyron. She moved on to announcing the next match.

Madison split her attention between the gladiators in the room and the ones on the screen. She learned a great deal about how the arena matches worked. Aside from Tyron, the gladiators tended to take moments to turn their backs on their opponents to play to the crowd. She guessed they did it to catch their breaths after furious bouts of intense fighting.

The fighting itself seemed real so far as Madison could tell. They used blades and they spilled blood, but none of the injuries appeared serious. One took a slice to the chest, another a cut along their arm. In both cases, the gladiator acted like the injury had mortally wounded them, but the slices looked shallow.

Halfway through the fifth fight, Madison whispered, "Do they use dull blades?"

"No. If anyone dies in the arena when they aren't supposed to, the incident is studied by Viriok and Overseer Neilan. They decide if the dead gladiator caused it or not by doing something stupid. If they did, the killer gets a minor punishment. If they didn't, the punishment is much more severe.

"About five years ago, two gladiators got into a serious hate grudge. One killed the other in the arena. It was ruled purposeful murder, and the other gladiator was fed to the monsters. That's the other way people die here."

Once again, something slapped Madison in the face with how much Viriok and all the pharedimi considered them property. They lived and died at the whims of their masters.

"I told you, I fight my way!" a man shouted from the door.

Tyron stormed into the housing area. He flung half his costume aside.

Overseer Neilan stepped through the door and let it swing shut. "So be it. I have given you more chances than you deserve, Tyron." He snapped his fingers and pointed at Tyron.

"What?" Tyron spun to face the overseer. Blurred figures leaped from the wall and seized him.

Two hevits shimmered into view, each restraining one of Tyron's arms.

"You're a failure, Tyron."

"Failure?" Tyron struggled against the hevits. "I have more wins than some of these other guys combined!"

"And yet, no one cares." Overseer Neilan waved for the hevits to remove him. "No one will miss you, Tyron. No one will remember you."

"I haven't lost a match in two years!" Tyron continued to resist.

Madison didn't blame him for struggling. Everyone in the whole room knew the overseer had sentenced him to death. She wanted to argue on his behalf, but the moment she moved, Lylla stopped her with a hand on her arm.

"There's nothing anyone can do. Not even his team leader can save him."

"Let this serve as a reminder to all," Overseer Neilan said, addressing the room as the hevits hauled a still-shouting Tyron through the door. "Losing with glory is better than winning with silence. A severe demerit has been assessed against Team Degrikar."

The overseer left. Murmurs engulfed the room.

"Everyone needs to watch their backs for the next few days," Lylla whispered. "Degrikor is going to try to goad other teams into doing stupid stuff to get their own demerits."

"Great. Just what we need." Madison decided she'd seen enough. She tapped Lylla on the shoulder and they slunk to the doorway.

Erryl reached it first and barred their passage with an arm. "You tell the savage to keep her temper in check. She's not going to screw my team because she's too stupid to keep it to defense."

Madison rolled her eye. "She wouldn't need to beat the kut out of people if they didn't keep poking her with a stick."

He slapped her. "Don't backtalk me. You're just a slave here."

Lylla hid behind Madison.

Madison rubbed her cheek. "You think you're not a slave?"

Erryl grabbed a fistful of her shirt and yanked her close. His breath smelled like rotting meat. "You're the new fish here. You toe the line or your toes get lined. Got it?"

"That doesn't even make sense. You're going to line my toes? With what? Bad breath?"

"Go ahead," the Degrikar lead purred. "Do it. Throw her against the wall."

Erryl's eyes narrowed and he let go of Madison. "Watch your mouth," he snapped. "And the savage girl." He turned and shoved the Degrikar lead out of his way.

Lylla yanked on Madison's pants. They slipped around the corner. The moment Madison couldn't see Erryl anymore, she realized how close she'd come to having her head cracked open like an egg. She and Lylla ran for their room and ducked inside.

"Why did you say that?" Lylla whimpered. She leaned against the door and covered her face.

Soft snores drifted in the room. Neither Jaco nor Shmar woke in the dim lights that flickered on.

"Because he's an ass."

"He's an ass who can kill you with his fist."

Madison covered her mouth to stifle nervous giggles. "If I let that stop me, I'd never say anything to anyone."

"Maybe that would be a good thing." Lylla kicked off her slipper-like shoes and crawled into the bed. "Try not to get beaten while Kirehe's gone."

That always sounded so easy and proved so difficult.

CHAPTER 20

KIREHE

In the mirror room, Madison helped Kirehe adjust her costume and test her ability to move in it. Leather pants clung to her hips and thighs, reaching to her knees. A band of more leather covered her chest. Smaller, narrow bands around her wrists, ankles, knees, elbows, and neck sported feathers in Skila's colors of green, rose, and gold.

Madison set a metal contraption bearing more feathers on her head. The band wrapped around her forehead and tied in the back. Thin, satiny ribbons in Zorileck's purple announced her sponsor's influence.

"This is ridiculous. I look like a fool." She waved her arm, making the feathers ripple.

"Yep. But unless it constrains your fighting, you're wearing it."

Kirehe scowled. "You do have a plan, right? This isn't a waste of my time?"

"I promise you're making a complete fool of yourself for a good reason."

"Kiki pretty," Skila said from her perch under Kirehe's hair. "Pretty like Skila."

"I'm glad someone likes it," Kirehe grumbled.

Madison kissed her cheek. "I think you look…" She wriggled her nose back and forth. "…unique."

The kiss confused Kirehe. She glowered at both the word and the strange tingling in her face. "That isn't a compliment."

Flashing a wide grin, Madison re-checked all the ties holding everything on Kirehe's body. "People want to see unique. Now remember, this isn't a death match. You're supposed to actively avoid hurting the other person. Minor injuries are okay, but not major ones. You're both supposed to walk out and fight again tomorrow."

"This is stupid and futile."

"Yes, but every fight where you wow the crowd gets us one step closer to victory. Just don't hurt them worse than bumps and bruises." She checked her infernal handheld screen, the master of all her tasks. "Time to go. Let's not keep Soallen or Overseer Neilan waiting."

"No, we mustn't do that," Kirehe muttered. She stalked into the common room and through the door to the bright light. Other gladiators in equally impractical outfits waited with several pharedimi.

Seeing the others with fur, oddly-placed metal pieces, and leather dyed in ridiculous colors made Kirehe feel better about her costume. At least she matched Skila.

"You remember what to do?" she whistled at Skila.

"Fly. Throw thing."

"Good."

"All here," Soallen told Overseer Neilen.

Among the group, Kirehe recognized Erryl, the leader of her team. She hadn't learned names for any of the others. Madison pointed to each one and listed their team. Three others from Corvik stood among the group of two dozen. Today's fights involved a sizable contingent from Ackrion. According to Madison, no one fought those on their own team, so Kirehe guessed she'd fight a member of Ackrion.

One of the other gladiators reminded Kirehe of Rho. He—or possibly "they"—lacked Rho's squat, wide body structure, but had similar facial features and the same short, tawny fur.

The overseer said a few words as he led the group to a small, empty room. Everyone packed inside blank white walls, including Soallen, the overseer, and a handful of other pharedimi. Kirehe didn't hear any hevits inside but knew several stood outside.

Once again, the overseer offered a short speech. These words sounded like encouragement.

Madison leaned close and murmured into her ear. "He's reminding everyone to make sure you play to the crowd. Winning isn't the only thing. Getting the crowd to love you is way more important, blah blah blah."

Kirehe nodded. She understood. Though she hadn't seen the incident with Tyron, Madison had explained it. "Who am I fighting?"

"I don't know. They haven't said yet." Madison raised her hand and asked a question.

The room rippled with exasperation. Overseer Neilan threw Soallen a disapproving glare. Soallen raised his hands and defended himself.

Though she didn't know what Madison had asked or would say, she reached over and covered Madison's mouth. Overseer Neilan flashed Kirehe an approving smile. Madison rolled her eye. The nearest fellow gladiator raised his hand like that one woman had. Kirehe smacked his palm. He grinned.

"Very funny," Madison muttered.

Overseer Neilan lifted his screen and read two names. Kirehe's was not one of them. All the gladiators glanced at her, then at the two who matched those names. Someone pointed at Kirehe and asked a question. The overseer waved off the question and repeated the two names, then jerked his thumb to tell them to go.

Those two fighters left with a pharedim escort.

"Everyone is confused about why you're not going out for the first match," Madison said. "Me included. The overseer told everyone to shut up and do their job."

Kirehe shrugged. She had no idea what to say.

One woman groaned and clutched her stomach. She traded words with overseer Neilan.

"She feels ill," Madison murmured. "The Overseer is annoyed

because this keeps happening, which is interesting. He thinks it has something to do with the local plants they mix into the food."

Food she'd grown up eating wouldn't cause Kirehe any problems, so she didn't care.

They waited. From the small room, they couldn't hear the crowd. Overseer Neilan kept his attention on his handheld screen.

Skila chirped her boredom. Kirehe agreed.

Overseer Neilan called out two more names, still not asking for Kirehe. Those two left. The first two fighters didn't return, but their escort did. When the overseer called the third pair and Kirehe wasn't one of them, the remaining gladiators, except for the two other Corvik members, flashed dark looks at Kirehe and Madison, then at each other.

Erryl crossed his arms over his chest and watched Kirehe with a tiny grin at the corners of his mouth.

"I'm not sure it's a good thing they decided to put you later in the program for your first fight," Madison said. "But Erryl likes it, so maybe it's not all bad."

"These people put too much energy into worrying about their status." Kirehe rubbed under Skila's chin and shifted her weight. Her stomach churned with tension she didn't understand. Her first experience in the arena hadn't bothered her this much. She felt the same pressure and nerves now as when she faced her fighting master for her final test to pass into adulthood.

Madison laid a hand on her shoulder and squeezed. "You're going to be great."

The fourth pair left. With eight people gone, including Rho's probable cousin, Kirehe had room to breathe.

Erryl prodded Madison and delivered a stream of words.

"He says to focus on your opponent," Madison said. "No one expects you to play the crowd perfectly in your first match. If you get nervous, jump up and down or run in a circle and wave your arms."

Her unease must've shown on her face. Kirehe nodded. Finally, the overseer called her name with another one. She presented herself and

Madison followed. Her opponent, an Ackrion man named Gordy with a neck thicker than her thigh, walked in front, with Soallen.

Soallen blathered things to Madison while Kirehe listened to the steadily growing crowd noise.

"Kirehe," Madison said as they reached the arena door, "when the arena goes dark, you run out there. Gordy here will show you where to stand. When you hear your name, wave to the crowd. You stay in your spot until he starts moving, then you fight. After this match, I'll teach you the right words to listen for so you don't have to count on your opponent for when to start. At the end, the arena will go dark again, and you'll run for the door. If Gordy needs help to run, you help him. If you need help, he'll do that. Got it?"

"Yes."

Kirehe stared through the metal bars. The previous pair still fought. They did numerous things her instructors would've smacked her for. Leaps and flourishes wasted energy for no reason. The crowd, though, cheered for every ridiculous motion.

If she wanted the crowd to love her, which Madison said she did, she would have to act like an idiot.

No one from her hapa and no dragoncallers would see any of this. She could handle making a fool of herself without their scrutiny. At least, she thought she could. Acting stupid in front of Madison bothered her, but not as much. Madison wanted her to act stupid.

One of the gladiators knocked down the other with a flurry of blows. Someone handed Gordy a spear. Madison asked Soallen a question. Soallen shook his head with a smirk.

"He says they aren't giving you a weapon this time because they don't trust you not to accidentally kill Gordy. I'm guessing that's why you don't get the maras either."

Kirehe glared at Soallen. "Fine. I don't need a weapon to beat this muscle-bound lump."

Madison grinned. "No, you sure don't. Kick his ass, Kirehe."

Oylesa's voice echoed as she announced the outcome. The crowd showered the winner, an Ackrion woman, with adoration. Gordy put a hand on Kirehe's shoulder. She chose not to make a fuss over it since he would guide her to her spot.

The lights died.

Gordy led Kirehe at a jog through the door and to the center of the arena in darkness. He patted her shoulder. She stayed in the spot while he left.

Overhead, screens showed replay action from the previous fight. Crowd noise fell to a dull murmur. Other images showed on the screens, some with text Kirehe couldn't read. Time passed slowly. Kirehe felt like she waited a while before anything of interest happened.

Finally, Oylesa spoke again. She jabbered for a minute or two, then she said Gordy's name. A spotlight shone on him.

Gordy raised his arms and turned in a circle. The crowd cheered for him. He planted the butt of his spear on the ground and shifted into a fighting pose.

Oylesa had more to say, then Kirehe heard her name. Bright light blinded her.

She'd expected light. The intensity hit her like a brick. Her last time in the arena, everyone had focused on Madison. This time, the attention poured on her.

The crowd screamed with the force of a hundred krata dragons.

Cringing from the light, she chirped, "Fly, Skila."

As Oylesa said something else, Skila launched from Kirehe's shoulder. She flew a spiral upward in the light, dropping the contents of a small pouch. Tiny flakes of what Madison called "glitter" sparkled in the light and drifted in the air.

Kirehe held up her hand and kept it motionless instead of waving.

Her ears hurt from the noise of the crowd. They loved her before she'd done anything. Aside from taming a pack of maras in front of their eyes and cameras, of course.

She lowered her hand and watched Gordy. They wanted a silly show, so she would give them a silly show. Like a mara readying for a pounce, she shifted one foot behind and swished it back and forth as if to dig it into the earth. Her foot scraped the thin layer of sand, accomplishing nothing.

Viriok stood from his chair and boomed his voice over the crazed crowd.

Kirehe watched Gordy. He shook his head only enough for her to see she shouldn't spring into action yet.

"Begin," Viriok said.

That word, Kirehe knew. In case she had missed some context, she waited for Gordy to move.

He lifted his spear and stalked to the left. The match had begun.

They wanted cheap theatrics. Kirehe would give them cheap theatrics. To that end, she needed to appear confused and disoriented by the noise. She also needed a goal to start with.

Keeping Gordy at the center of her attention, she turned her head and cocked it to the side several times. The crowd, she hoped, would think her afraid of the noise. Everyone wanted to believe she had an animal's savage brain, not capable of the same coherent thought as a full human. Why not play with it?

Reinforcing their beliefs might only work once. She could live with that.

For her goal, she chose to steal Gordy's spear. They didn't trust her with a weapon. Fine. She didn't trust them with anything.

She could either get him to throw it or take it from him. Gordy seemed smart and experienced enough not to throw his only weapon without extreme goading. Her chances of succeeding that way seemed low.

To get the spear, then, she needed to close the distance, get him to drop it, snatch it, and get away.

He took a step toward her, then continued his circle, turning it into a spiral with Kirehe at the center. Every few steps, he thumped the end of his spear on the ground.

Kirehe didn't think Gordy bought her dumb animal act. He didn't have to.

When he reached three long steps away, which took less time than she expected, Kirehe exploded into action. She charged Gordy.

His eyes widened and he hefted his spear, pointing at her. The crowd roared. Kirehe leaped to cover the third step. She planted her foot on Gordy's spear, between his hand and the tip. Gordy cried out in surprise. The spear came loose. As the spear landed, so did Kirehe.

Though she could have picked it up as she somersaulted along the spear's shaft, she chose not to. It would be more crowd-pleasing, she thought, to take it from his hand. Instead, she chopped the back of Gordy's knee with a flat blade of a hand and kept moving.

Gordy grunted and dropped to one knee. Kirehe stopped, turned, and faced him again. He picked up his spear and whirled to his feet.

When he saw her waiting for him, he raised his spear over his head and gave her a tiny nod of respect. She returned it.

Now he knew she understood the game.

He tensed and readied to fight. She followed his lead. They charged each other.

In the center of the arena, under blazing lights and covered with sparkling glitter, Kirehe and Gordy traded a flurry of blows, each telegraphing enough to let the other dodge. They danced in a circle, ducking, weaving, kicking, and throwing attacks.

"Breathe," Gordy whispered.

He lunged with his spear. Kirehe slid to the side, wrapped both hands around the shaft, and yanked it out of his hands while she turned her back to him. She finished the movement by twisting and sliding too far for him to keep attacking without closing the distance.

She held the spear with one arm looped around it. Like Gordy, she panted to catch her breath. They circled each other with slow, steady paces like two mara alphas preparing to battle over territory.

The crowd thundered their approval.

Now that she knew how Gordy moved, she had no doubt she could beat him with the spear. His technique relied on its greater reach.

With it, she could beat him senseless and never take a blow.

She stopped, took a step back and raised the spear. Though she'd wanted it, the weapon gave her an unfair advantage. This crowd didn't want an unfair advantage. Not for a battle like this. They wanted two warriors behaving like animals for their pleasure.

Kirehe considered breaking the spear over her knee. Since she didn't know if Gordy had any sentimental attachment to the specific weapon, she didn't do it. He'd done nothing to earn such cruelty from her. If anything, he'd won her gratitude for his help.

Turning her back on him, she threw the spear at the wall. Before it landed, she whirled to charge him again.

Crowd noise threatened to burst her ears.

She caught him by surprise. Her body slammed into his. They tumbled to the ground. With her doing the work, they rolled and separated.

Kirehe landed on her feet. Gordy only managed one knee. He swiped an arm across his face. She crouched and tapped her fingers on the stone.

Skila screamed a shrill cry of victory as she sailed overhead.

Startled, Gordy looked up. Kirehe darted close and punched his shoulder. He grunted and couldn't recover fast enough. She swept his leg.

Gordy fell to the ground. Kirehe slammed her fist into his gut.

She could've hit his face.

He swung his leg and tried to retreat on his back at the same time.

Kirehe caught his kick in both hands. Her grip firm on his ankle, she threw him aside.

Gordy groaned and landed on his face. He struggled to rise to his hands and knees.

Hoping he would forgive her, Kirehe slid close and kicked his stomach. She kicked him again as he tried once more to rise.

He stayed on the ground, gasping for breath.

Kirehe slid back a step to give him space. If he wanted to get up, she'd let him. This time.

The crowd's roaring evolved into chanting Kirehe couldn't understand. Oylesa's voice thundered over them, with Kirehe's name among the words she shouted. Skila fluttered to land on Kirehe's readied fist. Gordy's light snapped to Kirehe.

Guessing they counted Gordy down after some time limit, Kirehe raised her arms in victory. Skila had, in a sense, cheated. Next time, her opponent would expect such a trick. She preferred to win without tricks, but the crowd had loved it.

Madison had told her to do what the audience wanted. Kirehe had, it seemed, delivered.

CHAPTER 21

MADISON

Watching Kirehe's match had taken Madison's breath away. Powerful and amazing, Kirehe had put on a brilliant show. Viriok stood through the fight, then sat again as Oylesa filled some time with blather about the fight and other attractions. All this chatter gave the next fighting pair time to hurry into the arena while Kirehe and Gordy left.

Natalyais, fighting next, took the opportunity to kick the back of Madison's knee on her way into the arena. Madison fell forward and whacked her head on the wall with Natalyais's laughter ringing in her ears.

Madison grumbled a few choice curses for the qusamadi. She regained her feet by the time Kirehe reached the door supporting Gordy. He limped on one leg and couldn't stand up straight.

"Tell him I apologize for kicking him so hard," Kirehe said as soon as the door shut.

"Would you tell her to stop apologizing?" Gordy asked through a pained grimace.

Madison grinned. "Yes."

A pharedim shoved Gordy into a stretcher carried by two visible hevits. Soallen pointed for Kirehe and Madison to return to the gladiator housing area. Madison took Kirehe by the elbow and led her back to their prison pen.

"I think they'll let you fight with the maras now. You'll have to teach them not to kill in the arena."

"They'll need better conditions and food. They keep the maras so hungry and distressed they can't control themselves."

Madison nodded. "I'll tell Soallen. For now, you're going to eat, get out of this stupid costume, and sleep."

When they returned to the prison, Kirehe headed for the food.

Madison joined Lylla in the back. "What did you think?"

"She's amazing." Lylla's eyes sparkled as she watched Kirehe. She gabbled about the fight for several minutes.

Madison stopped listening to Lylla's gushing to watch the gladiator crowd. Several, including fellow new guy Hallor, gave Kirehe high-fives while she tried to eat. Others gave her venomous glares brimming with jealousy. Once she returned, Natalyais in particular looked ready to stab Kirehe's face, probably because she knew it would screw Madison. Bryor held himself with tight, stiff annoyance as he watched Kirehe.

At a point when Lylla paused to breathe, Madison pointed at a different man scowling at Kirehe, the one who Kirehe had beaten early to earn respect. He sat alone, and a puckered scar traced the line of his jaw. "Who's that guy with the ugly scar?"

"Wally. He hates everyone, especially when they do well. If he could, he'd probably kill us all in our sleep. He's on team Corvik with us."

"And her?" Madison pointed to another of Kirehe's anti-fan club. The woman had a long, thick braid of platinum blonde hair and tanned skin. The calculating hate on her face bothered Madison the most.

"Gigi. She's part of Team Bretikor. She and Bryor are showpieces. Bryor does a bunch of tricks with a huge whip-chain-thing. Gigi uses a bow. They don't fight other gladiators very often, and when they do, it's two or three against one. They step in as a diversion before the final fight. Executions also fill that slot. Monster tricks will probably do it too."

That explained Bryor's behavior. "They're worried they won't seem as exciting after Kirehe and her dragons, I guess?"

"Probably."

Madison scanned the group again and saw no one else with naked hostility. At least she had a small pool of people to worry about.

Someone screamed in rage from the hallway with the training and mirror rooms. Only a few glanced in that direction. Everyone else ignored it.

"What was that?"

Lylla sighed. "Tau. Every time he has a fight in the arena, he comes back and beats his hands bloody against the wall in the training room, then he screams like that. Everyone is used to it."

"Used to it." Madison already knew no one would ever help her, but she'd thought they would help each other, at least among teams. "What does this place even have teams for?"

"One more thing to bet on."

"Ugh." Madison hated this whole operation. "By the way, Tau's a they, like Rho."

"Oh. Sorry. Their hands, their blood, their screams."

The one other member of Rho's race stuck in the prison stalked from the training hallway. Strips of flesh dangled from Tau's hands. Blood dripped a trail on the floor as Tau roiled across the room like a storm cloud. Tiny white drones, each the size of Madison's thumb, skimmed the floor behind Tau and vaporized the blood.

No one watched Tau except Madison. She recognized anguish and wondered why Overseer Neilan hadn't chosen to execute Tau to end the obvious misery. Probably for the same reason he and Viriok did anything else—the crowd liked watching Tau.

Everyone else watched the fight on the screen.

Rho slipped through the door and headed after Tau. Madison got up to walk with Rho.

"Not now, Madison," Rho said, waving her off.

They both turned the corner together as a door shut at the end of the hall.

"I just want to help. Tau—"

Rho stopped and covered Madison's heart with their hand. "Tau is not right in the head. I told you our remica was killed. Tau and I survived. No one else did. And they took us so we couldn't find another family to join. As a nucri, I can handle living without her. Tau is a warrior. It is their purpose to give their life to protect the remica, and they failed. If you want to show Tau compassion, ask Kirehe to kill them in the arena. That's the only mercy they can handle."

Madison let Rho go. They understood Tau much better than Madison ever could.

So much anger and despair filled this place. More than ever, Madison wanted to find a way to destroy it on her way out. Most of the gladiators probably wouldn't survive outside it, but at least she could prevent the destruction of more lives.

By the time she returned to their room, Kirehe had shed her costume and climbed into her hammock. Jaco and Shmar slept in theirs, as did Oolaang. Madison climbed into her own and stared at the ceiling while her bed swayed. Lylla slipped inside before the dim light shut off.

Once darkness fell in a silence broken only by the chirping of Skila's crickets and Shmar's light snores, Madison thought of her uncle. Madman Wayward had probably seen his niece's failed execution. The Oligarchy had wanted it spread far and wide before they'd known she would survive. If Uncle Chris hadn't seen the original broadcast, he'd seen a recording in the days that had followed.

He knew who'd lived and who'd died. The entire crew of *Wayward Star* had seen it all. They'd watched friends suffer under the claws of monsters. Then they'd watched other friends live. How many would blame her for those deaths? Shmar still did. He barely had time to eat before collapsing from a hard day of manual labor, yet he still made sure she knew.

She pictured her uncle sitting in his armchair in the corner of his cabin with the lights off. He stared at a screen showing the stars off the port side, as he often did these days. Once upon a time, he'd spent most of his life in the cockpit, even when he didn't have to. Uncle Chris had watched the blur of FTL or the movement of planets and stars.

He'd dreamed more. He'd laughed with a spark of joy. For the last few years, since Madison had taken over as his primary pilot, he'd retreated. The fantasy of defeating the Oligarchy, of killing a single lakhan, had faded. At the ripe, old age of forty, he seemed to have lost all hope.

That deepening despair had pushed him into taking fewer risks. Christopher Wayward at twenty-seven had taken in his orphaned niece without hesitation. At thirty-two, he'd rescued Jaco. For the past few years, he hadn't paused once to look for lost souls. His crew hadn't changed.

Madison might not have taken the risk she did if he hadn't spent more and more time in the shadows, sinking deeper into that chair with each passing day. She'd done it for him as much as herself.

But only she had failed and caused nine deaths.

In the darkness, with everyone asleep around her, she cried for her lost friends. They'd placed their lives in her hands, and she'd let them slip through her fingers.

She'd never forget the last look on Dani's face, of terror, then surprise. The panic of the rest of the crew had etched into her memory.

Cradok needed to die. So did Viriok. Somehow. They had a weakness. Everybody had a weakness. Nobody was perfect. Not even Kirehe, the jungle princess dragon warrior. The lakhans had flesh and blood. They could bleed. In theory.

Madison fell asleep fantasizing about shooting Cradok. She dreamt of her uncle's chair swallowing him, and of running through his ship, trying to find him.

Not enough hours later, Skila chirped loud and bright, waking everyone. They all grumbled. The whole room shuffled to stuff their faces under Kirehe's protection. Rho had returned at some point and accompanied them to the food line.

Jaco, Shmar, and Oolaang left together, all three under escort by

Ilai. Rho assisted a different pharedim checking on those who'd suffered injuries in the arena the day before, then left with the pharedim to handle her other duties. Lylla lurked in the common room. Madison spent her day following Kirehe from one training to another.

The days plodded by. Kirehe fought again three days later, this time with a machete. At her grandstanding lesson the next morning, Madison decided Kirehe had enough status to make more demands.

"Overseer Neilan?"

He sighed as he dismissed his gladiator students. Kirehe and the two other newer gladiators all tried with earnest effort as far as Madison could tell. The overseer seemed to regard working with them like banging his head against a wall.

"Yes?"

She hurried to keep up with him on his way out of the housing area. "I'd like to ask for something."

"Ask your patron. Despite the arrangement between you and me, I am not here to get things for you."

"It's not on the list of approved boons he can provide."

Overseer Neilan raised his brow. "And that's stopping you?"

Madison snorted. "No, of course not. It's just not something he has any say over. I'm hoping you'll reduce the workload for the other slaves in our group. They're practically walking dead, and if you keep them going at this rate, they'll become really dead in a few months, of exhaustion. Which would make Kirehe very upset. Why not avoid that by cutting back on their work a little?"

"I see. And what do you propose to trade for this boon?"

She'd hoped he would agree without asking for anything. She should've known better. "I'm prepared to negotiate."

Overseer Neilan waved for her to follow him out of the housing area. "Get into the cage."

Madison sighed and shuffled into the cage in the overseer's office. He stepped through the door a few moments later and sat in his chair. The moment he seemed settled, a green light flashed on one of the consoles behind him.

The overseer checked whatever had flashed. His mouth twisted into a scowl. "This will have to wait." He tapped a screen. A force field crackled into life between the cage and the overseer.

Madison could no longer hear anything, but she could still see him.

Another pharedim, this one in a maroon and black uniform with gold trim, stormed into the room. She didn't notice Madison, or she dismissed Madison as nothing more than a wretched slave unworthy of notice.

Madison remembered the colors. Cradok used those colors. She'd never forget.

The new pharedim shouted at Overseer Neilan. Madison could tell by how much effort she put into verbally assaulting him. The overseer bowed to her, then fidgeted with the hem of his shirt. While Cradok's pharedim raised her arms in frustration and turned her back on Madison, the overseer gestured for Madison to turn away or leave.

The furtive nature of his gesture gave Madison the feeling she needed to do what he wanted. She couldn't leave, though. Hevits outside had shut the door, locking her in until Overseer Neilan gave a signal to release her. Madison sat with her back to them.

For a long time, she stayed on the floor. Then she heard a crackle of energy.

"You can get up now."

Madison stood and found Overseer Neilan sitting on his chair, rubbing his temples.

He tapped on a screen. "Which slaves did you want to have shorter duties?"

"Jaco, Shmar, Oolaang, and Rho." If he wanted to skip the negotiation part, Madison had no cause to question his change of heart.

"Each of them will have their hours of work reduced by half starting with their next shift. If Kirehe loses her next match, I'll increase their hours again."

The door buzzed open. Madison blinked at him. "Yes, Overseer. Thank you." She fled for the safety of Kirehe's room to wonder over what had just happened. On the way, she heard the overseer call for Ilai.

Overseer Neilan hadn't wanted Cradok's representative to see her. He'd done what she wanted without an argument.

Madison sat on the edge of the bed in Kirehe's room. As she pondered possible reasons for those two things to fit together, Ilai burst into the room. "Get up. Patron meeting."

She jumped to her feet, all thoughts of the overseer and his visitor banished. Without a word, she followed Ilai and stepped obediently into the elevator. Ilai, she noted, eyed her as if she expected Madison to explode or grow an extra head.

Establishing a reputation for backtalk and balking had its uses.

Zorileck already had his drink by the time the elevator stopped. He gaped his mouth, which Madison couldn't decide how to interpret. Maybe he smiled?

"Mister Zorileck," Madison said with a bow. "What can I do for you today?"

"Kirehe is amazing."

"I agree with you."

He laughed. "I'd like to know if her feathered monsters are in a good condition to fight in the arena with her yet."

Zorileck wanted insider information? Madison stared at him. "Is it cheating to tell you? Am I going to get into trouble if I say it'll be after her next fight?"

"Probably." He gaped his mouth wider. Considering the conversation, she guessed it approximated a grin.

Madison clasped her hands behind her back. "Then it wouldn't be wise of me to tell you. Kirehe is a handful, and the pharedimi can't manage her without me."

"You're a clever one. Does Kirehe like my gifts?"

"Yes, very much. She especially appreciates the continued cricket deliveries."

"Good. I don't know how she manages to perform so superbly with how much time she spends in the brothel, but I approve."

Madison blinked at him. Kirehe spent no time in the brothel. She didn't go there. Between the maras, the overseer's training, eating, sleeping, and the stupid kut Soallen made her do, Kirehe barely had five minutes to herself on any given day.

Zorileck slurped his drink and tossed his glass. "Kirehe is the best investment I've ever made. Her simple pleasures and needs are so cheap. Perhaps I can find something for you? As her manager, your continued well-being is also my concern."

"Me?" The wheels in Madison's head spun at high speed. If she asked for the right kind of thing, she could figure out where Zorileck kept his ship, which would be helpful for her plans. She made a note to ask the group to brainstorm a way to accomplish that.

For the moment, she thought of something else useful. "I'd love a small tool set, actually. I like to tinker with things. Keeps my hands busy while Kirehe is, you know, busy."

"An interesting request." Zorileck stood. "I'll see what they'll let through."

"Oh, and I could also use a replacement eye. It's a little dangerous to have a blind side in here."

"Ha!" Zorileck nodded. "I'm sure it is. Send me the specifications. I can't imagine anyone would have a problem with that request."

"Thank you, sir." Madison bowed and watched him leave as the elevator carried her down. Tools in Oolaang's hands would make a big difference in her planning calculations.

CHAPTER 22

KIREHE

The days blurred. Fights provided an anchor to remember how much time passed, but nothing else did. With Madison having worked magic, not only did she have a new cybereye, the rest of her crew spent more time among them. This pleased Madison, and also the other four. Kirehe had preferred to avoid them, but she liked making Madison happy.

Regular food and a shared cage had improved the maras' health and well-being tremendously. After her third fight, she told Soallen they wouldn't kill in the arena. In a few hours, they'd join her for a battle against two or three others.

She stood at the food conveyor with Madison and Jaco, mentally running over the strategies she'd devised to keep the mara pack under control. Despite her confidence when facing Soallen, she worried they might not obey. Worse, she feared they would react poorly when a gladiator hit one. The concern of taking a hit while handling the maras also lurked in the back of her mind.

Kirehe had learned more of the language in the time since her first match than she'd let on. This meant she heard someone grumble about having their foot stepped on. She turned her head as she reached for a serving spoon.

As usual, Natalyais "stumbled into" Madison, causing her to slosh her plate and lose some of her meal. Everyone had given up confronting her about it.

Someone else waiting for a spot at the food line threw a punch at the woman standing next to Kirehe. The woman dumped her plate on the man next to her. Kirehe ducked to the side. As she moved, she had to hop over an outstretched foot. Meat flew off her plate and smacked someone else in the face.

Madison squeaked and fled with whatever she had. Kirehe couldn't evade the brawl. Bodies bumped into her. Voices shouted. She shoved someone. Flying plates and utensils winked in the light.

Sharp, white-hot pain slashed across Kirehe's right side. Clutching it, she stumbled out of the melee. Hands pushed and pulled, bodies fell over each other. People squawked, grunted, and groaned. Jaco appeared at her left elbow and helped guide her out of the brawl.

Hevits waded into the throng. Bodies flew. Kirehe reached a wall and panted to catch her breath. Jaco leaned against the wall with her, gasping for air.

Madison jumped in front of her and tugged at her hand. "Is this your blood?" She also pointed to Jaco.

Kirehe lifted her hand and turned her hip. Blood covered her palm and oozed through her fingers. It stained her shirt.

"I was trying to help," Jaco said. He seemed surprised and distressed by the red smears across his hands.

Ripping open a hole in Kirehe's shirt, Madison paled. "You've been stabbed." She turned and shouted at the room.

Jaco blanched. She thought he might vomit as he stumbled to the side. Gordy appeared. He swept Kirehe into his arms and carried her someplace she hadn't visited before. Too much bright light shone off too white walls and a too white bed.

Rho stepped into view. They covered Kirehe's forehead with their hand while other figures inspected the wound in her side. Things happened around Kirehe too fast and too slow for her to comprehend. People shouted.

Once the pain faded, the world returned to normal speed. Kirehe couldn't breathe without wheezing, but she could comprehend her surroundings again.

"She can't fight like this," the pharedim with the mask said. "She needs a few days to recover. The moment they see her, no one will bet on her match."

Soallen checked his handheld screen. He tapped on it several times. "What would it take to get her back on her feet in one hour?"

"Access to…" He used several words Kirehe didn't know. "High Priest Oylesa or His Benevolence Viriok has to authorize that. No one else can."

"Prepare to use that. I'll get it authorized." Soallen left the room.

The masked pharedim sighed. "Fine." He gave Rho instructions to prepare foreign things.

"Madison?" Kirehe asked between gasps for air.

"That's her translator-manager," Rho said. "Madison is good at keeping her calm."

"No." The masked pharedim stepped away.

Kirehe fumbled for whatever she could reach. Her hand hit a tray of tools and sent them flying. Rebellious fingers clamped around something long and thin. The masked pharedim turned at the clatter of his tools on the floor. She threw her stick-thing at him.

The masked pharedim dodged into the stick-thing and squealed. "Stay still! Get her to stay still!"

Rho draped their body over Kirehe. "Calm down, Kirehe. They're going to fix you."

"Madison!" Kirehe struggled against the warm weight on her chest. She didn't want to hurt Rho, though, so she avoided hitting them as she flailed.

The masked pharedim skittered to the door. "Fine! Get Madison before she rampages!"

Certain they understood and would comply, Kirehe subsided. She let Rho help her adjust so she lay on the bed without her leg dangling over the side.

Madison sprinted into the room. "Is she dying?"

"No!" The masked pharedim pointed at Kirehe. "She's being difficult. Fix it."

After a moment's pause, Madison burst into laughter at the masked pharedim. "Okay. Yeah. I'm here to save the day. Everyone relax."

"This isn't funny," the masked pharedim snapped. "She tried to kill me." He bent and picked up the stick-thing, then brandished it at Madison.

"Gosh, wow, yeah, that is absolutely the scariest thing imaginable. The fear is so real and raw."

He pressed his thumb against the side while glaring at her. Red light sprang from the end in a short beam. Growling at Madison, he told her the name of it, which Kirehe didn't understand.

Madison crossed her arms, unmoved by the light. "And does that thing actually work if one of us slaves touches it?"

The masked pharedim jabbed a finger at her. His mouth opened and shut. He made the light stop. "That's not the point," he said, his words sharp and staccato as he tucked the stick-thing into his pocket. "Deal with her."

"That's my job," Madison said with a nod. She stepped close to Kirehe and softened her expression. "Hey. Are you okay?"

"I'm fine," Kirehe said. She couldn't feel anything across her torso, including her heartbeat.

"Sure you are, jungle princess dragon warrior. I just want to tell you right now that I have no idea who stabbed you. Overseer Neilan already handed out a giant pile of demerits. They found the bloody weapon on the floor. I caught a glimpse of it before they shouted for me. Long, thin knife, made for a sharp, deep stab, and I think it was all plastic.

"I got the feeling weapons in the prison doesn't happen very often. I'm not sure what the security is, but Overseer Neilan trusts it. So someone smuggled it in somehow. And stabbed you. I'm going to assume they targeted you on purpose. And I'm going to figure out who did that so you can beat the kut out of them."

Kirehe smiled. "I knew you'd fix things."

"That's what I do." Madison brushed Kirehe's hair with the back of her fingers. Her new eye didn't match her real one, giving her an odd, lopsided feel. Standing beside a pharedim, she seemed more tangible, more approachable. The pharedimi seemed more remote than ever.

The gesture soothed Kirehe and gave her flutters in her belly at the same time. "Yes. And you're good at it."

Soallen returned. "The treatment has been authorized by Viriok. Do it."

"What are you doing to her?" Madison asked.

"Getting her fit for the arena with methods normally reserved for guests."

Madison whistled. "I take it there are already bets on her fight?

"Correct." Soallen turned and left the room.

Rho ripped off the bandage, which Kirehe didn't feel. The masked pharedim stuck a thick needle into her wound. A tube connected to the end pumped green liquid through the needle. The liquid spread cool pressure through her gut.

"This will heal the wound fully in about three hours," the masked pharedim told Madison. "In fifteen minutes, she'll be in good enough condition to get up and prepare for her fight."

Kirehe would fight with a half-healed stab wound in her side. She would have preferred to postpone her first match involving the maras. No one cared what she wanted. More to the point, Viriok and his pharedimi didn't care.

The numbness drained from her body in a rush. She groaned at the dull ache in her side.

Madison darted to her and leaned over her. "What's wrong?"

Kirehe scowled. "There's a hole in my side."

A grin sprouted on Madison's face. "So long as it's nothing serious, we're okay." She kissed the end of Kirehe's nose.

That irritating flustered feeling swirled in Kirehe's belly again. She didn't understand it, and it didn't fix the ache, so she didn't like it. Rho kept holding her down, preventing her from getting up and leaving to avoid it.

"Relax," Madison cooed. "You have to wait for the medicine to work enough so you don't make it worse."

"I'm not a baby," Kirehe grumbled.

"Of course not."

Scowling at Madison, Kirehe waited. The time took too long to shamble by. Finally, when she wanted to scream for everyone to stop fussing over her and let her go, Rho said she could leave.

The ache persisted. Kirehe sat up. She held her side and stood. Pain flickered across her entire body, all the way to her fingers and toes.

Madison hovered at her good side. Rho hovered behind her. Kirehe hated how much effort walking took.

By the time they reached the gladiator staging room, sweat soaked Kirehe's clothes. Half the gladiators had arrived, including Natalyais. No doubt, the moment Kirehe turned her back, Natalyais would shove Madison, or prod her in the ribs, or whatever else she thought she could get away with.

Overseer Neilan frowned at her over his handheld screen. "She can't fight in that. Where's her costume?"

"I'll get it." Madison sprinted out of the room.

"You will have the monsters in the arena today," Overseer Neilan said.

"Wait," one of the others said. "We're fighting those things?"

At Madison's request, Kirehe had stopped acting like she didn't understand anything at all. She nodded. "Trained. No kill."

"They better not," someone growled.

Madison returned with Kirehe's costume and helped her into it. She used spit and cloth to wipe away blood so no one would see it. Then they waited.

This time, Kirehe didn't fight until the second-to-last bout. She would face three warriors, each using a different weapon. The match presented a member from each team, giving the audience something extra to bet on. Her opponents included Tau, Rho's familymate.

As she stood in the darkness, waiting for Oylesa to announce her name, Kirehe wondered when the pain would fade. Her side still ached. Hadn't that masked pharedim claimed she'd feel better in an hour? At least that much time had passed since he'd dosed her with green liquid. Maybe he'd delivered the medicine to the wrong part of her body.

Oylesa shouted Kirehe's name last. The spotlight flared into life over Kirehe. She spread her arms. Thanks to the stabbing, Skila hadn't accompanied her, so she had no glitter to dance in. At the moment when the crowd might have rumbled their disappointment, the large gate opened.

"Today, Kirehe fights with her beasts by her side," Oylesa said.

Chana burst through the gate, followed by the rest of her pack. They screeched their defiance at the crowd. The crowd roared in returned.

"Final wagers close in one minute," Oylesa boomed.

The mara pack rushed for Kirehe and stopped in a formation around her like a squad of loyal guardians. Kirehe petted Chana's neck.

"Remember. No killing. Chase, threaten, scare. No killing. No eating."

"Not hungry," Chana chirped. "Good meat. Enough."

"Good." Kirehe had no weapon for this fight. Soallen had said she could only have it when she fought without the maras.

"Wagers close in ten seconds," Oylesa said. "Gladiators, begin."

"Wooni, harass the one with the big stick. Fobi, the one with the small stick. Heetay, the middle one. Don't let them hit you with their sticks. The sticks bite. Chana and Rila stay with me."

Three maras surged at the other gladiators. The other two screamed at the three men. Kirehe stood between Chana and Rila, not sure what Viriok expected her to do.

The man with the staff raised it and shuffled backward while Wooni stalked toward him at a sedate pace. Fobi leaped at the man with the shorter blade. Heetay streaked past Tau in the middle, whapping them with his tail on the way past.

All three fighters scrambled to put their backs together. Kirehe remembered Gordy circling her and how the crowd had liked it. Her side still ached, so she needed something easy to do anyway. She took Chana and Rila for a walk around the edge of the arena. Since she had no real need to watch the three men and their three maras, she waved to the crowd as she walked.

From the noise, the audience enjoyed this. As she, Chana, and Rila reached the spot where they'd begun, she assessed the three-on-three matchup. Fobi, Heetay, and Wooni kept the three men pinned together, taunting them with growls and rhythmic movements. To the men, the maras probably seemed angry and ready to pounce.

Kirehe recognized the typical mara mating dance from the trio and had to stop herself from laughing. They flashed their claws, swished their tails, and stomped their feet. Their frills raised and lowered.

"Return to me!" she whistled, her voice not audible to anyone but the maras.

The three maras stopped their dance and rushed to form a pack again. Kirehe stood in the center of them and beckoned for the three men to come get her.

Her opponents glanced at each other. They didn't move toward her. Kirehe wished they would close the distance and attack so she didn't have to stress her injury.

The men took one step together. They all knew the overseer would punish everyone for failing to do their job. Kirehe hadn't yet discovered the penalty for one substandard match. She didn't want to find out.

"All charge the man in the middle with me." Kirehe turned her whistles into a long, drawn-out shout. She took one step, then another. Her maras stayed with her, matching her speed.

The three men scattered. Kirehe and the maras chased the one with the sword. Wooni reached him first. He smacked the man's back with his lowered head. Chana knocked him aside. Kirehe swept his foot. The man fell to the ground. Rila turned around and screeched at the audience as Kirehe had taught her. Fobi pounced on the man's feet, wrapping her claws around his ankles. Heetay snatched his wrists.

Two maras held the gladiator like a rope. They swung him back and forth. Kirehe leaped over him and charged the man with the long stick.

While her maras acted silly with their prey, Kirehe crashed into her opponent. She noted Tau moving in to challenge the maras. Then she paid attention to the man trying to brain her with his staff.

She spun and slammed the back of her fist into his chest. He sliced his staff through the air where she'd stood a moment earlier. She snapped her foot at his knee. He slid back and swung his staff. She leaned away from the staff's arc.

Kirehe's wound kept her from leaning far enough. The staff clipped her arm and knocked her off-balance. She fell on her knee and cried out as she turned it into an unexpected somersault. Launching herself to her feet at the end proved challenging. Luck and nothing more kept her out of her opponent's reach. His staff whirled close enough to ruffle the feathers on her sleeve.

"I thought you were good," he taunted.

"I think you smell bucket." Those words didn't sound quite right, but Kirehe liked the effect.

Her opponent paused and squinted at her. She leaped at him. He started with surprise. Holding her side, Kirehe spun and kicked, missing on purpose. As he slid back and swung his staff, she landed a step behind him. She slammed her elbow into his chest.

He grunted, his attack foiled. She snatched his staff and whirled to whack his knee from behind. As he groaned and dropped that knee to the floor, she held the staff aside, slid close, and punched his kidney.

One of the men screamed. Kirehe snapped her head up to see the maras' prisoner flying through the air. He landed and slid across the floor, curling around his arm. The crowd roared with approval.

Kirehe's opponent flung his fist into her side, smashing into her wound. She groaned and twisted. He kicked her knee. She fell. Lying on her side, she raised the staff faster than she intended and slammed it between his legs. The impact caused a solid crack.

Wincing in less pain than she expected, he bent and clutched at his privates. Kirehe rolled to her feet and slapped his butt with the staff. Audience laughter disgusted Kirehe. She tossed the staff aside and charged her opponent. They fell together in a tangle of limbs. Her momentum carried them in a slide to the man still lying on the floor.

"Are you hurt?" Kirehe asked as she punched her opponent in the face.

"I think my arm is broken."

"Stay down," the former staff-wielder said. He jammed his knee into Kirehe's side.

"Stop hitting my stabbing," Kirehe snarled as she curled up, then kicked at his chest to fling him to the side.

He grinned as he rose to one knee, gasping for breath. "Anything for the win, honey."

Kirehe narrowed her eyes at him. She could no longer ignore the pain in her side and held her elbow over the wound. "Chana! To me!"

His amusement vanished. His eyes widened and he said words Kirehe didn't know. They sounded like panic.

Standing with all the dignity of a queen, Kirehe glared at him. "Anything for the win."

The man on the ground laughed.

Kirehe turned her back on her opponent as Chana sped past her. The mara plowed into the man at full speed.

In the center of the arena, Tau displayed admirable acrobatics in evading the tails and balled fists of the remaining four maras. They played as Kirehe had taught them. To them, no killing meant no reason to hurt their prey.

She walked into the mesmerizing rhythm of four dragons and one warrior dancing to unknown music. Another time, she would've joined their strange dance. With her wound throbbing, she walked to Tau and punched them in the gut.

Tau lost their balance and fell under the maras' assault. The dragons pretended to pounce and rip him apart. Their performance made even the gladiator shriek. The spotlight on the group shut off.

Behind her, Chana squealed and gurgled. Kirehe whirled to see blood spurting from Chana's neck. The staff-wielder staggered back, drenched in blood and holding the broken-arm man's sword.

Kirehe froze. She watched Chana stagger and slump. The mara's blood soaked the floor.

The pack left their prey to cluster around Kirehe. She draped her arms over them. Together, they watched Chana die. Her death took moments that stretched into eons. Kirehe heard nothing beyond her own heartbeat pounding in rage, drowning the pain under a wave of hate so fierce she needed to rip that man apart.

As one, the pack and Kirehe shifted their attention to Chana's murderer.

"Kill," Heetay growled.

The rest of the pack murmured their agreement. Kirehe wanted to allow it. At last, she had someone to spew her vengeance at. One man had turned himself into a focal point for all the frustration she'd experienced since losing Nihan.

Behind him, she saw the door. A figure stood in silhouette, watching them. Though she couldn't tell who she saw, the shadow reminded her of Overseer Neilan.

This gladiator didn't deserve any of her wrath. He'd probably acted in fear of Chana's claws and teeth. After seeing his fellow fighter fall under the pack's assault, he hadn't trusted Chana not to kill him, so he killed her first.

"No. Not his fault."

"Blood on him," Fobi protested.

"The bad masters made him do it."

All four maras growled deep in their throats, producing a low, rumbling purr of a noise. The maras couldn't be trusted not to kill this man.

"Sit. Stay. I am alpha. He is mine."

Her maras sat on the floor. Kirehe paused and watched to make sure they followed her command. She noticed blood on their claws and snouts. "What happened to the other one?"

They looked away. Rila said, "Man stab self on claws. Blood smell thick. Man die. No eat."

She frowned. Kirehe would be punished for this. At least Tau had found peace, as Rho had wanted. Whatever the overseer chose to do in retaliation, she would endure it knowing that much.

Kirehe turned her attention to Chana's killer and stalked forward. As she passed the broken-arm man, he whispered, "Don't kill him."

She didn't respond. If her pack saw her lose to Chana's killer, they would never respect her again. They needed a strong protector, not a pathetic weakling who couldn't even defeat one of her own.

When she reached the man covered in Chana's blood, she stopped outside his range with the sword and waited.

He met her gaze with no apology. In the arena, she didn't think he'd show anything else. Instead of launching an attack, though, he tossed the sword to the side and used both hands to beckon her closer for a fistfight.

The crowd, which Kirehe had blocked out the moment Chana had shrieked, roared with delight.

Kirehe took one step. He took one step. They glared at each other close enough to throw punches.

Oylesa's voice rose above the crowd, but Kirehe didn't care what she had to say.

"If you hit my stabbing again," she murmured, "I will rip out your spine."

"Fair," he grunted. "First to land a solid blow wins?" Following her lead, he avoided moving his mouth much so the audience might not realize they spoke.

"First on the floor stays down."

"Agreed."

They fought. Each displayed their skill with punching, kicking, and blocking. In the shared glare of two spotlights, they danced in circles. The pair bounced together and apart. Kirehe forced herself to twist despite her injury. She kept moving, the fresh memory of Chana's death goading her.

He matched her, blow for blow. Kirehe had no Skila to distract a man with equal skill. In time, she knew he would win for lack of an injury like hers. She needed to do something unexpected.

Desperate to prove herself to the mara pack, she let him hit her in the shoulder. Knowing it would land and choosing how she took it let her prepare her return blow. Her fist connected with the side of his neck.

He lost the fight. She swept his leg and shoved him to the ground. He stayed down.

Kirehe bent over double, clutching her side and her shoulder. She gasped for breath, deafened by crowd noise.

She shambled to Chana's corpse and lowered her knee to the ground. Oblivious to the spotlight still trained on her, she touched Chana's face and pressed her eyes closed. The rest of the pack joined her.

As one, the pack and Kirehe raised their heads and loosed a keening wail.

"Truly a magnificent death for a magnificent creature," Oylesa said.

The light shut off.

CHAPTER 23

MADISON

More than once, Madison had thought Kirehe would lose. She released a breath and a load of tension when the last guy dropped. Then her heart broke. The dragons cried their anguish, and Madison had no idea how anyone with a shred of empathy could hear that sound and not feel their loss.

"You have to let them mourn," she said to Soallen as the final two gladiators for the day slipped into the darkness of the arena. "They're animals. They might go berserk if you don't."

"I'll pass on your request."

The spent gladiators returned. Kirehe dragged Tau's body. The other two men supported each other in a shamble.

"I'm sorry," the last man down said between panting for breaths. "Kirehe, I thought—"

"I know what you think," Kirehe snapped. She sounded ready to drop any moment. "Tau is kill on claws," she told Soallen. "They good. They try hard no hurt. Tau sit up. Claws scrape. Accident."

Madison slipped under Kirehe's arm the moment she surrendered Tau's body.

Kirehe raised a weary arm. She pointed at Soallen and jabbed him in the chest. "I go to pack now."

Soallen lifted his chin. "No. Every death must be investigated.

There will be no rewards for one who used her weapon to kill a fellow gladiator."

Kirehe narrowed her eyes. They held a wild, dangerous glimmer.

"It happened in the dark," Madison said. "What footage are you going to check? She didn't tell them to kill Tau, and you know Tau was messed up in the head."

Overseer Neilan emerged from the darkness. "In this particular case, Soallen, I accept Kirehe's account. Madison is correct. Tau has, on multiple occasions, attempted to throw himself at his opponents' weapons. That he finally succeeded in the dark, against creatures not equipped to evade his effort, should not surprise us."

"Yes, Overseer," Soallen said. "Kirehe should still be punished."

"I agree, but it can wait." The overseer pointed at the arena. "I will allow this mourning activity after the last fight if you will do whatever you intend before the crowd. Otherwise, the corpse will be removed and disposed of immediately."

Madison didn't think Kirehe would agree to that. In fact, she suspected Kirehe took a breath to spew obscenities at him. She stepped in to prevent that. And to show Kirehe that she cared. "We agree, but only if the rest of our family group can come. Including me."

Kirehe scowled at her. Madison ignored it.

The overseer flicked his gaze between Madison and Kirehe. "Only if you and your people stay out of the spotlights. This is about Kirehe and her animals."

"Deal." Madison braced for Kirehe's tirade the moment Overseer Neilan disappeared into the darkness.

"Honoring a fallen packmate isn't meant to have an audience," Kirehe muttered.

"I know." Madison took Kirehe's hand and kissed it. "But either you do it with an audience or you don't get to do it."

Kirehe's scowl faded. "Help me take off these stupid feathers."

While they fussed with Kirehe's costume, Skila found them. She carried a glitter packet and twittered at Kirehe. When Kirehe chirped in return, Skila drooped.

"She can still use the glitter," Madison said. "It might seem silly and garish, but I think it'd look nice in the light."

Nodding, Kirehe sighed. "He killed her. He didn't trust me, so he killed her."

Madison squeezed her hand. "He didn't know you." She could've pointed out that the maras could scare even a giant slab of muscle with their claws. Or that the gladiators always knew they could die in the arena, even if they didn't expect to.

Maybe she'd bring up those points later. For now, she offered Kirehe her support. And considered who benefited from trying to kill Kirehe.

The overseer gained nothing if Kirehe died. The same held true for Viriok. No gladiators gained anything directly from Kirehe's death unless a patron had convinced them to do it. Even then, she thought anyone sane would balk at the possibility of punishment when the overseer determined the culprit.

Not that all the gladiators retained their sanity.

Wounding Kirehe, on the other hand, could serve a purpose. Anyone might want her to lose a match. At this point, Kirehe probably had good odds, so payouts for betting on her would be low. Anybody wanting to bet on her opponent with long odds could see value in convincing a gladiator to stab her.

Even Viriok might see a benefit to having her wounded, depending upon how he profited from the betting itself. But then, if Viriok wanted her injured, he wouldn't have authorized a treatment he expected to bring her back to perfect health by the time of her match.

One suspect cleared, a bazillion to go.

Madison greeted Jaco, Rho, Shmar, Lylla, and Oolaang as the final match ended.

Rho collapsed with tears of relief and gratitude at the news of Tau's death. "May I see Tau's body?" they begged Soallen. "Please."

Soallen raised an eyebrow and sneered. "No."

Rho sobbed into their hands. Jaco draped an arm around their shoulders and held them close.

Madison wanted to punch Soallen in the face. He could've allowed it if he'd wanted. Doing so would've cost him nothing. His refusal carried the stench of superiority.

Oylesa announced the winner of the final match while the two gladiators left the arena in the dark. "That concludes the fight schedule for tonight. Remain seated if you'd like to witness a special event."

Soallen waved for them to return to the arena floor. Kirehe let go of Madison and loped inside. Madison took Rho's hand and led the group at a more sedate walk. They had to stay back, so she didn't go far.

"Tonight, for the first time in Rikor Six history, we present to you, our guests, the unique experience of a local savage ritual to honor a fallen warrior. Your favorite wild gladiator, Kirehe the Untamed, offers this exotic performance for all. Behold a one-of-a-kind experience, revealing secrets of this primitive culture beyond our walls."

Some of the crowd left. They'd come for blood and guts, and didn't care about dead dragons or cultural enrichment. Or whatever they wanted to call it.

Among those who remained, murmurs and whispers rippled through the crowd. Jaco squeezed Madison's hand. Shmar touched her shoulder. She clutched Oolaang's shoulder as he stood in front of her. Rho squatted in easy reach beside them and with Lylla.

The spotlight clicked on. Its pool of light wandered the center of the arena until it found the mara dragon corpse. Kirehe stepped into the light. She knelt beside the body. The rest of her pack joined her, two on each side. They squatted and sat still.

For the next ten minutes, Kirehe and the pack touched the body. Skila flew overhead, dripping glitter over them. They sang together in whistles. Each of them dipped their muzzles in the blood, including Kirehe. During several short sections, they clearly continued to sing without making a sound.

Halfway through, Oolaang spoke the names of their dead. People they had cared about and watched die, and never mourned. Madison repeated the nine names and added Tau. Jaco also repeated them, then Shmar. With one breath, they repeated the names together, even Rho.

"They didn't die in vain," Madison whispered.

"Didn't they?" Shmar asked.

"No. I have a plan."

Shmar huffed. "Your plan got them killed."

By now, Madison had stopped wrestling with her guilt. It wouldn't drive her. She could still take chances when they needed taking. They wouldn't all die in this hellhole. "My mistake got them killed. I'm taking more time with this plan to prevent mistakes like that. I just need to figure out who attacked Kirehe, then I can work around our enemy on the inside."

"Everyone hates her," Jaco said. "Or you. Or both."

"That's not true. Hardly anyone hates her." Madison thought she could count all the names on one hand. "Only one person in there really hates me. The rest all think I'm getting away with something and don't deserve to be there. That's not a reason to attack Kirehe."

"You're not going to figure it out standing here and speculating," Shmar said.

"True." Madison quieted and watched the rest of Kirehe's ceremony in silence.

When she finished, Kirehe stood, bowed to the corpse, and stepped out of the light. Her pack retreated with their heads bowed.

"Let's go." Madison made sure everyone left the arena.

On the other side of the door, Lylla kept staring back at the darkness. She walked with her hand in Rho's. "I felt Mom's ghost," she whispered.

"I'm pretty sure a lot of ghosts haunt that place," Shmar said.

"Probably thousands of them." Madison's thoughts turned back to the matter of finding Kirehe's attacker. She knew how to watch people, and she knew how to research things. Making plans worked for her, but unraveling plans made by other people sounded like a challenge.

She glanced at those walking with her, trying to decide how far she trusted each of them. She barely knew Lylla, but the girl had proved reliable and knowledgeable. In return for Kirehe's protection, Lylla would do anything. Rho owed Kirehe a debt for saving their life and had made clear they wanted to repay it. Oolaang didn't have a dishonest or aggressive bone in his body. Madison trusted Jaco with her life.

Shmar…

Madison glanced at the man. He kept blaming her for everything here. When Kirehe had stumbled aside, Jaco had shown up and helped, but Shmar hadn't.

No, he wouldn't have wanted to see Kirehe hurt. Madison, he'd like to beat to a pulp, but not Kirehe. Even if she hadn't saved everyone in that initial execution, she'd still saved him.

They reached the gladiator housing area without Kirehe. Madison checked behind them and didn't see her.

"She went with the beasts," Soallen said from the darkness. "Viriok approved it. She will endure punishment for Tau's death afterward."

Kirehe probably needed to spend some time with the dragons. Madison nodded. She took Lylla's hand. The others returned to the room. Jaco and Rho both needed to wash off blood. Madison did too, but she'd survive.

She and Lylla sat in their usual spot.

"Did you see the brawl?" Madison asked.

Lylla lowered her voice until Madison had to lean close to hear her. "Yes."

"Who started it?"

"Wally."

A member of Kirehe's own team had thrown the first punch. "Who did he hit?"

"A mid-card Degrikar woman."

"Wally just hates everyone, right? So him throwing a punch takes a pretty thin excuse. Do you know if she did anything to him recently?"

"Not that I've seen. He hasn't fought her in a while, and he doesn't mix with anyone. He spars with Soallen, his handler."

Wally and Kirehe shared the same handler, which maybe meant something. "Who else does Soallen handle?"

"About half of team Corvik. Each team has three handlers. One takes care of the top person, then the other two split the rest of the team."

"Is Ilai the other Corvik handler?"

"No. She's a regular slave handler assigned to just the group of us. But." Lylla moved close enough for Madison to feel the girl's breath on her ear. "Ilai and Soallen are a thing."

"Huh." All the pharedimi acted so disdainful and arrogant that Madison hadn't imagined them capable of love or anything approximating romance. She supposed they treated each other better than they treated slaves. Baby pharedimi had to come from somewhere, after all.

"If one of them wants something, the other will probably help," Madison said. "I don't suppose you actually saw who stabbed Kirehe?"

Lylla shook her head. "Too many bodies in the way."

"Did you see Gigi in the mess? Or Natalyais? Bryor?"

"Bryor was in it. Natalyais got out right away. Gigi walked in when the fight started. She turned around and walked back out." After a short pause, Lylla said, "Soallen is also Bryor's handler."

Madison had a feeling Soallen had brought in the weapon himself. Ilai also could've done it. Soallen and Ilai took orders from only one person—Overseer Neilan. Or, she supposed, Viriok.

The motive for Viriok to have a gladiator injured in such a roundabout way didn't make sense. If he wanted someone handicapped in some fashion, she thought he'd have it done on purpose, without any question he'd done it. He even seemed like the kind of person who'd do it himself to make sure no one screwed it up. Stab her like this, so she's disabled this much and not killed.

Besides, she reminded herself, he'd authorized a medical intervention that should've healed Kirehe more than enough to overcome the injury by the time of her match. That it hadn't worked as advertised didn't mean he'd sabotaged it. More likely, the one who'd relayed the request—Soallen—hadn't explained the full time required.

"Madison?" Lylla wrapped her arm around Madison's and held on like she thought a strong wind might carry her someplace worse.

"What?"

Lylla wiggled every portion of her body before settling and saying anything else. "I only saw four people with blood on them. You, Kirehe, Jaco, and Gordy. Gordy only got blood on him when he picked up Kirehe."

"That just means you didn't see the attacker. Which is okay. I'll figure it out." Madison nudged her and they stood. "Thanks for keeping your eyes open. You're a big help."

Lylla nodded. They returned to the room.

Along the way, Madison considered that anyone could've washed off blood in the time between Kirehe's stabbing and the start of the gladiator matches. For someone who hadn't fought today, they'd had even more time to clean up.

She hadn't seen Shmar, Bryor, or Gigi after the attack.

"Wait," she whispered with her hand on the doorknob. "Shmar has no motive to hurt Kirehe. Without her, we're all screwed. She's the reason we're all in here instead of dead. And you said they reward killing with death here, right? Unless it's provably an accident?"

Lylla nodded. "No one would be able to call that an accident, no matter what."

"No," Madison said, "they wouldn't." Soallen or Ilai had given a weapon to the attacker. Madison couldn't see any other reasonable possibility. A gladiator would have to reach well past stupid to stab someone without assurances of protection from consequences.

Once they had a weapon, any idiot could convince Wally to throw a punch at anyone else.

Would Soallen or Ilai do something like that on their own? Soallen found Kirehe annoying, but he probably gained prestige from serving as her handler. Trying to kill or injure his path to a promotion sounded stupid.

Overseer Neilan had no reason to sabotage his stable of gladiators.

Except that he'd taken a visitor from Cradok. That pharedim in maroon had stormed in and shouted at the overseer. About what, Madison had no idea. After the pharedim had left, Madison remembered the overseer calling for Ilai. Then Ilai had come to tell Madison about Zorileck's arrival.

What if Zorileck had nothing to do with the reason the overseer had called for her?

Madison opened the door. Oolaang sat on the floor, fiddling with the three tools Zorileck had sent. Given privacy and some time, he could use them to get into a lot of trouble. They had precious little of either commodity.

Shmar lay in his hammock, one leg dangling to keep his bed swaying gently. Jaco sat on the end of the bed, his arms crossed over his chest and staring at the wall.

Lylla slipped around Madison to climb onto the bed and curl up against the corner of the wall.

Madison stared at Jaco. He seemed more distressed than he had been after all the crew deaths.

No, that didn't make sense. Jaco wouldn't have attacked Kirehe. Would he?

He had no more incentive than Shmar. Without Kirehe, he'd suffer the same as Shmar, and Madison would die. As her closest friend ever, he had no reason to work toward her death. They'd played together on her uncle's ship. He'd helped her figure out she liked girls. She'd helped him get dates in bars.

And yet, he sat there, staring into space as if he'd lost something. As if he'd suffered with Kirehe over the death of that mara dragon.

Sure, they'd all recognized the dead, but Madison felt more like she'd laid them to rest than stirred up their memories. Shmar and Oolaang also didn't seem more upset than before.

Only four people had blood on their hands after the attack. Madison frowned at the one who, now that she thought of it, had stood on Kirehe's left side, suggesting he'd never come into contact with the wound on Kirehe's right side.

She slipped in front of Jaco and touched his cheek. "What did the overseer promise?"

Jaco gulped and shifted his stare to her belly. "He said he'd let us go," he whispered. "You and me."

Cradok naturally would've complained about Madison surviving his execution order. With Madison having made herself necessary for Kirehe to fight, Viriok would've refused to eliminate his newest money-making toy. At his refusal, Cradok sent his pharedim to deliver threats or promises to the overseer. Overseer Neilan had seen Jaco and judged him willing to do anything to save Madison, thus solving a problem without angering Viriok.

With Ilai's access to Jaco, Soallen might not have known anything about it, which would explain why he'd informed Viriok about the request for medical intervention. Dishonesty about the effect or time required might've had a lot more to do with saving his own neck than any desire to sabotage Kirehe. Even if he'd known, he could've decided to abandon the plan once the doctor got involved.

"You idiot."

He gulped.

"Did you really think I'd never figure it out?"

"I..." He blinked like a moron.

"How did you think it would play out? That once Kirehe was down, we'd escape together in a zippy little ship made of rainbows and dragon farts? Did you forget about Cradok?"

He paled and covered his face.

She sighed and hugged him. "Why won't you trust me?"

"I'm sorry. He made it all sound so..."

"Plausible and reasonable?" She punched his arm. "Jaco, you dumbass, I'm not the one you need to apologize to."

He let out a slow, quiet breath like he thought he could die on the spot to make everything better.

At least he understood. "For right now, we're going to pretend like I don't know. I want the overseer to think you failed but weren't discovered. He's going to think you're eager to find another way to do your job."

"Why?" He peeked between his fingers.

"Because I have a plan."

CHAPTER 24

KIREHE

The next day, Kirehe stomped through the light corridor with Soallen as her escort. She clenched her fists at her sides, hoping she'd find something else to hit besides a wall or Soallen. The former would hurt her hand and the latter would get her into worse trouble.

Punishment for her maras killing someone who wanted to die didn't seem fair.

"I know spending the night with your beasts would be a reward, so you get to stay with this monster instead." Soallen pointed at a door with dim light on the other side. "Get inside. You can come out in the morning. Overseer Neilan wants you to fight tomorrow."

Kirehe glowered and stormed through the door. She walked into a large, round room with stairs against the circular walls, leading upward. Dappled light shone from above. The heat felt normal, and the air smelled almost right, like this room had access to the outside. Overhead, trees grew sideways from the walls to point at the sky.

Not sure what she'd find, Kirehe climbed the stairs at a slow, steady pace. Something in the air reminded her of home and hope. Until she saw a drape of smooth green flesh marred by a new scar over a diagonal tree trunk, she didn't recognize it.

"Nihan?"

Her beloved krata moved his head into view. "Kirehe?"

Kirehe forgot about Tau and everything else. She ran the rest of the way to reach Nihan. He shifted to meet her. Metal clinked with his movements.

Chains held Nihan in place and kept his wings from unfurling. Kirehe didn't understand the point of his prison until she looked past him.

The round cage had glass walls. On the other side, people passed by and milled in halls made of white stone. A cluster of people with a similar appearance to that pilot who'd shot her, some child-sized and others not, paused at the wall and stared into the large cell. One child pointed at Nihan and bounced with excitement.

They'd turned Nihan into an exhibit. He lived on display for these wretched people who came to watch blood spill and whatever other madness Irondoom offered. As if she hadn't hated them enough, she'd found a new reason.

Careful to avoid letting anyone see her face, she hugged Nihan's neck. "Can you climb down?"

"No. Stuck."

With her gaze, she traced the chains to the walls. Nihan had enough slack to turn around or move from one tree to the other. One pair ensured he couldn't climb lower. Another pair kept him from reaching the top of his cage. Even if he could get there, though, thick bars crossed the top, preventing his escape.

Kirehe, on the other hand, could fit through those gaps. When night fell, she would do so and see if she could find anything to help him escape.

For the moment, she sighed and climbed under Nihan's wing. She liked Soallen's punishments. When he collected her in the morning, he'd probably realize the situation.

"I may not see you again after this. We're going to try to escape, but I don't know the details yet. When we do, you'll come with us."

Nihan tucked his head close to her and purred. The sound

rumbled in her chest. Kirehe inspected his collar. On the top, where Nihan couldn't reach with his claws, she found a hole too small for her finger. Though she tried sticking a variety of nearby objects into that hole, including sticks and leaves, nothing made the collar loosen or fall off.

Unable to come up with any other ideas, Kirehe settled under her krata's wing. Madison would find a way to remove the collar and chains. Kirehe trusted her to think of something.

Nihan's heartbeat, slow and thunderous, gave her the best rest she'd had since their crash. Knowing he lived, even if he suffered in a prison like she had, changed everything.

When Soallen came for her the next morning, she waited on the floor below.

He smirked. "I trust you slept well?"

"Yes. Much sleep. Quiet. No snores." Kirehe breezed past him. "Monster in trees good neighbor."

Soallen caught up and escorted her back to the gladiator housing. He resumed his more usual annoyed expression. Kirehe took satisfaction from seeing it.

"I suppose I shouldn't be surprised you enjoy time with beasts since you're practically one yourself."

She stopped and waved her hands at him like curled claws, mock growling at him. "Kirehe beast," she said. Chomping her teeth together made him flinch.

He grumbled under his breath.

She returned to her room to find everyone there. Madison leaped off the bed and hugged her. Lylla and Rho sat with the handheld screen, their attention fixed on it. Many pieces of an unknown device surrounded Oolaang. Shmar sat beside him, holding two more pieces while Oolaang used his tools on them. Jaco swung in his hammock, watching Oolaang.

Kirehe let Madison hug her. Madison seemed to need that kind of contact and Kirehe didn't mind. She had little practice doing it, though.

"You smell different," Madison said.

"Their scary monster is my krata, Nihan."

"Your krata?"

"He's a big dragon. I was riding him when they captured me. I thought they might've killed him, but instead they have him chained in a prison of glass so the enemy can gape at him. He's restrained by chains he can't break, but if you can find a way to free him, he can help us escape. Skila can take messages to him."

Madison lit up with contained excitement.

Kirehe's belly flickered with warmth, fuzziness, and other, stranger things. These things seemed good?

"That's amazing. You're amazing. I know what to do now!" Madison planted a swift kiss on Kirehe's mouth. She squeezed Kirehe's shoulders and bounced back to the bed, all moving so fast she couldn't have noticed Kirehe's confusion at all of it. "Okay. Huddle up so we can talk." She put her head together with Lylla, Oolaang, and Rho, speaking softly so any recording equipment couldn't catch their words.

Unable to think, Kirehe blinked. She backed out of the room, stumbling like an idiot, and shut the door. Leaning against the wall beside the door, she touched her mouth. Madison had kissed her.

It had felt like an expression of unrestrained joy, passing too swiftly for restraint to get in the way. Regardless, Madison had kissed her.

In the village, no one kissed anyone in public, except on the hand. She'd seen many men kiss women on the hand. Sometimes, they tugged the woman by that hand into a hut and didn't emerge again until later.

Kirehe did understand what they did inside those huts. She knew about sex and babies. Even if no one had explained those things to her, she'd seen enough between dragons to get the idea of how such things work.

A few times, she'd seen a man kiss another man's hand. Mothers in the cave kissed their children on the forehead or cheek. Kirehe's mother had stopped when they discovered she had the dragoncalling gift, saying she didn't understand Kirehe anymore.

Never had she seen a woman kiss another woman's hand.

Never had Kirehe wanted anyone to kiss her hand, or any other part of her person.

Never had anyone tried after her mother stopped.

She frowned at her hand as if some disease or visible mark might have transferred to it from her lips. Seeing nothing, she wondered what Madison wanted from her. They couldn't cause babies together. What did two women even do inside a hut? How did it work?

She frowned and tried to imagine what would happen in such a situation. Nothing made sense.

Though she liked Madison, and could see that Madison had a great deal of affection for her, she didn't understand.

Dragons made sense. People did not. After a night with Nihan, she wanted to return to him as soon as possible. But Soallen wouldn't make the mistake of using that as a punishment again, so she didn't know how to make it happen.

At a loss for what else to do, she jogged to the common room and gathered food. Eating would stop the thinking. Several gladiators waved to her. Most had accepted her as worthy. Even Bryor and Gina seemed to stop glaring at her. She hadn't caused any of their deaths, and she'd treated everyone she faced with as much respect as possible. Doing so had produced the desired effect of reducing their distrust of her.

As she sat, Natalyais joined her.

"What do you want?" Kirehe asked.

Natalyais slurped from her cup of white liquid. She said nothing.

Kirehe ignored her and ate. She liked the vegetable dish they prepared every few days. It incorporated local roots and seed pods with local herbs. The flavors reminded her of home.

"Where's Madison?" Natalyais said after she finished her drink.

"Other where."

Natalyais curled her lip. "A shame whoever stabbed you didn't do a proper job of it."

"Do you wish for me to reveal how you cheat in the arena?" Kirehe knew nothing. She merely wanted to annoy the irritating woman who seemed to delight in shoving Madison at every opportunity.

To her great surprise, Natalyais paled. "What do you know?" She used a harsh whisper, as if the words scalded her tongue on their way out.

Since she had no idea how Natalyais cheated, Kirehe had no idea what to say. She shrugged and hoped for the best. "Enough."

"What do you want?"

"Leave Madison alone."

Natalyais bared her teeth. "That Stardrifter chit got me in here."

"She may also get you out." Kirehe echoed the woman's feral snarl.

"Is that a threat?"

Kirehe shrugged again. "I do not know this word."

With a growl, Natalyais leaped to her feet and shoved Kirehe's tray off the table. "Watch yourself, Beastmaster!"

The tray hit the floor with a clatter, spraying food in every direction, including onto Kirehe's leg.

Certain the woman wanted to provoke her, and unwilling to take the bait, Kirehe glanced at the tray, then sighed and stood. "I hear they do not punish much for a gladiator punching a gladiator. Not like punching a slave." She crouched to clean up and watch Natalyais's legs through the table.

"It's true," Natalyais snarled. She slipped around the table on the balls of her feet.

When she reached Kirehe, she punched down.

Kirehe ducked to the side and threw the tray at Natalyais's face. The food she'd collected splattered across Natalyais's chest. Eager to avoid hevit interference, Kirehe sprang to her feet and backed out of range. Natalyais would have to close the distance if she wanted to fight more.

Across the room, Erryl set aside his lifting weight and strolled toward them.

Natalyais flung sticky food aside with a sharp swipe of her hand. She showed every intention of continuing to fight.

This qusamadi had done nothing good since Kirehe arrived. Kirehe saw a chance to deal with her and took it. She raised her voice. "Cheat is bad, yes? Madison say this. Do not cheat. No worse thing here but kill."

Natalyais froze. "What?"

Erryl's brow raised and he picked up his pace. Other heads turned.

"Are you accusing Natalyais of cheating?" Erryl barked.

Kirehe pointed at Natalyais. "She say. I hear."

Natalyais stopped and stared at her. "I didn't," she said, her voice breathy and stunned.

"Maybe she is liar?" Kirehe shrugged.

Hevits approached, machine hum preceding them.

"Don't call me a liar!" Natalyais realized too late how this sounded. "I don't cheat," she snapped.

Erryl reached them and laid a hand on Natalyais's shoulder. "You'd better be sure there's nothing the least bit questionable on camera or in recordings."

"Everything is questionable when they scrutinize you!" Natalyais jerked out of his grasp. She bumped into a solid mass of hevit. Panic exploded across her face. "This is your fault," she gasped, pointing at Kirehe.

"Accusing someone of cheating is very serious, Kirehe." Erryl glanced between them. "Are you sure that's what you heard?"

"She say." Kirehe crossed her arms. "I hear." She waved one hand in the gesture everyone had come to understand meant she couldn't figure out how to explain something.

Erryl nodded at the hevit no one could see. "I trust Kirehe."

"You what?" Natalyais sputtered. The hevit must have draped an arm across her body, because she couldn't move. "I've been here months longer than her! Those monsters under her control killed someone! How can you take her side?"

"She's never tried to stab me in the face." Erryl pointed to the thin scar beside his eye. "In fact, she's never tried to stab anyone. Her beasts may have killed Tau, but he's tried to throw himself on swords more than a few times, so that's not a shock. Kirehe is a thousand times more the team player than you are. I wouldn't be surprised if you've been cheating this whole time, with your record."

The hevit picked up Natalyais. She struggled. Kirehe heard a second hevit arrive. A blur swiped across Natalyais's face and she sagged. They carried her out of the housing area.

Kirehe watched them extract her with Erryl. He leaned close.

"Did she really say she cheated?"

"Yes."

"Figures. Damn qusamadi are all broken cogs."

Though she didn't know what Erryl meant, she grasped the sentiment. "If not big, she back?"

"It's possible, but I doubt it. Cheating is cheating. Given how she wound up here, I'd say it's a safe bet she was doing something shady."

Madison probably knew more details. If not, she could find out and explain it later. Kirehe had a feeling any explanation would take time and many words.

CHAPTER 25

MADISON

Sitting on the bed, Rho rubbed their thumb over some brown object Madison couldn't identify. They hadn't seen the nucri since Tau's death a few days earlier. With everyone else working and Kirehe training, Madison considered backing out of the room to give Rho privacy. The hunch of their shoulders, though, made her hesitate.

Madison knew complicated grief when she saw it.

"Tau's torment is over," Rho said.

Talking to her felt like an invitation. Madison sat beside Rho on the bed. "Yes."

Rho opened their hand, revealing a small fang made of dark wood. The polished surface gleamed. "Our remica gave them a token like this. The real one had glyphs for strength and fortitude inlaid with dark stone. They told me they'd asked their patron for this to try to remember her. If they closed their eyes and pictured her, they could almost feel normal."

Not sure if she could offer comfort, Madison raised her arm as if to hug them.

Rho leaned into the offered shelter. "Tau was a good friend before. They liked watching the children, especially the prasilor ones. I remember their laughter as infectious." Rho curled their hand over the fang, concealing it again.

"That's a really good way to remember someone," Madison said. She still had nightmares with Dani's dead, empty stare. "I try to remember Dani's eyes. So full of life and always sparkling with something. Wit, mischief, joy, whatever."

With a heavy sigh, Rho said, "I killed them. All of them."

Guilt wrapped itself around Madison's throat. "So did I. It's my fault they're dead, and it's my fault we're here. But it wouldn't have happened if not for the damned hevits. I hate them. They're so—"

"No."

Madison blinked. "No?"

"Don't hate them." Rho shook their head. "Hate the qusamadi and pharedimi, who joined the Oligarchy because they wanted to. Or the vreesliik, who truly deserve it. But don't hate the hevits. I have yet to prove it, but I'm certain they don't serve out of choice. Pity them."

At this point, Madison didn't think she had much pity to offer anyone on the lakhan side of the equation. Telling Rho as much wouldn't help anything, though. "We could blame the lakhans, then. If not for them, the universe would be a much better place."

"Yes, that I agree with." Rho covered their eyes with one hand. "Without Tau to care for, and no hope of escape, I have nothing left to live for."

Madison wished she had another language to use when talking about escape. She leaned close and whispered, "There's always hope. I have a plan. I just need another few pieces to slide into place. Can you hold on a little longer?"

Rho lowered their hand and met her gaze with resignation heavy on their brow. "Whatever you need me to do, I'll do it."

They needed something to cling to. Though she didn't need anything from Rho, Madison could give them that much.

"Keep an eye on whichever of the pharedimi you can. The more I know about their movements, the faster I can put everything into place, and the sooner we can get out of here. But don't take unnecessary risks. We don't want them figuring anything out."

Leaning away from Madison, Rho took several deep breaths. "I can do that. I will do that. We will get out of this place. Their deaths won't mean nothing."

"No, they won't." Madison stood, thinking she needed to talk to Oolaang soon. He had a critical role to play in the escape plan. As soon as she could corner him for a few minutes, she would. Besides, if she thought about talking to him and the plan, she didn't think about everyone she'd lost. "Aside from why, I'm glad you're here with us."

"I feel much the same." Rho patted her hand. "Thank you. You're a good person, Madison. In this place, caring about others is a strangeness."

She grinned. "Happy to be a weirdo."

Rho nodded with a ghost of a smile and laid back on the bed.

Madison took that as a silent request for privacy and left them in search of Oolaang. Though she didn't find him immediately, she did later manage to explain his part in her plan away from the rest of the group. He needed two extra items from Zorileck to do it, which Madison had no trouble getting a few days later.

Without Natalyais in the common room, everyone found it much more pleasant. After a week without the qusamadi, Madison declared victory. A few offhand questions to Soallen and Overseer Neilan revealed that Natalyais had actually cheated. In addition to uncanny betting on other gladiators by her patron, they'd discovered vials of a weak poison in her room.

She'd dosed people before matches, then her patron had bet on their opponent. If they dug more, Madison suspected they'd find more, at least partially linked back to the Isokovria family and business.

It couldn't have happened to someone nicer.

Another week slogged by before Madison assessed the situation again. She had what she needed, Kirehe had fought the day before, and everyone shared a table in the common room. Jaco and Shmar seemed rested and in reasonable spirits. Rho had shed some of their despondence in favor of determination. Lylla kept watching everything and everyone. Oolaang had asked for a specific amount of time, and that number of days had passed.

Overseer Neilan seemed to buy that Madison and Kirehe hadn't figured out Jaco's betrayal. He wouldn't understand all of them accepting Jaco after discovering it. That would defy his ability to comprehend. Viriok's too. In their minds, such a gross breach of trust would create an unbridgeable rift. They would've cast him out of the family group.

Human predictability governed every policy and procedure they'd put into place. Madison had crafted an audacious plan to use that to her advantage.

As long as the pharedimi and Viriok acted as expected, everything would work perfectly.

They would. The overseer had lots of experience, but based upon how he ran things, Madison doubted he'd ever encountered someone like her. Slaves allowed to serve as gladiators relied more on muscle than brain. No one else had as much freedom, which she knew from watching Jaco and Shmar suffer. If they'd ever caught someone like Madison before, they'd either worked that person to death or given them a horrifying execution long before they could've thought up a good, solid plan like hers.

"Kirehe isn't on the fight list today, so we're going to try the plan."

"Should we talk about this out here?" Shmar asked.

"Eh. Why not?" Madison shrugged. "They listen everywhere. Out here, there's more noise to filter out. Besides, we've spent the last week discussing stupid kut here to throw off suspicion."

"Is that why we talked so much about feathers?" Rho asked.

"Yes. And because Skila is adorable and enjoys being the center of attention."

Skila, sitting on the table, chirped and whistled at the sound of her name. Kirehe rubbed under her chin, which made Skila purr.

Madison grinned. "Oolaang, your door thing is ready, right?"

"Yes." Oolaang patted his pocket. "It will perform as requested."

He had another object she knew he'd completed, though she didn't ask about it.

Lowering her voice, Madison leaned in so she could get more specific. "Everything else is ready, so now it's just about us reaching the mara dragons. We free them, they go berserk and cause a whole lot of distraction. We head the other direction once they're loose. I've already set things up so we can reach a cargo ship on the docks where we can hide in the loading bay. Everyone go do something for half an hour. Meet at the door." She tapped Jaco on the shoulder. "Stay back for a minute. I've got to give Kirehe some extra directions, then I have an extra thing I want you to do."

Jaco gulped and nodded.

Everyone else except Kirehe stood and left. Kirehe picked up Skila and deposited the tiny dragon on her shoulder. Oolaang gave Madison a long, slow, significant nod because he had special instructions already.

Madison scooted her chair closer to Kirehe. Even though she didn't have to anymore, she switched to Kirehe's language. All evidence suggested the overseer hadn't bothered to have anyone try to translate it. "Do you trust me?"

Kirehe gave her a long, slow blink. "You are part of my pack."

Grateful Kirehe saw things this way, Madison nodded. "I know Nihan means a lot to you. I promise I'll get him free. But not immediately. We have to get the maras loose first. That's critical."

To her relief, Kirehe didn't look angry. "I understand."

"One other thing." Madison rubbed under Skila's jaw like she'd seen Kirehe do a thousand times. "I want you to have Skila ride Oolaang's shoulder. He's small and has a hard time in bright lights. With her keen eyes, he'll be better off. Just ask her to stay with Oolaang and point if he gets lost."

After a short exchange of whistles and chirps, Kirehe nodded again. "She agrees and will stay with him."

"Thank you. Before we do this, I want you to know that, whatever happens, I think you're amazing."

"You've said that enough times to make me think you mean it." Kirehe crossed her arms, displaying her usual discomfort when they spoke about anything other than fighting, escaping, or food.

Skila chirped, which made Kirehe frown.

"Skila says she's ready to do her part as soon as Oolaang returns."

"And she also said…?" Madison knew that frown. It happened at odd, random moments, usually right after Madison said something complimentary.

Kirehe shook her head and looked away. "Nothing."

"You know what? You're a pretty good actor in the arena. With me, you're terrible at it." Madison grinned and touched Kirehe's cheek. "Big, strong jungle princess dragon warrior is confused about feelings for weak, skinny girl with machine eye."

The frown deepened into a scowl, telling Madison she'd hit the truth, or close to it. Kirehe seemed so awkward and confused about it all the time, Madison suspected she'd never had a relationship with anyone. Other people had probably found the dragoncaller thing intimidating.

They didn't really have time for this, but she couldn't leave it as is. "If you don't want me to touch you anymore, I'll stop."

Kirehe crinkled her brow. The confusion had returned. "You are pack."

Madison opened her mouth, then thought better of what she'd intended to say. She raised a finger. "I can see this is going to be complicated. I'm attracted to you. Whenever you decide if you're attracted to me or not, let me know. Okay?"

This had the effect of deepening the furrows in Kirehe's brow and making her squint with even more confusion.

They needed time to sort through this. Lots of time. She still had things to do to prepare for the plan, so it would have to wait.

Madison patted Kirehe's shoulder. "Good talk. I'll get everything else set up. Maybe half an hour?"

Skila chirped.

Giddy about her plan, her dragon warrior, and the prospect of freedom in the near future, Madison giggled and left Kirehe to sort through things. She took Jaco by the arm and dragged him out of his chair.

"There's something special I need you to do for us. For the plan."

"Absolutely." Jaco leaned his head closer so they could whisper.

"If you screw this up, you'll get us all killed. Follow my directions exactly. Okay? Are we clear?" If he deviated even a hair, she had strong doubts about this whole effort accomplishing anything. His guilt would keep him honest, she thought, or she wouldn't bother giving him this task.

He huffed. "I'm sorry. You were right, and I didn't trust you enough. How many more times do I have to say it before you believe me?"

"Probably three, but never mind that." She guided him out of the room and gave him instructions. This plan would work. It had to. If it didn't, she had no other hope left to give.

CHAPTER 26

KIREHE

When Madison walked away, Kirehe remained standing in the food area. She hated this feeling of confusion and incompetence. Her annoyance made her growl at the floor and consider tossing Skila in the air.

"Kiki like Madad," the tiny dragon kept repeating.

"Enough," she snapped.

Skila twittered with laughter.

She noticed Gordy leaning against the wall and smirking at her. Ready to punch him in his smug face, she stalked in his direction.

"You look like you could use a sparring partner," Gordy said as she neared him.

When she nodded, he led her to the room with the sticks. He tossed her one the right length to stand in for a spear and picked up another of the same thing.

Kirehe caught the stick and swung it around her body. Heavier than a real spear, it reminded her of a practice staff.

"I can't wait to watch you fight with a spear in the arena," Gordy said. He grinned and held his staff ready.

On that day, she hoped she could find a way to stab Viriok. "This is also my want." She clacked her staff against his and bounced to the balls of her feet.

Gordy spun his staff and danced in a circle. Kirehe tracked and followed him, keeping her distance. They each tested the space with their weapons. After three empty swipes, Kirehe lunged at him and slashed her staff downward. Gordy caught her blow on his staff and counterattacked.

As they had in the arena, they traded blows without touching each other. Their staves met in the middle over and over, filling the air with wooden thunks.

Kirehe's mind cleared, leaving her with the blessed blankness of mock battle.

"Gordy," Madison barked from the door.

He turned. Kirehe pulled her blow enough so she only swatted his thigh. Gordy grunted. Skila chirped her amusement.

"Thanks," he spat at Madison.

"You're welcome." Madison bowed as if she'd performed for them.

Kirehe rolled her eyes. "I don't need you to cheat for me," she said in her own language. Gordy wouldn't understand it, but he'd hear her chiding Madison.

Madison grinned. "I know, but it's fun to watch when it works."

Taking Kirehe's staff, Gordy huffed. "This is why no one likes you."

"I'm pretty sure that's actually because I'm not a gladiator." Madison batted her eyes at Gordy. "But I came because I need Kirehe. Time to go. Things to do, people to beat up, and all that."

Gordy held up his hand to Kirehe. "You're a good opponent. I kind of wish I was on your team, but that would mean we'd never get to fight."

After a moment of considering his words, Kirehe grasped his hand in camaraderie. "You are also a good opponent. Thank you for the working." She wished they could take him for the escape. "Many luck for your next battle."

"You too." Gordy turned to practicing on his own with both staves.

Kirehe waved and followed Madison out of the room.

"We're all set. Follow my lead." Madison looped her arm around Kirehe's and strolled to the main room. She acted casual, like they had nothing interesting planned for the rest of the day.

The sparring had settled Kirehe enough for her to behave the same way. She followed at the same sedate pace.

"This touch is good," she said.

"Yes, it is. Very pleasant."

When they reached the main room, Oolaang and Lylla entered and headed toward them. Jaco and Shmar followed a few moments later. Rho waddled behind them.

Madison produced the tablet with Kirehe's schedule and consulted it. "Oh, there's a new message," she said. Putting out a hand to stop Kirehe in front of the door, she consulted the tablet.

Oolaang slipped behind Madison and Kirehe.

Forcing herself not to glance at Oolaang, Kirehe peered at the tablet. She watched while Madison tapped and swiped. Though she'd learned to understand a great deal of the alien language as spoken, Kirehe had no idea how to read it. The symbols meant nothing to her.

"Done," Oolaang whispered.

"Let's go," Madison said. She turned and led Kirehe through the door. "Funny how Soallen wants to meet us but didn't come or send an escort." She spoke louder than she needed to, and in the alien language. "I guess it's not critical. We only have to go to the arena anyway. I think he wants to explain some new 'savage' ritual thing they've cooked up for you since that first one went over so well."

Kirehe shrugged. Whatever Madison felt she needed to say to make this plan work, Kirehe wouldn't spoil it. The hevits she heard nearby made no move to intercept them, which suggested it fooled them.

"He probably wants us to carry stuff whenever we do the real thing," Jaco said as they strolled down the corridor of light together. "Can't see any other reason he'd ask for all of us."

Crowd noise from the ongoing battles grew as they approached the arena. Halfway there, when Kirehe could hear no hevits, Madison turned down the corridor leading to the mara cage.

Kirehe checked behind to make sure no one followed and noticed they'd lost Oolaang and Lylla. "Skila," she whistled.

The kukiri didn't respond. Kirehe frowned. She hadn't heard any hevits stepping closer as they passed.

"Oolaang and Lylla are missing with Skila," she whispered to Madison.

"It's fine. They're doing a thing for the end game part."

Madison knew, which eased Kirehe's concern. Oolaang could ask Skila to take him to Kirehe. She'd made certain of that. Therefore, he would find them again.

"Who's down there?" Soallen called. Kirehe recognized his voice.

For a moment, Madison grinned, then her face shifted to surprise. "Run!" She sprinted for the room holding the maras.

Kirehe sprinted down the rest of the corridor to reach the mara cage door first. She knew how to open it from watching her escorts. With a press of a button and a pull of a lever, the door swung into the cage.

Four mara heads raised from the pack pile in the back of the room. They lounged on woven mats, surrounded by mangled logs the maras liked to scratch and gnaw.

"Inside," Madison snapped.

Kirehe dashed through to her maras. Jaco followed her, though he didn't approach the dragons. Rho did the same.

Shmar stopped at the doorway. "I thought we were going to unleash the dragons and follow their carnage."

"Not yet," Madison said. "Trust me."

"Guards!" Soallen shouted.

Shmar scurried inside. Madison leaned through the door, watching for something.

Though she didn't understand, Kirehe hugged her maras and kept them calm. The pack could shift to bloodthirsty on a moment's notice.

Madison stepped aside. Skila darted into the cage. Oolaang and Lylla followed her. Stunner blasts flew across the room. Madison shoved the door, causing it to clang shut.

"Did it work?" Madison asked.

Oolaang kept running until he reached the back of the cage. He attacked a spot on the wall with his tools for no reason Kirehe could understand.

Lylla panted to catch her breath and nodded while she flashed a thumbs up.

"Should the maras prepare to attack?" Kirehe asked.

Shaking her head, Madison held the door shut. "Not yet."

"Not yet?" Shmar demanded. "What are you waiting for? Them to rip the door off its hinges and stun us all?"

Rho held up a hand to quiet him. Shmar swatted it aside.

Madison grinned. "Just a little longer."

Jaco, Kirehe noticed, leaned against the wall and covered his face like he'd expected failure.

"Then what?" Shmar snapped.

"Tell the maras to listen for your call," Madison said in Kirehe's language, ignoring Shmar.

Kirehe nodded. She had elected to trust Madison, no matter how wrong or strange her instructions sounded.

Oolaang raised a hand. "It's set!"

"This part will suck," Madison said. She let go of the door and stood with her finger pointed as if she had a laser or projectile weapon and intended to shoot it.

"What are you doing?" Shmar gasped. "Have you gone completely mad?"

The door flew open. Stunner bolts slammed into Madison's body. She crumpled to the floor. Hevits poured into the room. Skila shrieked her fright and hid among the maras.

Kirehe had no interest in suffering the effects of the stunners again. Holding up her hands, she stood and chirped for the maras to wait for her call, as Madison had instructed.

No one resisted.

"I'm glad the rest of you can see reason," Soallen said. He crossed his arms over his chest and held his nose high as he pointed to Madison's unconscious form. "Take her to examination room three. The rest go to the execution pit while I consult with the Overseer."

"Wait," Jaco said. "What about me?"

Kirehe raised her brow.

Soallen regarded him with a cold, calculating stare. "What about you?"

Jaco glanced at Kirehe. His body vibrated with discomfort. "What's that supposed to mean?" He took a breath. Then he pointed at Kirehe. "I did what Overseer Neilan wanted! I stabbed her and I told him everything."

Anger churned in Kirehe's belly. "You did what?"

Smirking, Soallen shook his head slowly. "The Overseer was not impressed with your efforts and does not consider your side of the bargain fulfilled."

"Bargain?" Shmar said.

His chest heaving with panicked gasps, Jaco leaped at Soallen. A hevit intercepted him. Jaco slumped in the machine-creature's arms.

"Don't kill him," Soallen said. "He can stew with them."

"There's gonna be stew all right," Shmar grumbled.

Soallen's choice left Kirehe free to take care of Jaco herself.

The hevits brought them to that blessedly warm pit with the dead water. Kirehe entered the room last. Jaco lay on the floor in a heap. Everyone else had suffered a blow to knock them unconscious after reaching the cell, probably to keep them from trying to escape. Their captors clanged the door shut behind Kirehe, leaving her unharmed.

She stared at Jaco. The man loved Madison with all his heart, yet he'd betrayed her. She had no idea what would have possessed him to do such a thing.

As she sat and tried to understand, she alone heard Madison's first screams. For Madison's benefit, she would let Jaco live.

A few minutes later, no one else witnessed Viriok stepping

through the darkness and crouching in front of her. His cold breath in her face smelled sweet and fruity.

"You would have been great," he murmured, his face within centimeters of hers. "Alas, letting that girl infect your mind with hopeless escape plans has made you a liability. Which is a shame. Now I see that I can't afford to keep you here. Like your beasts, you're a wild creature that must be broken to serve. And like them, once broken, you'd no longer be worth it."

Madison screamed in the distance.

Viriok sniffed the air around Kirehe as if he wanted to remember her through scent alone. "I appreciate your nobility, and admire your spirit. As such, you have earned the chance to live forever as my opponent. If you accept this boon, you can wait while these fools die and instead walk out with Erryl to face me."

Kirehe remained passive and still. "I will eat your liver."

He chuckled. "Yes, an incredible spirit. Such a waste. Ah well." Viriok stood, his cape swishing against his legs. "You were certainly profitable in your short career. I don't think I've ever made more money in this short a time on anyone. Enjoy your remaining few hours. You all die together in tomorrow's matches. If you change your mind, the overseer can arrange a retirement." He turned his back on her and left.

She waited.

Madison had failed to accomplish something no one had ever accomplished before. Kirehe could accept having tried and lost. At least she hadn't taunted Nihan or the maras with the idea of a true escape attempt.

Shmar awakened first. He groaned and rolled to lie flat on the floor. When Madison's next scream reached them, he raised his head and checked the room. Then he lowered his head to the floor and lay in silence for a short time.

"She deserves all that pain," he growled.

Kirehe said nothing.

"All our deaths are on her pokken head."

Jaco groaned and stirred.

"And you." Shmar rolled onto his side and stabbed a finger at Jaco. "You betrayed us. All of us. Kirehe should snap your pokken neck."

"I'm sorry," Jaco mumbled.

Kirehe narrowed her eyes. Something didn't add up about Jaco, but she couldn't put her finger on what.

The others woke slowly. With unspoken accord, they left Jaco to sit by himself.

Rho sat up and leaned against the wall. "Back where we started," they murmured. "It was interesting while it lasted."

Oolaang huddled beside Rho, hugging his knees. They'd left him with his goggles this time, at least.

"We could have lived! She's killed us all." Shmar struggled to his feet.

"Don't be stupid," Jaco grumbled. "Once Cradok caught us, we were done. She bought us some time. Maybe she even made a mistake on purpose to put us all out of our misery."

Kirehe had no idea why he spoke and called attention to himself. He sounded as if he'd forgotten what he'd done.

"Shut up!" Shmar stalked to Jaco and kicked him in the side. "At least she only made mistakes!"

"Stop shouting," Rho said.

Lylla scooted close to Kirehe. Since she seemed to need comfort, Kirehe draped an arm over the girl's shoulders.

"I don't want to die," she whispered as she leaned against Kirehe's side.

"No one does," Kirehe said.

Shmar stalked across the cell, back and forth, rubbing his temples and muttering. Every few steps, he threw another glare at Jaco.

Jaco lay by himself, holding the side Shmar had kicked.

Madison's screams, the gap between them growing, peppered the quiet for a long time. Shortly after it seemed they'd ended, Madison's body flew into the chamber to land in a crumpled heap.

Her deranged, hoarse giggles filled the air. "That was fun. Let's do it again."

Kirehe and Jaco rushed to her side.

"Do. Not. Touch. Her," Kirehe snarled.

Jaco recoiled. "I did it—"

Kirehe slapped him hard enough to leave a handprint. "No one cares."

Holding his face, Jaco scooted back to isolation, where he belonged.

With Rho and Lylla helping, Kirehe straightened Madison's body so she could lie flat with her head in Kirehe's lap. Lylla brought her water. Shmar's pacing turned to storming and stomping.

The kukiri flock joined them as the day's dim light waned. Their happy, inane chatter about mating season made Kirehe consider joining Madison's mad laughter.

"What now, brilliant tactician?" Shmar sneered.

"Recover. Relax." Madison grinned. "Close your eyes and think of Havenport."

"We're all going to die, and you're cracking jokes. Again." Shmar raised his hands in exasperation.

"And you panic," said Kirehe. "Again. Be silent."

Shmar jabbed a finger at Kirehe. "You're even worse than she is. You enable her. You make her think she's some kind of genius or something. Ooh, Madison is so smart because she's smarter than you. It's not that hard to be smarter than a rock!"

"Shut up," Oolaang said. "Just shut up." He used the wall for support to stand and point at Shmar. "From the beginning, you've been the worst team player ever. Maybe if you'd thought for one second about someone other than yourself, more of the crew would still be alive. We all decided to back Madison while she took a risk. We all accepted that risk might get us killed. And we all did it because we want to believe.

"We want to believe that the lakhans can be defeated. Like Captain used to say, stories don't come from nowhere. There's truth in that myth, even if we don't know what it is. If we'd succeeded, we would've given hope to everyone. But we failed. That's how it is. Yelling at Madison won't change anything now. So just stop. We've all heard your tired, worn whining before. Enough. She's in it with us. She didn't cut and run or save her own hide and leave us to hang."

Kirehe had never heard the small man say so many words at one time. "Rest now. Fight later."

Oolaang nodded and sat.

Shmar tuned his back on everyone and sat. He hunched his shoulders.

Lylla crawled to him and set her hand on his knee. "It's okay to be scared. Everybody else is too. If we die tomorrow, we'll die together. No one will be alone. That's worth something, isn't it?"

When he didn't respond, Lylla hugged him. She murmured to him too quiet to overhear.

"Sleep is a good plan," Madison croaked. "Don't forget to tell Skila what a good little dragon she is." She closed her eyes.

Skila left the flock to land on Kirehe's shoulder. "Leave now?"

"No, not yet. Eat. Sleep."

With a bright, happy chirp of understanding, Skila returned to the flock. Kirehe leaned back and thought about what to expect in the arena. She drifted to sleep knowing Jaco couldn't do anything else to them with the hevits lurking by the door.

CHAPTER 27

MADISON

By the time Madison woke, everyone else had already awakened. Oolaang sat beside her. Kirehe crouched at the water pool with the tiny dragons. Shmar paced. Jaco leaned against the wall in a miserable lump. Rho and Lylla sat together, playing games with their hands and scraps of cloth.

"Thanks for what you said before," Madison murmured. She lifted her head, decided it didn't hurt anymore, and sat up.

"I still believe in you." Oolaang removed his goggles and showed her the key he'd fabricated and hidden there. "Even if your plan doesn't work, I'll die knowing we tried instead of sitting back and never challenging how things are."

She took his hand and squeezed it. He passed her the key.

"You should know that after they stunned you, Jaco said he betrayed us."

"Yep."

Oolaang cocked his head in surprise and confusion as he replaced his goggles.

Kirehe joined them and offered Madison water from her hands. After she sipped at it, she handed the key to Kirehe as covertly as she could.

"Give it to Skila," she said in Kirehe's language. She had a strong suspicion none of the hevits or pharedimi had bothered to try and understand any of it. Why would they? Kirehe had proven she could learn Lakhan Basic. If they ever snatched another local, they'd know what to do. "Tell her to use it when we leave this room for the arena. Maybe also explain how, though Oolaang tried to show her."

Her amazing dragon warrior nodded and took the key to Skila without asking questions. After all this, Kirehe didn't complain or accuse her of anything. Amazing.

She waved for Jaco to join her. Jaco glanced around the room, then shook his head.

"Guys. Everyone." Madison gestured for them all to huddle around her.

No one moved, except Shmar, who kept pacing. Kirehe jabbed a finger at Jaco. "He stabbed me."

Madison sighed. Her plan had worked so well it had put her crew at odds with each other. "Yes. I know."

Kirehe narrowed her eyes from across the room. "You knew this?"

Shmar stopped pacing to scowl at her. "I hate you," he growled.

Madison sighed. Of course he hated her. She'd killed everyone, including him, after all. And Kirehe wanted to gut Jaco, and probably her too. Lylla and Rho probably didn't know what to think or who to trust. "That's fine. But do you trust me? Do you all trust me?"

Shmar frowned at the floor and opened his mouth to speak. Nothing came out.

Lylla and Rho scooted closer. Kirehe's brow wriggled like she had too many competing thoughts to understand anything.

The moment Jaco leaned toward Madison, Kirehe bared her teeth and growled at him.

Madison raised her hands between them. "I need you to trust me. And also move closer." She tapped her ears. Whether someone listened or not, they would act as if the room had microphones.

Shmar stopped pacing to stand in front of her with his arms crossed. "This had better be good."

Jaco crawled toward her and stopped out of reach. "I'm sorry. I am truly, deeply sorry. He made promises, and I didn't think." He covered his face. "It was selfish and stupid. I should've trusted Madison."

"Jaco was trying to help me." Madison put a hand on Kirehe's shoulder. "It wasn't about you."

Kirehe's gaze flicked from Madison to Jaco and back. She closed the distance and pointed at him again. "I watch you."

"That's it?" Shmar said. "We're going to die, and before we do, we should forgive him for betraying all of us? Twice?"

"Once. Poorly." Madison held up both hands and watched them absorb this correction. Lylla grasped it first. She could tell by the way the girl's expression cleared, then she put a hand on Jaco's arm.

Oolaang nodded. "I knew something was up when you told me what you wanted. At least, I hoped so."

"You have a plan?" Rho asked.

Madison nodded. "Now will you trust me?"

Kirehe kept glaring at Jaco, which was fair. "You," she said to Madison, "I trust."

The unspoken part didn't need clarification for Madison to grasp it.

Shmar crouched in front of her, his eyes brimming with fearful hope. "Will it work?"

Madison nodded. "If we all do our parts." If it didn't work, they'd all die and no one would care anymore. Hope would make them try to survive in the face of execution. "Once we're in the arena, I'll need everyone to buy time for Kirehe however you can."

"What is my part?" Kirehe asked.

The time for secrecy had passed. She couldn't say much to the others, because the pharedimi would overhear, but she could say plenty to Kirehe. "When we get to the arena, call the maras. The cage door should open for them, but the one in the arena may not. You'll have to get it open for them."

"The key? Is it for Nihan?"

Pleased Kirehe had caught on so fast, Madison nodded. She had to stifle her grin for the sake of appearances.

Kirehe patted Madison's shoulder. "Did everything happen as you expected?"

"It sure did." Madison smirked and wanted to taunt whoever stood in the hallway. The pharedimi and Viriok had played their parts according to predictability. She'd used them against themselves, the best kind of revenge.

"I wish you would've told me about Jaco," Kirehe said.

Madison understood. "When we've escaped and are safe, I'll explain why I didn't. For now, we have to focus on teamwork."

Kirehe gave Madison a curt nod. "I trust you," she said in Lakhan Basic.

With this, the tense despair in the room eased in favor of anticipation.

"Get up," Soallen barked from the darkness. "Get moving. You know the way. Troopers line the corridor, so don't bother trying anything."

"Follow my lead," Madison murmured. "And act beaten. We're going to our deaths, remember?"

The group stood together, helping each other.

Even Shmar. "I swear, if—"

"I know." Madison squeezed his shoulder and strode out of the cell as if summoned to preside over her domain.

Kirehe chirped at Skila, who fluttered to the metal grate in the wall and slipped outside.

They shuffled down the corridor of light one last time as a group. Soallen stopped them at the door to the arena, where the crowd cheered for the ongoing match. Erryl, wearing his costume, stood nearby.

Madison had a feeling Soallen would happily kill any of her friends early as retaliation for being difficult. She stood and waited, watching Gordy trounce Wally with flair. Everyone touched her, with their hands on her shoulders and arms.

For Soallen's benefit, she said, "It's been an honor serving with all of you." She wished she could tell both him and Ilai what she really thought of them.

The rest of her group murmured their assent. Except Lylla, who burst into tears. Jaco put an arm around the girl's shoulders and hugged her close.

"I miss Mama," Lylla whimpered, sounding younger than ever.

"I got this," Jaco mouthed to Madison.

As Madison had done for Jaco once upon a time, Jaco did for Lylla. He murmured into her ear, and she wiped her face. He looked like the big brother he'd never had.

Erryl reached for Kirehe and set his hand on her shoulder like he considered her a young student he needed to lecture. "Make sure she understands," he ordered Madison. "I'm here in case you change your mind about the retirement match offer."

Kirehe stared at him. As Madison opened her mouth to explain and protest, her jungle princess warrior held up a hand. "I understand. What does he give for this?"

Straightening, Erryl crossed his arms. "Wiping the demerits you cost us with her stupid stunt." He nodded at Madison.

If Viriok hadn't offered Erryl an extra reward for talking Kirehe into this, Madison would eat her boot. The guy represented everything Viriok did right to keep his moneymaking pit running smoothly.

"He'll even add the beasts to the statue of you for the garden. You'll have a good spot, and there's probably enough video for a decent compilation. He'll prolong the battle to make sure there is. You'll have the glory of the longest duel ever fought against him."

To think Viriok had a garden of statues cast from all his best gladiators. Madison hadn't expected that level of creepy, but it made sense. She imagined him taking a favored pet for a walk through it during off hours to discuss the matter of their own retirement and statue. He put stars in their eyes, then murdered them in front of a crowd.

Lakhans considered humans the inferior barbarians.

Leaning close, Kirehe sneered at Erryl. "You are a slave," she growled, enunciating each word with care.

Erryl shrugged. "You're dead already. Why not gain glory from it? Otherwise, you're just another corpse on the floor to be forgotten. Like Tyron. Fed to the beasts in the dark of night and never heard of again."

Much to Madison's alarm, Kirehe appeared to consider this. She leaned closer to make sure Kirehe heard her. "You don't—"

Kirehe held up her hand again. "Do you like chain on your neck, slave? Is feel like silk, but is chain."

For one terrifying moment, Madison had thought Kirehe might reject her in favor of a statue for the maras. To have the aliens acknowledge the local fauna might have swayed her. The moment those words came out of Kirehe's mouth, though, Madison realized how stupid that thought had been.

Soallen rolled his eyes and waved for Erryl to leave. "I told you she wouldn't listen. Get back to the pit."

In the arena, Gordy put Wally on the ground with prejudice. Oylesa announced him as the winner. Crowd cheering made further talking impossible. The lights died, and the door opened. Soallen shoved Madison forward.

A spotlight flared into life, following Madison as she straightened and swaggered into the arena on her own. Complete silence greeted her.

Kirehe whistled into the eerie quiet, the sound echoing off the walls.

Oylesa's voice boomed through the arena. "Welcome back to Madison Wayward, of the notorious Stardrifter ship, *Wayward Star*. Today, she faces certain execution at the hands of the Arena Master's own finest troopers. Her co-conspirators join her to meet their grisly fate."

More spotlights compounded the light beating on Madison, swelling until it made Oolaang groan. Somehow, they didn't notice Kirehe's absence among the group. Then again, this part was all about Madison, not the crowd's favorite savage. Viriok might even approve of Kirehe staying out of the light so the crowd stayed focused on Madison.

Or he might have thought she took his offer at the last minute.

"Madison Wayward," Viriok thundered. "For your many crimes against the Lakhan Oligarchy, you have already been sentenced to death. It is now time to carry out this sentence. You may run if you wish."

Titters of laughter ran through the crowd.

Though she hated to do what Viriok suggested, Madison had minimal control over this part of the plan. Running might help. She'd expected an execution without knowing how he'd set it up. In fact, if Viriok hadn't taken her bait and also condemned Kirehe, she had no idea how any of them could survive.

After seeing all the precautions, decisions, and procedures in place for the past few months, Madison had figured out Viriok's one and only weakness.

He didn't have to anticipate anyone's every action by watching them. He'd lived more than long enough to see so many people do so many things that he knew what to plan for. All contingencies had foils. All options had safeguards.

But Kirehe had surprised Viriok by failing her assessment on purpose. She'd proven that he'd never seen someone throw a fight with their life on the line. Knowing that tidbit had led Madison to a particular conclusion.

In Viriok's world, everyone wanted to win. No one in the entire ecosystem wanted to lose or to earn demerits, or to do anything to jeopardize their life or status. Every facet of the arena and its back end worked together to ensure everyone understood how to gain and lose privileges, status, glory, and other rewards.

Viriok had constructed a foolproof prison by distracting his gladiators from the fact they lived and died in a prison.

Madison hadn't forgotten. She saw it every day. On *Wayward Star*, she'd lived through some of the most boring periods of time imaginable while the ship traveled or hid from Oligarchy cruisers. Those days had dragged much worse than any time in this prison. But they ended. The ship reached its destination, or the cruiser moved on. They docked on backwater worlds and explored the local scenery.

They'd picked up strays like Jaco.

This prison trudged onward with every day the same as the one before. Nothing would ever change. The overseer or a handler made a point to remind all the slaves of their minimal value every so often. As if Madison could forget.

The Stardrifters fought because they didn't believe one being could own another. They could've done what the qusamadi and vreesliik did, and acquiesce to the Lakhan Oligarchy in return for citizen status. But they didn't. Because they believed in freedom.

What Viriok didn't understand was the ability to accept failure as the first step of a plan. She'd set them up to fail on their first escape attempt on purpose. Viriok's entire worldview couldn't handle that.

He had no idea she'd used that mad dash to the mara cage as a diversion. His entire being couldn't comprehend her intent to make sure she and the others earned an execution. To Viriok, none of this made sense.

More spotlights clicked on, revealing hevit troopers making no effort to camouflage themselves. They held rifles.

"Troopers, stand ready!" Oylesa shouted.

Madison dove to the side, trying to get out of the spotlight. The others reacted a moment later and followed her lead. Like she'd asked them.

The spotlights moved, trying to track them. Ducking, weaving, and otherwise moving erratically, Madison kept out of the spotlight. Kirehe would do her part and save their lives.

Viriok's laughter echoed off the walls. The crowd laughed with him.

"Laugh all you want, pokkentoff," Madison muttered. She paused to catch her breath.

"Troopers," Oylesa barked, "fire at will."

A spotlight blasted Madison in the face.

CHAPTER 28

KIREHE

The maras came at Kirehe's call. They met her with the arena gate between them. No one had bothered to give the gate a latch. Its own weight held it down. Between Kirehe and the four maras, they lifted the gate enough for the maras to dart through.

With a few soft chirps, Kirehe unleashed them to hunt the bad masters. They streaked through the darkness soundlessly. No one knew about them until Rila pounced on a hevit about to shoot Madison. She tore it apart, creating an explosion of tiny feathers and blood.

In a wave, the maras shredded through the line of hevit troopers. Kirehe followed them, making sure the hevits on the ground stayed there.

More light flooded the arena, rendering the spotlights pointless. Camera drones swirled overhead, following the mara carnage. The crowd buzzed with confusion.

Kirehe took a moment to look up. Viriok stood on the edge of his platform, watching.

Certain she needed to keep Viriok's attention on herself, Kirehe screamed a wordless war cry and pointed at him. As long as Madison and the others kept moving, the maras could handle the hevits.

Viriok flung aside his cloak and raised his spear. He stepped off the edge of his platform and fell to the floor. As he'd done when facing Anya, he landed on one knee with a fist punching the floor.

Kirehe's attention narrowed to Viriok. She'd seen him fight. His skill demanded her respect.

He straightened and thumped the end of his spear on the floor. The sound resonated in Kirehe's chest. "I accept your challenge," he rumbled.

Watching his shoulders and face, Kirehe shifted closer. In her head, she estimated the reach of his spear. To snatch it from him, she'd have to goad him into thrusting it with full intent. That required using herself as bait.

The Arena Master had watched her fight. Silly tricks wouldn't work on him. She'd noticed, though, that he hadn't expected the key Oolaang had made. The small man must've done that during the run for the mara cage when Kirehe had noticed him missing.

Had Viriok or Overseer Neilan considered the possibility of Madison's escape attempt as a ruse, they would've searched everyone. They might also have executed everyone other than Madison on the spot instead of making it a spectacle.

He couldn't see past the spectacle.

Kirehe circled to the left.

Viriok turned to follow her with an extra flourish of his hand. He still wanted a show.

Her attack would have to appear foolish. Like Madison's escape attempt had done, she'd have to make him think she faltered by accident instead of on purpose.

She slid a pace closer. When Viriok didn't react, she took two more.

He swept his spear at her. The arc swung low, offering her an easy dodge by jumping. Though she took what he gave, she used the chance to leap at him. His reflexes shifted him out of the way. She missed colliding with his body on purpose, skewing to the side.

The follow-through for his spear ended where Kirehe landed.

Setting both hands on the spear, she tried to tear it from his hands and continue on her way. Viriok held firm. The spear twisted. Kirehe's momentum scraped the point across Viriok's thigh.

Since she couldn't have it, Kirehe let go and danced out of his reach.

Viriok righted his spear. He touched the wound on his thigh and raised his hand. Dark blue blood, gleaming in the light, painted his finger. The sight seemed to confuse him for a moment. Then his expression changed to a feral grin of glee.

Kirehe's heart raced as wondered if she'd picked a fight with a krata.

He rushed her. She dodged his spear and threw a punch. His arm swept aside her fist. Ducking to avoid the spear again, she kicked his knee. The blow hurt her foot more than his leg.

Speed like nothing she'd seen before propelled Viriok's attacks and blocks. He seemed to have six arms and ten legs. His flurry of blows battered her and drove her backward, step by step. A slap to the leg flung her body to the ground. She rolled to evade a stab with his spear.

Viriok laughed and let her scramble to her feet. "For a moment, I thought you might be a worthy adversary. My mistake."

Before she could slide out of his reach, he snapped his foot against her hip in a blur. The force of his blow knocked her down and sent her sliding at least a meter.

"Get up, savage," he snarled, "so I can defeat you properly." He stalked toward her.

Kirehe struggled to breathe and force her beaten body to stand. Her arms hung from their sockets, leaden and protesting. She shuffled backward until she hit the arena wall.

If she died now, she hoped she'd at least given Madison and the others enough time to escape the arena with the maras.

"You are not hero," she managed between gasps for air.

"You will die here, by my hand, as expected." He held up a hand and gestured for her to attack.

Kirehe bared her teeth. "You mean by spear. Hands not good enough."

Viriok laughed again. "So be it. With my bare hands." He stamped the end of his spear on the ground again, then tossed it aside. The metal winked and flashed in the light as the spear clattered on the floor and rolled to a stop too far for Kirehe to try snatching it.

They glared at each other. With every passing moment, Kirehe caught her breath and more pain crept into her body. Nothing felt serious or sharp, but if she closed with him, he would win.

Skila streaked into the arena. "Nihan coming!" she chirped several times.

Stone exploded from a section of the audience seating behind and above Kirehe. Nihan bellowed his rage into the arena. People screamed.

Wide-eyed surprise flashed across Viriok's face. Kirehe grinned.

Nihan leaped over the glass wall and smashed his tail against it. The glass shattered, sending shards flying at the fleeing crowd. More glass showered Viriok and Kirehe. Viriok watched the massive krata pass over his head.

If she'd had the spear, Kirehe could've slammed it through Viriok's chest.

Suddenly filled with adrenaline, Kirehe sprinted to the side. She waved for Nihan to attack Viriok.

The krata landed and snapped his jaws around Viriok.

Kirehe snatched Viriok's spear and held it ready to attack as needed.

Viriok squawked. The low, guttural sound reminded Kirehe of a risi dragon mauled by a mara pack.

Nihan crunched. He whipped his head to the side and flung Viriok at the far wall of the arena. The krata roared again, shaking the building.

"Nihan!"

Her krata lowered his knee for her to climb onto his back. "Free," he chirped.

Kirehe scrambled onto her beloved krata. She wanted to sit and savor the moment.

Near the gladiator exit, Madison and the others had stacked hevit corpses to use as cover. The maras lurked behind the escapees, protecting their backs. Everyone had rifles taken from the corpses, even Oolaang. They traded fire with the enemy through the door.

"Save small man," Nihan said. He ran on all four legs with his wings tight against his body.

Kirehe laughed. Skila must have told Nihan to trust Oolaang, and he must have figured out Oolaang's task. Kratas had much larger brains than kukiris.

Close behind the escapees, Nihan stopped and bellowed through the door.

Everyone ducked and covered their ears. The enemy stopped firing too.

Madison flashed Kirehe a thumbs-up.

"Now what?" Kirehe called.

Madison flashed a giant grin. "How many can your dragon carry?"

"One more and still fight. Two and still fly. Everyone and run."

"Take Oolaang and meet us at Zorileck's ship!"

Kirehe leaned down. So did Nihan. Oolaang squeaked as she lifted him to sit behind her. For Madison and the rest to meet them at the ship, they had to escape the arena first. Beyond that, she had no doubt they could find a path through the complex.

"Rila, lead a charge! Oolaang, hold on. Nihan, we leave."

Nihan rose on his hind legs. He flared his wings and flapped hard enough to send debris slamming against the wall and shooting through the door.

Oolaang squealed one long, shrill note of terror as Nihan screamed his rage again and lifted off the ground. The maras flowed over the corpse barricade and through the door, echoing his screech with their smaller voices.

Kirehe noticed Viriok to the side, rising to his hands and knees. Did his body repair itself? Everything he'd suffered should have killed him. But they needed to escape, not to kill Viriok. She liked to keep her promises, and eating his liver would make her happy. It could also delay her long enough to ensure their final escape failed as poorly as their initial one.

Madison led the bipeds in a charge behind the maras. As Nihan turned to use the hole he'd made on the way in, Rho waved to Kirehe. They ducked through the door, the last of the group on foot to escape the arena.

Nihan and Kirehe shot through the gaping hole in the wall.

No one had designed Irondoom to withstand krata dragons from the inside. Why would they? So long as they couldn't break through the outside, it made no difference.

They streaked past Nihan's round prison. Glass and bodies littered the floor around it. He'd smashed through the glass walls to escape it.

With the hallways too narrow for Nihan to fly, he landed and loped. They passed garish art with grotesque, unnatural colors. Nihan charged through grand archways of white stone. Screaming people scattered before him. Those not fast enough to escape him fell beneath his claws.

Had anyone in Irondoom other than Madison treated Kirehe or the dragons with kindness, she might've felt some remorse over all the deaths. These people, though, deserved none.

Ahead, someone opened large double doors to the outside. At this point, she would've wanted the krata in her home to leave too, no matter the cost. Nihan charged the sunshine and leaped into the air, trilling his delight at finding open sky again.

Lasers cut short his joy. He swerved. Oolaang shrieked. Kirehe reached behind and grabbed the small man as he fell. She reseated him in front of herself and let him hold the bony knobs at the base of Nihan's wings.

"Hold on tight." She jumped off Nihan's back to land on top of a gun emplacement as the dragon flew over it. Using Viriok's spear to break her fall, she cried out her anger at those who would defend Irondoom.

Qusamadi and pharedimi alike fell to her furious attacks.

When she'd dispatched all the soldiers, she stabbed the gun until it made screechy noises and belched smoke.

Across the way, Nihan ripped a second gun off the roof and threw it, soldiers and all, to the side.

Kirehe waited until he could see her, then ran to the wall edge and leaped into the air.

CHAPTER 29

MADISON

With a clear path and all signs pointing to Viriok not dying from a krata dragon assault, Madison led a charge out of the arena. "Guys, we need some direction here!"

The mara dragons charged down the corridor, apparently chasing enemies.

"I know how to get out of the basement," Lylla shouted. "After that, I'm not sure."

"Lead the way." Madison fired her stolen hevit rifle into the darkness. She hoped the mara dragons survived and found them again later. Kirehe would hate to leave them behind.

The others followed her lead, shooting ahead. Someone grunted. Blood spritzed from the edge of the light. A hevit fell, its feathers no longer providing camouflage.

Though Madison knew the hevits had lined up to kill them all, and they'd already killed some, the troopers' deaths still surprised her. She carried a deadly weapon. When the crew boarded ships, they normally carried stun weapons. The crews of their targets didn't often die. They lost cargo and got hurt, but Captain Wayward didn't like leaving corpses in his wake.

Every single person here, aside from most of the slaves, deserved to die. That didn't mean Madison wanted to make it happen. On the other hand, she knew they all wanted her dead. If she didn't kill them, they'd happily murder her first.

Shmar kicked the hevit corpse as they ran past it.

They reached an intersection. Voices rang out in a confused mess of shouting and screaming. Madison and Lylla leaned forward to check for guards. Overseer Neilan stood in the center of the corridor to the left, tapping on his handheld screen.

Lylla pointed in that direction.

Madison sighed. Of course they had to go that way. She checked her gun. Half the charges remained. No problem.

Stepping into the corridor, she pointed her rifle at him. She could've shot him from the corner, and he never would've seen it coming. But she wanted him to know. For the short time between seeing her and dying, he'd understand his grave mistake. Besides, he probably had access codes or something they'd find useful.

"Overseer Neilan," she said. "I expected you to hide in your office and watch everything like a coward."

He glanced at her, then he raised his hands and gave her his full attention. "Madison Wayward. The unique case that has caused a unique problem." Peering behind her, he smiled. "You seem to have forgotten to stay with your group."

Madison suspected hevits hid nearby. "Sure does seem that way, doesn't it? Kind of like how you seem to be alone yourself."

"You know what's funny here?" Gordy asked from the darkness. He stepped into the light, wearing his usual green and gold slave clothing, and slammed an ordinary spear into the overseer's gut. "Nothing."

Skila chirped, though Madison couldn't see her. Then she saw a hevit, sparkling with glitter, shift into the light. Madison shot it.

"Skila is the best bird ever." Madison jogged forward and offered her hand to Gordy. "I don't know how many we can take on our escape, but you're welcome to come with us."

Gordy yanked his spear out of the overseer's shuddering corpse and grasped Madison's forearm. "Thanks. I'll do that. Erryl opened the door when your execution went sideways, so I think we'll find plenty of chaos to slip through."

More guns fired, hitting glitter-covered hevits. Madison waved an arm to get everyone to join them.

"Have you seen Soallen?"

Gordy shook his head. "No, but I haven't been checking corpses."

"Let's keep moving. Lylla, which way?"

The girl took them up one tunnel and down another. They skirted around groups of gladiators fighting with hevits and pharedimi. Gunfire erupted in random bursts. Screams, grunts, and groans echoed through the corridors. Down Lylla's preferred path, they discovered a fire blocking passage. She kept going, finding another option.

Madison hadn't appreciated how much of a maze they'd lived in. She wondered if they'd done it on purpose to help prevent mass escapes? Probably.

Thank goodness they had Lylla to navigate it.

Around one more corner, they reached a dead end.

"There's a door," Lylla said, pointing at the darkness shrouding the end of their path. "I swear."

"There better be." Madison panted to catch her breath.

Gordy ran to the end and stabbed the darkness with his spear. The metal tip thudded against the wall. Everyone else followed him.

Madison watched behind them with Rho and Lylla while the men stepped out of the light to figure out the door.

Soallen and several glittered-doused hevits ran past their hallway. Madison waited with a hand up to keep Rho from shooting. Maybe they hadn't noticed the group.

Maybe, Madison thought, the three of them shouldn't stand in the light like idiots while the guys felt up the walls. With a frantic wave, she jumped into the darkness along the side of the tunnel. Lylla followed her.

Rho planted their feet, held their rifle ready, and a glared at the intersection. The moment a shimmer of glitter crossed back into sight, they opened fire. One hevit dropped.

"This isn't a winning strategy," Soallen called from around the corner. "No one has ever escaped Rikor Six, and you won't manage the become the first. Even if you can get out of the dungeon, which you can't through that wall, you won't make it to anything that can take you offworld. Surrender now and you'll go back into the gladiator program with no penalty. All will be forgiven."

Madison barked a laugh. "Maybe that would work on a bunch of dumb, overmuscled gladiator slaves, but it won't work on us, you voidsucking broken cog."

"That kind of hurts," Gordy said.

"I say it with sisterly love."

Someone, probably Jaco, snorted.

"Ah. Wayward. In that case, never mind."

Glitter-covered hevits rolled into the light. Soallen leaned around the corner, holding a pistol. Everybody opened fire. Rho screamed as they darted to the side and filled the tunnel with rifle rounds. Madison crouched to shoot.

"Got it," Gordy said. "Low ceiling. Soallen's side."

Madison skittered backward. Blasts tagged the floor and walls. Someone grunted with pain. Hevits fell. She reached the empty gap and slid through, still firing along the wall.

"Gordy here and fine."

"Jaco here. Fine."

"Shmar here." He gasped. "Hit in the leg."

"Madison here. Jaco, help Shmar."

"Lylla here. I'm fine."

"Rho, on the floor. Fine."

"That's everyone." Madison found the open door. "Hey, Soallen!" She watched, hoping he stuck his head out enough to shoot it.

"Yes?" He failed to do anything stupid, leaving Madison with no opportunity to shoot him.

"Good luck with that zero escape record." Madison slammed the door shut. "Move. They have to know where this leads. And an ordinary door won't stop them."

They ran in the dark. Madison kept one hand on the wall and the other on someone's back. Someone else kept a hand on her back and fired shots behind them every half minute or so. Shmar's pained loping made a weird shuffle noise among all the clomping boots.

The group turned a corner, then stopped. Light flooded the narrow passage from above. Screams echoed in large, airy halls. Glass shattered. Stone thundered. Metal squealed. People scurried.

Gordy climbed up a ladder built into the wall at the end. He popped his head through the hole, then ducked down again. After flashing a thumbs-up, he climbed out. Madison helped Jaco haul up Shmar. Rho fired behind them. Lylla scurried up and fired from the top to cover Rho.

Madison grinned as she surveyed their situation. They'd emerged in an empty hallway slathered in bright purple, pink, and green. Chunks of broken glass and plastic littered the floor, along with random scraps of cloth. That lump of stuff in a puddle of green goo might've been a severed body part.

Someone had already used this path, because the thick, heavy cover for the passage lay a meter to the left as if tossed there.

"The Rikor Six Luxury Resort might need a new paint job." Madison patted Shmar on the back. "How bad is your leg?"

Leaning against the wall and gasping for breath, Shmar shook his head. "I can't run on it anymore."

"He's limping at best," Jaco said.

"Okay. From here, we need to get to Luxury Dock Sixteen. Kirehe is securing a ship for us." Madison pointed to a screen across the hall.

"What ship?" Jaco asked. "How does she know where to go?"

As if they had time for thorough explanations of everything. Madison sprinted across the hall and tapped on the screen.

She heard Gordy say, "Really? We're talking about Kirehe here. I believe she could do just about anything with the right directions."

There is currently an emergency situation. Everything is under control. Please proceed to the nearest evacuation point and await further instructions.

Madison read the message twice before laughing at it. At least the map showed her everything she needed to know. Pointing for the group, she got moving. Gordy half-carried Shmar.

The decorations for the guest portion of the place made Madison cringe. They used terrible colors, smashed everything together, and didn't seem to understand the concept of restraint. Even the big halls with huge arches had distracting designs on the floors and decorations dripping from the walls and ceiling. They passed a seating area with at least two hundred cushions in piles four or five deep, in addition to the plush chairs and couches.

In the distance, Madison heard a really big dragon screaming. She picked up speed. Something hit her shin. She sprawled across the floor and slid past the nearest corner. Her rifle slipped out of her grip to land several feet ahead of her.

She twisted her body to see Soallen straightening from a hiding spot around that last corner with a staff in both hands.

Beyond him, everyone else huddled together. Shmar lay in a heap on the floor. Jaco raised his rifle. Gordy stabbed a glittering hevit with his spear. Lylla hid behind Jaco. Rho sprayed fire in an arc.

No one could help Madison. They couldn't even see Soallen.

Except Skila. The little dragon landed on a neon pink spike sticking out of the wall. She watched Madison and Soallen.

"Madison Wayward," Soallen said. He glared at her.

"Back to the full name thing." Madison knew she couldn't reach her rifle without lunging for it. If she glanced back to check for it, she'd draw Soallen's attention there. "It's like a fetish or something."

"It's a reminder that this really has nothing to do with you. You don't matter in the slightest."

If she kept him talking long enough, someone would stop him from killing her with a long stick. "Sure. It's all about Captain Wayward." Madison sat up, scooting her butt backward instead of forward to get closer to the rifle.

Like she'd said a magic word, Soallen's face screwed up with a surprising amount of anger. "Captain Wayward," he growled. "Responsible for my sister's death."

Madison blinked. "Uh, what?"

Soallen sneered at her. "Of course his precious niece would have no idea about something that happened ten years ago."

Ten years ago, a ship crash had killed Madison's parents. Her uncle had rescued her. "Maybe because his precious niece was only nine at the time and had bigger problems? Like losing my parents. You know, no big deal."

Soallen laughed. "He killed your parents and my sister in one fell swoop. Did you think he was a hero?"

Captain Wayward had always made clear he blamed himself for those deaths. He'd told Madison the story, and she didn't think it fell entirely on his shoulders. But then, she didn't have anyone else's story to compare it to. Maybe he'd told her part of the truth to help him absolve himself.

Guilt pushing him down could explain his steady loss of optimism and enthusiasm over the years. Failure could also explain it. So could loneliness, since his wife had died in that crash too. Even if guilt did crush him under its heel, that still made sense. He'd survived when the rest of his family hadn't.

"Yes, now you see." Soallen held out a hand to her. "All this time, you've devoted yourself to a lie. This man told you what you wanted to hear."

Soallen thought the look on her face meant she considered betraying her uncle? Madison could work with that. She wished she had a knife to stick between his ribs, but she could manage something without one.

"You and I, we can work together to end the madness."

Madison stood without his help and kept her frown intact. "He was like a father to me."

"Of course he was. He's a myth, a story. Nothing he's ever said has been real. Everything he's ever done has been calculated to bring you further under his control." Soallen held his staff aside, the end planted on the floor.

Though she had much less skill reading fighting body language than Kirehe, Madison knew Soallen's options. She also knew what Viriok and Cradok wanted. If Soallen produced her for an on-camera execution, he salvaged something from this fiasco. His ideal outcome from this moment involved Madison walking under her own power for as long as possible. At some point, he knocked her unconscious and took her to Viriok.

After all the chaos and damage she'd caused, Madison imagined Viriok wanted to rip her apart with his bare hands. Soallen had enough brains to figure that out too.

Hoping her face reflected a conflict inside her, she took the last step into his reach. "I just want to be free."

"Don't we all." Soallen gestured down the hall with his staff.

Madison nodded and turned her back on him. Any moment, he'd deliver that strike to knock her down. She reached up to rub her nose and took the first step. Skila watched her. As Madison lowered her hand, she pointed past her face, indicating Soallen as clearly as she could without giving herself away.

Skila leaped off her perch and opened her wings, a silent flower drifting on the air. She turned and dove at Soallen's face.

For a tiny thing, she could move like lightning.

Soallen screeched and pawed at the dragon assaulting his face.

Madison whirled and snatched his staff. She had no idea how to use it properly. She did, however, know how to hit someone with a stick. One solid thwack to the backs of his knees drove him to the floor.

Skila let go, her claws dripping with blood. Soallen wheezed in pain and flailed his arms in every direction. Madison winced at the sight of his eyes dribbling blood and goo down his cheeks.

Madison had lost her eye ten years ago, in that crash. She still remembered the desperate agony of losing her sight. For one eye, that loss had been temporary. Not so much for the other.

Soallen deserved it, ten times over.

Four mara dragons slammed into Soallen, appearing out of nowhere as far as Madison could tell. They shredded him until he couldn't scream anymore.

Gordy arrived with his spear ready as Soallen's severed arm flew to the side. "Sorry I took so long, but I think they covered you."

Jaco and Rho dragged Shmar, who groaned. Lylla watched their back with a rifle held ready.

"I'm okay. It's okay. That's really gross, but it's otherwise okay." Madison took a deep breath and noticed her limbs shaking. She stopped watching the maras. "He still wanted the public execution, I think."

"I'd love to stand and chat for a while," Jaco said, "but we're kind of in a time crunch and Shmar needs medical attention. He took another hit."

"Yes!" Madison stamped the butt of Soallen's staff on the floor. It made a satisfying clunk that reverberated up her arm. The sensation made her feel strangely powerful. "No wonder everybody does that," she murmured.

Skila landed on Madison's shoulder and chirped. The maras raised their bloody snouts. One whistled to Skila.

"Right. Yeah. Moving. This way." She led the group as fast as they could go while still hauling Shmar.

They plunged into a crowd as they neared the spacedock. Madison saw dozens with bandages, and dozens more sheltering as if something terrible had happened in the dock and no one wanted to chance it happening again. Of course, the maras running through terrified the crowd again.

The roar of a big dragon made everyone whimper and flinch.

Everyone, that is, except Madison, her crew, and the maras. They picked up speed and stormed the spacedock. Two ships, each cracked and broken, burned. More fire burned in scattered clumps.

At the far end of the dock, Kirehe's dragon reared on his hind legs, his wings outstretched. Kirehe stood at his feet, shielding Oolaang with her body and holding Viriok's spear aloft like a goddess.

Kirehe slammed her spear into someone or something on the ground.

Madison sprinted to reach her. All four mara dragons outpaced her in moments. The others stayed in a group, moving slower to keep Shmar safe.

While she ran, she watched Kirehe spin and skewer a hevit. She ripped her spear out of that one to shove the butt end into another. Nihan dropped to all fours and snatched two hevits at once in his jaws. He flung them into the distance. Her mara pack destroyed another three.

By the time Madison had reached Kirehe and her dragons, bodies littered the ground around them.

The immediate area seemed safe. Madison charged to Kirehe, who flipped her onto her back and froze in the act of stabbing Madison through the chest with wide-eyed horror.

"Madison!" Kirehe stooped and took Madison's hand, then yanked her onto her feet. "I thought you an enemy."

Her brain scrambled by yet another scrape with death, Madison wrapped her arms around Kirehe and hugged her.

Kirehe had no idea how to hug someone. They'd fix that. Later.

Oolaang squeaked. Kirehe shoved Madison aside and hauled Oolaang with her to avoid blaster fire. The attack stopped in a moment because Gordy reached the shooter.

"Right! To the ship!" Madison pointed at a slim, sleek ship near the size of the *Wayward Scout* parked nearby. It would hold all the dragons. She'd already run more than enough to gasp for breath, but she hauled her ass into and through the ship to the cockpit.

The ship had a logical design, and finding the controls took nothing more than following her instincts. Unlike Captain Wayward's ships, which people lived in and called home, this one felt empty and hollow. It reminded her of the Oligarchy cruiser, except without Cradok laughing at her.

Zorileck sat at the controls, flipping switches in a frantic effort to get the ship moving. In a moment, Madison figured out he had no idea how to make the ship go. The guy probably employed a private pilot who hadn't reached the ship yet. Maybe they never would.

"Hi, Zorileck. Nice to see you again."

He cranked his body to see her. "Madison!" Rolling his body out of the pilot seat, he grinned at her. "You or one of your people knows how to pilot, don't you? The whole place is collapsing! It's under attack by a horde of those flying monstrosities."

"Yes it is." Gordy stepped to her right.

Kirehe matched his pose on her left.

Two spear-wielding guardians made Madison feel like she could do anything. These people could defend her against anything.

Skila chirped on her shoulder, reminding her that she had a lot more backup if she needed it.

"Tell you what, Zorileck." Madison smiled at him. The guy hadn't harmed them. In fact, he'd helped. Without his patronage, Madison would've needed months longer to set up her plan. "Get off the ship now and we won't kill you."

Zorileck's face fell. He held up his hands. "Now, wait a minute. I was nothing but good to you. And I have a lot of money! With my help, you can accomplish so much more."

Madison wanted to pinch his cheek. "Do you really think we want your blood money?"

His grin fell. "But you're Stardrifters."

"He's got a point," Jaco called from behind them.

Madison nodded. "I'm not saying we'll turn down blood money." She waved for Gordy and Kirehe to get rid of him. "I'm just saying we don't need him to get access to it. Like he said, we're Stardrifters. Stealing is what we do. And now we're going to steal this ship."

CHAPTER 30

KIREHE

Gordy took the strange, ugly man to the back of the ship. Kirehe watched Madison pop out her artificial eye and climb into the cushioned seat surrounded by glass and many of those damnable screens. She plugged a cable into her eye socket.

Every light in the area flickered to full power.

The floor rumbled.

"You've probably never been on a ship before," Madison said. "This is normal. I'm starting up the engines. We'll lift off in a few seconds and leave."

"Leave the complex?" Kirehe thought she knew the real answer. Her belly fluttered.

"Leave the planet. Viriok might object to that, so they'll probably shoot at us. This ship has no weapons, which means you might want to strap in because I'll have to maneuver faster than the artificial gravity can compensate."

Kirehe didn't understand many of those words. But she understood leaving the planet. The idea made her panic. She raced back to the big part of the ship where Nihan and the maras waited for her with Skila. Gordy hit a button on the wall, and the big door shut, locking them all inside. The floor became unstable and gravity pushed down on Kirehe's shoulders.

This machine with its noise threatened to carry her from her home. Space held nothing but cold and darkness. She wanted warmth and light. Things made sense in the jungle.

"I let him live," Gordy said.

"Open the door," Kirehe said as she climbed onto Nihan's back.

"What happens?" Nihan asked.

The maras huddled against a corner, chirping fear and distress.

"I can't open the door now. We're lifting off." Gordy raised his hands. "It's okay. Don't panic. We're escaping."

"Open the door or I stab you with spear!"

Gordy wrapped his arm around a post and hit the button.

The door opened.

Through it, Kirehe saw the ground fall away at high speed. Her maras would never survive the jump. Madison could take care of them well enough.

"What's going on?" Madison's voice said from everywhere. "Close the door!"

"Go," she told Nihan.

Nihan leaped out of the ship. He snapped open his wings. They flew unhindered for five seconds before a pair of flyers lifted from Irondoom. Two more joined them. Another two followed.

Madison had said the ship had no weapons. Six flyers against one unarmed ship sounded bad. Even if Madison could fly that thing like Nihan, it wouldn't last long. The ship offered too large a target and the flyers could shoot too many times.

"Attack," she told Nihan.

The krata roared for help from the jungle below.

Four of the flyers aimed for them. The other two lifted to follow the ship. Lasers filled the sky.

"Those two first." Kirehe pointed at the two aiming for the ship. Whether any kratas came at Nihan's call or not, Madison and the others would escape.

Nihan wove through the laser blasts to soar over the two flyers.

The other flyers stopped shooting long enough for Kirehe to leap off Nihan's back.

This time, Kirehe had a lakhan spear and two fully functional arms. She drove the weapon into the cockpit with the full force of her landing. The shaft pierced the canopy and the pilot inside. Kirehe tore her spear free and leaped off the faltering craft. Dozens of meters off the ground, she used her arms, legs, and spear to aim for the next flyer.

Her spear hit the next flyer in line, slamming through the right wing. Kirehe dangled from the end, in front of the flyer's leading edge. The craft veered to the left. Using the new angle, Kirehe swung onto the flyer and landed on all fours. She leaped at her spear and wrenched it out of the craft.

The pilot ejected. That meant the flyer would crash. It had already strayed too far for her to leap to the next.

"Nihan!"

The krata streamed overhead, snatching the ejected pilot from the air with his jaws. Two flyers remained, both chasing the big ship.

Kirehe jumped off the machine. Nihan flipped and dove to catch her. He tossed the dead pilot aside. She dropped onto his back.

"Two more." She pointed to make sure he knew where to go. "We attack together. One at a time."

"Then home?"

"Then home." Why did those words fill her with a queer dread? Kirehe shook it off. She needed focus to land on the flyer.

Madison's ship swerved. The flyers followed it, shooting in rapid succession. With their focus on the big ship, Nihan had no trouble reaching the first machine. He spun to fly upside-down. Kirehe let herself fall to the flyer. She landed on the wing.

As Nihan flew across the flyer, she ran over the surface. The machine angled, turning toward its partner. Kirehe stopped, braced her feet, and stabbed her spear into the machine's wing. Nihan passed her and slammed his claws into the other wing.

The pilot ejected.

"Let him go!" Kirehe wrenched free her spear and leaped.

Nihan caught her.

"Throw it into the other one."

With a gleeful roar, Nihan pounced on the damaged flyer and acted as a sail for it. They rode the machine into the last pursuing flyer.

At the same moment that Nihan let go, the last pilot ejected.

They watched the two flyers fall from the sky. Nihan pushed himself into a smooth, slow glide.

Ahead, Madison's ship had slowed. The large door in the back slid open again. Madison expected her to return with Nihan.

"Home?" Nihan asked.

Kirehe peered past his neck to the jungle below. Under the canopy, everyone had abandoned all thought of her as anything other than lost. If anyone had mourned, she doubted they'd done so for long. When she returned, she'd find another dragoncaller tending her route. If Lipa's pack remained near the village, that other dragoncaller had taken control of it by now.

She hadn't left much behind. Everything she'd kept in her small home belonged to the treehouse itself. It had all been there when she arrived. What little she'd added had no value to her. Skila would shed more feathers. Nihan would shed more scales. This new mara pack would do both. They'd all bring her bones and other strange gifts.

And then she had Madison. The feelings Madison inspired in her made no sense. At the same time, Kirehe decided she liked them. Sometimes. No, wait. At first, she hadn't liked them. The more often she experienced it, the more she liked it.

She liked Madison in ways she'd never cared about anyone else. Even her mother had left an impression of distance. Among her people, Kirehe might never find someone who inspired the same feelings in her that Madison did.

What would she do when Madison's ship left without her? Return to flying? Knowing what she knew about Irondoom, she saw no other option than to raise the dragoncallers in an assault against the place. They would refuse. She knew it with certainty deep in her bones. All Iwans had avoided Irondoom since the offworlders had come and destroyed the lost hapa.

When they refused, she would stew in frustration. Then she would lead her own dragon assault on Irondoom. Many dragons would die. She might also lose her life.

Madison intended to continue pursuing the fight against Viriok and his kind. Kirehe's people would never do the same. If she left with Madison, she had a better chance of protecting and helping her people than if she died trying to assault Irondoom on her own.

The idea of Viriok finally standing over her corpse settled the matter in her head.

"I'm going on the ship with them. We'll leave the planet." She patted his neck. "You can drop me in the ship and go home if you want. I'll miss you, but I'll understand."

Nihan flapped his wings to catch the ship. He landed on the edge, making it impossible for Gordy to shut the door again.

Kirehe slid off his back. She raised her arms. Nihan lowered his head. He touched his snout to her head. His scales felt warm under her hands.

Nihan snorted heated air through his nostrils, ruffling her hair.

"We have to close the door!" Gordy shouted. "He needs to move!"

He drew back and checked the view of the jungle behind him.

"Go if you want." A piece of Kirehe's heart broke again. This time, at least, he chose to leave her.

Turning to face her again, Nihan cocked his head. "Meat on ship?"

Kirehe laughed and gestured for him to move out of the way. The door whirred shut with Nihan inside the ship. She patted his flank and hurried to comfort the maras.

A strange new world awaited them all. It promised cold, dark, and empty stretches of space. At the same time, as the maras gathered around her and Nihan settled close at hand, she knew it also held warmth.

Enough warmth made light, and light filled the hollow spaces.

OTHER BOOKS BY THE AUTHORS

STARDRIFTERS

Dragoncaller
A Foundation of Gravestones (coming soon)
The Last Armada (coming soon)

OTHER TITLES BY BOTH AUTHORS

Nova Ranger Academy
Unnatural Dragons: a science fiction anthology
Swords, Sorcery, & Self-Rescuing Damsels
Working the Table: An Indie Author's Guide to Conventions
Clockwork Dragon (coming soon)

WRITERPUNK ANTHOLOGIES

'punk adaptations of classic works
Sound & Fury
Once More Unto the Breach
Merely This and Nothing More
What We've Unlearned
Hideous Progeny
Taught By Time (coming soon)

LEE FRENCH

Spirit Knights series
Maze Beset trilogy
The Greatest Sin series (with Erik Kort)
Harper Revolution series
Darkside Seattle collection (as L.E. French)
Damsel In Distress
Al-Kabar

JEFFREY COOK

Dawn of Steam trilogy
Airs & Graces trilogy
Fair Folk Chronicles
Gothcraft series
The Accidental Inquisitor series
Unchosen

If you'd like to keep up with Lee, Jeff, and the rest of the Clockwork Dragon crew, sign up for our monthly newsletter on our website, www.clockworkdragon.net.

ABOUT THE AUTHORS

Lee French is a *USA Today* bestselling author living in Olympia, WA with two kids, two bicycles, and too much stuff. She's a frequent visitor to Myth-Weavers, an online RPG site, and also trains in taekwondo. Best known for her young adult urban fantasy series Spirit Knights, she is an active member of the Science Fiction and Fantasy Writers of America and a NaNoWriMo Municipal Liaison.

Jeffrey Cook lives in the wilds of Maple Valley, WA now, but has lived all over the U.S. (and a little bit of Canada.) His mother insists he's wanted to be an author since he was six years old, but he didn't get his official start as a novelist until 2014. He now has 16 novels, many with frequent collaborator Katherine Perkins. He also heads up charity press Writerpunk Press, which currently has 5 anthologies out, benefitting PAWS Animal Rescue—a charity near and dear to Jeffrey, as the place he met 3 of his rescue dogs.

When not reading, researching, writing, or gaming, he is also a passionate football fan. (Go Hawks!)

Thanks for reading! If you enjoyed this book, please take a moment to post a review on your favorite book site. Every review matters, and we appreciate the effort.